IF YOU WERE MINE

JENNIFER SUCEVIC

If You Were Mine

Copyright© 2017 by Jennifer Sucevic

This is a work of fiction. Names, characters, businesses, palaces, events, locales, and incidents are either the products of the author's imagination or used in a fictitious manner. Any resemblance to actual persons, living or dead, or actual events is purely coincidental.

Cover Design by Mary Ruth Baloy at MR Creations

Editing by Evelyn Summers at Pinpoint Editing

Home | Jennifer Sucevic or www.jennifersucevic.com

ALSO BY JENNIFER SUCEVIC

<u>The Campus Series</u> (football)

Campus Player

Campus Heartthrob

Campus Flirt (free novella with newsletter)

Campus Hottie

Campus God

Campus Legend

<u>The Barnett Bulldogs</u> (football)

King of Campus

Friend Zoned

One Night Stand

If You Were Mine

<u>The Claremont Cougars</u> (football)

Heartless Summer (free novella with newsletter)

Heartless

Shameless

<u>Hawthorne Prep Series</u> (bully/football)

King of Hawthorne Prep

Queen of Hawthorne Prep

Prince of Hawthorne Prep

Princess of Hawthorne Prep

<u>The Next Door Duet</u> (football)

The Girl Next Door

The Boy Next Door

<u>What's Mine Duet</u> (suspense)
Claiming What's Mine
Protecting What's Mine

<u>Stay Duet </u>(hockey)
Stay
Don't Leave

<u>Standalones</u>
Confessions of a Heartbreaker (football)
Hate to Love You (hockey)
Just Friends (hockey)
Love to Hate You (football)
The Breakup Plan (hockey)

<u>Collections</u>
The Barnett Bulldogs
The Football Hotties Collection
The Hockey Hotties Collection
The Next Door Duet

CLAIRE

I watch him with narrowed eyes from my covert position inside the house. Even when we're nowhere near one another, the man is still able to burrow deep under my skin. Like an itch I just can't scratch. It's irritating as hell.

No, *he's* irritating as hell.

Someone needs to explain to me why he even bothered to show up today.

This is hardly his scene.

He's lounging on the patio in a pair of vibrantly colored board shorts. His thickly muscled legs are stretched out lazily in front of him. Even though there's a smile curving his lips, he can't possibly be enjoying himself. He's probably bored out of his ever-loving mind. This is a G-rated, Disney-esque family barbecue. Not a wild, drunken orgy where women will be abandoning their bikinis in an hour or two once they're liquored up.

In case you were wondering, JT Higgins is definitely more of a drunken orgy kind of guy. Trust me, my conclusions haven't been drawn from a few questionable lapses in judgment on his part.

It's taken *years* for him to cultivate this kind of reputation. He was already making a name for himself at whatever Big Ten university he attended before being drafted by Green Bay three years ago. He may play professional football, but he's even more notorious for his alcohol-induced antics, bar brawls, and, of course, the females who flock to him in droves.

For the life of me, I can't figure out why any self-respecting woman would actually want to be with him, let alone broadcast it to the world at large. It's a well-known fact that the guy dips his wick in anything that moves.

Gross.

It's not just groupies who lose their minds over him. He's been linked with his fair share of actresses and models as well. I think he was even seeing two chicks from the US Women's National Soccer Team last year.

At the same time.

From what I read online, it didn't end well.

The only possible upside I can see to all his *activity* is that he's probably keeping some clinic in business with penicillin and swab tests.

"Why is *who* here?"

Not realizing that I muttered the question out loud, my brother's wife, Gia, steps beside me and scans the backyard as if she can pick out who I'm talking about, all the while bouncing four-month-old baby Max in her arms.

Yanked from my thoughts, I attempt to cover my slip up. "Hmmm? What? Did I say something?"

Since her arms are full, she nods toward the patio where roughly seventy people are enjoying the early September sunshine. They're definitely a loud, boisterous group. It's football players and their wives or girlfriends along with offspring. People are lounging in the pool or playing bocce ball in the sand pit. A volleyball net has also been set up on the wide, expansive back lawn. Others are hanging out at the many tables that have been scattered around the brick paver patio.

My roommate, Holly, tagged along with me today. She's busy soaking up the sunshine on a lounger near the pool and enjoying all the man candy on display. This is our second year living together. We spent last year in the dorms and recently moved into an apartment off campus.

It's a tradition for Liam to host a Labor Day party at his place. Everyone from the team is invited. Since it's an open house, friends and teammates will drop by throughout the day. The party starts around two, lasting well into the night before ending with a professional firework display.

It's something I look forward to all summer long. Everyone always has a good time. Liam and Gia are gracious hosts and go out of their way to make everyone feel welcome and included. There's plenty of food and drinks being served. If you walk away hungry at the end of this party, it's your own fault.

Gia gives me a knowing look before asking again, "Who were you talking about?"

A slight blush creeps its way up my cheeks as the fib slides off my lips. "No one. Just mumbling to myself."

She narrows her blue eyes and gives me one of those deep, speculative stares that would normally leave me squirming. It's a relief when she doesn't push the issue.

As far as I'm concerned, JT is a complete ass and not worth wasting my breath on. Especially when there's a party in full swing. I'm just going to ignore him. Should be simple enough. It's not like I haven't had lots of practice.

Out of all the players on the team, why did my brother have to take an interest in JT Higgins?

It was bad enough when I occasionally ran into him at team events and functions, but now he's hanging around all the time. It probably wouldn't be so bad if he weren't always trying to strike up a conversation with me.

But that's exactly what he does.

Even though he knows perfectly well that I don't care for him.

I'm so lost in thought that I don't realize I'm still staring until clear green eyes collide with mine. A jolt of electricity spears through my body as my breath gets lodged at the back of my throat before I rip my gaze away.

Gia points toward a group of football players. "Looks like Ryan is here."

Careful to avoid JT's gaze, I cautiously glance back out the window, only to find my boyfriend standing in the midst of all that testosterone.

He looks completely awed by the company he's keeping.

I'm not sure if I should be miffed that he couldn't be bothered to find me first and say hello.

I met Ryan freshman year. His dorm was situated next to mine, so I'd see him frequently in the cafeteria or walking to and from class. He introduced himself after the first few weeks of school, and occasionally, we'd get together to study. Sometimes, he would invite me to a party, but I always declined.

Ever since I can remember, school has been a challenge. I'm not one of those people who can cram for a few hours and sail through a test with an A. In fact, that's a surefire way for me to flunk an exam. I've always had to work harder and longer than my friends to get the same grades. And I knew college was going to be more rigorous than high school. Instead of getting caught up in all the social stuff, I concentrated on my studies.

This semester, I'll start student teaching. I'm excited to finally step into a classroom. Now that I'm in the program and have the first three years of college under my belt, I feel like I can finally loosen the reins just a smidge. Maybe even have more of a social life than I've allowed myself in the past.

It's the reason I finally caved to Ryan after three years. We've been seeing each other for two months. We're definitely not the kind of couple who has to spend every waking moment together. Since we're both busy, we usually see each other a few times a week. We go out to dinner, grab coffee, see a movie, or hit a few parties.

I've yet to invite him to stay over at my place now that I finally have an apartment off campus, even though he keeps hinting at it.

I almost snort.

All right, he does way more than hint.

Up until this point, I haven't been ready to take our relationship further. I don't know what's holding me back, but something is. Maybe it's just first-time jitters.

I certainly didn't set out to save myself for someone special. I've been so focused on school and spending time with my brother and his family that sex was never a priority. But now, suddenly, I'm a senior in college. It's like I blinked and realized that I'll be graduating this spring.

Just as I'm about to respond to Gia, my gaze is ensnared by green ones for a second time. Another reluctant shiver shimmies down my spine as I yank my attention away yet again.

I really wish he would stop staring.

"I'm going to head out and say hello to Ryan." I force a bright smile before tickling the chubby baby in Gia's arms.

At this point, Max's eyes appear to be a gorgeous, deep gray. Even though they could still change, I don't think they will. Both Liam and I have the exact same shade.

"Want me to take Max?" There's nothing I love more than spending time with my niece and nephews. The two older kids are bundles of boundless energy. I don't know where they get it from. They're exhausting, but in the best way possible.

The question isn't even all the way out of my mouth when she drops the baby into my arms. "Sure, why don't you give him to Liam so I can get more food out onto the table? Looks like things are running low."

"No problem." I cuddle his wiggly four-month-old body close to mine before inhaling a great big breath of baby. As I do, everything inside me settles, just like it always does.

Max is like taking a handful of Xanax.

Totally addictive and completely necessary.

Especially when JT Higgins is in the vicinity.

JT

I bring the bottle of ice-cold water to my lips and take a long swig. Not once does my attention deviate from her. I don't think I could yank my eyes away even if I wanted to.

Just to be clear, I don't.

Now that I've pulled on a pair of aviators, I can sit back and stare to my heart's content.

Kind of like a creeper.

I should probably be a bit more conspicuous about my interest. Liam would kick my ass right out of the state of Wisconsin if he knew I was sitting here with dirty fantasies of his little sis rolling around in my head.

My gaze rakes over her for the umpteenth time.

What the hell is she wearing?

A teeny-tiny bikini, by the looks of it.

The lower part is submerged beneath the crystal-clear water. She shouldn't be wearing something like that in front of all these horny dudes. I straighten and glance around to see if anyone else is scoping out her hot little body. Once I realize that no one else is paying attention to Claire, my muscles loosen.

You'd think her brother would have something to say about what she's got on, but apparently not. Liam seems completely oblivious to the fact that his sister is practically naked in front of his teammates. Of course, the guy does have three kids running around.

At the moment, Claire is in the pool with Charlotte. The kid has floaties on and is splashing around like she might be drowning. There's a wide circle around her and the child because some of the women hanging out in the pool don't want their blowouts to get wet.

Guess they shouldn't be in the water.

I'm half tempted to climb in myself. It's hot as balls out here. Even though I'm relaxing in the shade, the sun continues to beat down. I don't think there's a single cloud in the cornflower sky today.

I glance at the guy who I've recently learned is Claire's boyfriend.

I'm not just saying this because I'd hate any guy who she brought around, but this one specifically has *tool* written all over him. For one, he's not paying a damn bit of attention to her. He's too busy yapping with some of the guys from the offensive line. I almost snort. He looks like a child standing next to them. We're talking about three-hundred-pound dudes who could stop a freight train in its path. My guess is that Claire's boyfriend weighs a whopping buck sixty.

Soaking wet.

I think if Collin McTavish or Grady Bradford asked him to lick the dirt off their shoes, he wouldn't hesitate before dropping to the ground and doing exactly that. If I wanted to be a real dick, I'd go over there and mess with him.

Can't say I'm not tempted.

But I'll restrain myself.

It's just too damn hot out to put forth that kind of effort.

If that guy had any brains whatsoever, he'd be glued to Claire's side. Not yipping and yapping the ears off those guys.

If she were my girlfriend, that's exactly where I'd be.

Stuck to her side.

I sure as shit wouldn't be hanging out with a bunch of dudes who won't remember my name in the morning. Hell, McTavish won't remember his name thirty minutes from now, if he even knows it to begin with.

I glance over at him again.

Yup, still transfixed. I almost shake my head. There's nothing sadder than watching a grown-ass man go all fangirl. I'm more tempted than ever to get in the pool and try striking up a conversation with Claire.

Except I know exactly how that will go.

It's the reason my ass is firmly planted in this chair. I've never met a woman who despises me more than Claire Garrison. I can't be totally sure about this, but I'm willing to bet that hitting on her over the last few years could be the reason for it.

I'm not going to lie—in the past, I've usually gotten pretty shit-faced before finally working up the courage to approach her. It's an unspoken rule on the team that everyone stays away from Liam's sister. It's the reason I hit on her when I'm drunk off my ass. I know all too well that Liam would beat the piss out of me if I laid one solitary finger on her.

That knowledge alone should be enough to keep me from eyeing her up.

It's not.

When my ass was in a sling at the end last season, it was Liam who stepped up and offered to help me out.

And you know what?

The last eight months have gone surprisingly smooth.

When I was first drafted by Green Bay, I went a little crazy. Okay, the entire city went nuts. It was like the prodigal son had returned home. I'd already earned quite a reputation the four years I spent playing in college.

My family is Green Bay royalty. My father, Joe Higgins Senior, played for the team back in the day. My older brother, Joe Jr., plays for Minnesota. He's the golden child of the family while I'm more the black sheep, which suits me just fine. My parents expect me to fuck up, and I sorely hate to disappoint them.

The conversation with Stu, the GM of the organization, at the end of my third season was a real kick in the balls. Since I had another year left on my contract, they grudgingly agreed to give me one more season to pull my shit together. If I couldn't stop creating PR nightmares for the team and being a constant source of embarrassment, they would cut ties and trade my ass.

That's when Garrison, our QB, took me under his wing. He kept me out of trouble and invited me over for family dinners. I don't think it was his intention, but he gave me a glimpse into the kind of future I could carve out for myself if I controlled all of the bullshit in my life.

The man is settled in a way I can only imagine. A beautiful, supportive wife. Cute kids. A rising career. Nice home. Comfortable lifestyle. For all intents and purposes, he's living the dream.

For whatever reason, it's Claire's face that pops into my head whenever I think about settling down. Which is ridiculous. That chick hates my guts. In fact, I'd go so far as to say she hates every damn thing about me.

Fuck it, I'm getting in that pool.

As I rise to my feet, ready to peel off the T-shirt that's sticking to my back with early September heat, Garrison plops himself down in the chair next to me. He's not alone. There's a baby in his arms.

The newest addition to the Garrison clan.

Max.

I can't help the disappointment that surges through me as I lower myself down again.

"It's freaking sweltering out here, man."

"Yeah, I'm pretty sure my sweat is sweating at this point," I say easily in response.

He glances at the little man in his arms.

I do the same before taking another slug of water. "So, this one do it for you? You finally gonna let your wife relax for a while?"

A huge grin lights up his face and he leans closer as if we're conspirators. "I'm gunning for at least one more." He gives the infant in his tattooed arms a gentle kiss on his downy head. "Usually right around the one-year mark, Gia starts missing the newborn stage. So for now, I'm biding my time, waiting for the right moment to spring it on her."

I'll admit it...watching them together has something loosening within me. I'm not made of stone after all. That being said, does it make me want to go out and impregnate the first woman I see?

Hell no.

"You're freaking nuts," I say with a snort. "Look around you, dude. You're already overrun with kidlets. They've outnumbered you. Mark my words, you continue to procreate and you'll have a coup on your hands."

He glances at Claire in the water with his daughter and Ty, who's running around with a water gun. "One more," he muses. "Maybe two."

Five freaking kids…

That's some craziness right there. I can't even begin to imagine it. Total and utter chaos.

Unable to stop myself, I change the subject by nodding nonchalantly toward Claire's boyfriend. I have zero idea what his name is.

"Looks like your sister caught herself a cleat licker."

And just like I suspected, that comment has the smile dropping clean off Liam's face as his gaze arrows to the guy in question who is still, as we speak, chatting up a few of our teammates. I haven't seen him give Claire more than five or ten minutes of his attention the entire afternoon. And her roommate is right there beside him.

The longer Liam stares, the more his lips flatten.

I'm not going to lie, I'm kind of loving it.

Does that make me a shitty person?

Probably.

Liam is crazy protective of his sister.

Just as he should be.

Claire Garrison is stunning. Straight mahogany colored hair that flows down her back like a thick, rich curtain. Piercing gray eyes that I get lost in whenever we come into contact. Legs that start somewhere in the general vicinity of her armpits. They're ridiculously long. I'd be lying my damn ass off if I didn't admit to fantasizing as to how they'd feel locked around my waist as I pumped into her.

She's got curves, but they're more subtle than a lot of the other women I'm used to going out with. And she's tall. If I had to guess, I'd say around five foot nine. Rather surprisingly, I like the height.

It's sexy.

Especially since I'm six foot three. I like that when she looks at me, she doesn't have to get a crick in her neck to hold my eyes. Mine might burn hot when I'm gazing at Claire, but hers are usually stone cold.

Liam's voice turns grumbly when he mutters, "Yeah. I've met him a few times. He seems to like Claire well enough. Treats her all right, from what I can tell."

Umm, why shouldn't he?

The girl is absolutely perfect. There's no reason for him to treat her any other way.

Although, I'm smart enough to keep that opinion to myself. The guy would flatten me if he caught me looking sideways at his sister. He's let it be known to everyone on the team, *repeatedly*, not to mess around with her.

And me...

Well, I don't have the best reputation.

I'm trying to rectify that, but it takes time.

Liam's voice drops to a hushed whisper. "She, ah, doesn't have much dating experience. So, I'm hoping this guy doesn't stick around for long. She can do better. I wanted to say something, but Gia told me that I'm not to open my mouth. Apparently, who Claire sees is *Claire's* business. Not mine." He shoots me an exasperated look.

One that says, *Can you believe that crap?*

Those last words are muttered as if they're stuck on repeat inside his head, but I'm not thinking about them. I'm more interested in the whole *doesn't have much dating experience* part.

I can't help but raise a brow.

Not much experience?

What *exactly* does that mean?

Just because I personally have never seen Claire with anyone, it doesn't necessarily mean anything. Up until six months ago, I only saw her sporadically when we were at team functions, or when Liam invited everyone over for a get-together.

I assumed she'd been dating people all throughout college. She must have a legion of guys trying to get with her on a daily basis.

All right…

We're going to shut down that particular line of thought before it pisses me off.

Even though it's tempting to bombard him with questions, I don't.

Nope.

I have to play this cool and not give myself away.

The last thing I need is for Liam to catch on that I'm interested in his sister. That would definitely be bad for business. Can't imagine the guy would be extending any more invitations if he knew just how much I wanted to bone her. Plus, Claire can barely stand to be in the same room with me. So, there seems little point in trying to get anything going with her.

But I'll tell you this, if that douche does anything to hurt her, I'll break both his legs. Then Stu can bitch about what a real freaking PR nightmare looks like.

I can't help but snort at that thought.

When Liam cocks a questioning brow in my direction, I clear my throat and refocus on the conversation.

Right.

Claire's dating habits.

Or lack thereof.

My cock twitches at the thought.

"That's, um, hard to believe."

There.

Perfectly executed, if I do say so myself.

A completely innocuous statement.

Nothing that reveals my true thoughts or feelings.

Liam is quiet for a long, speculative moment. I can't tell if he's picked up on something in the tone or if he's just mulling over the comment.

"Claire has always been focused on school to the exclusion of almost everything else. Up until this point, she hasn't allowed herself to have much of a social life." He nods toward jackwad.

"I think this is the first guy she's seriously dated."

I frown.

This guy is the first one Claire has dated?

Ever?

What the hell does that mean?

Like…are we talking *ever-ever?*

I'm doing my damnedest not to leap to conclusions, but is he suggesting that Claire Garrison is a *virgin?*

My dick stirs at the idea as my eyes narrow again on jackwad.

If what I *think* Liam is trying to say is the truth, then it'll be over my dead fucking body that the cleat licker is her first.

Over.

My.

Dead.

Body.

CLAIRE

"*D*id you have a good time today?"

Why am I even bothering to ask the question?

I know Ryan did. He was totally in his element, standing around all afternoon with the guys from the O line. Ryan is a huge Green Bay fan. His family has been season ticket holders for two generations.

Ryan grew up playing football and was on the team at UW- Green Bay for the first two years before calling it quits. He said it was because he needed to devote more time to his studies, but I suspect it's because he wasn't getting much play time. Being part of a college athletic team is both grueling and time consuming. You have to absolutely love it and be a hundred percent committed, otherwise there's no point. I saw that with my brother when he played at Barnett University.

Football was his life.

Well, it was until he met Gia his junior year of college, a few months before the NFL draft.

Then his focus shifted to her, and she became his life.

With a glance, Ryan squeezes my hand as we drive toward my apartment near campus. Liam lives in a high-end, gated subdivision on the outskirts of Green Bay where each house has a few acres of land. When I decided to move out of the dorms at the end of junior year, Liam *suggested* that I move in with them.

All right, it was more than a suggestion.

I was, for all intents and purposes, browbeaten.

In the kindest, most loving way possible, of course.

As much as I adore being with them, I need my own space. And with a five-year-old, a three-year-old, and a four-month-old, it's crazy time all the time at their place.

After spending nearly ten hours at their house, I'm sweaty and tired. I helped Gia with food preparation and making sure everyone had what they needed, or I was in the pool with Ty and Charlotte.

The party was a massive success. Just like it always is. It turned out to be a gorgeous day. Everyone had a great time playing lawn games my brother set up or hanging out in the pool. Holly flirted with a couple of football players. Both Ty and Charlotte were mesmerized by the fireworks show at the end of the night.

The only fly in the ointment, so to speak, was JT.

For the most part, he kept to himself and didn't bother me. Sure, he tried striking up a conversation toward the end of the night, but I shut it down.

What bothers me most about JT is the way my body comes alive whenever he's in the vicinity. Especially when I feel his green-eyed gaze on me. It would be easy enough to brush off the situation, just like I have in the past, if I didn't find myself unconsciously responding to him.

Ryan squeezes my hand as his brown eyes drift toward mine as if he's waiting for an answer. That's when I realize I spaced out for a moment and didn't catch what he said.

Damn JT Higgins!

Even when I'm nowhere near him, he's still able to mess with my head. I grit my teeth in frustration. He's the last person I want to feel this way about.

It takes effort to shake away the irritation as I admit, "Sorry, I didn't catch that. Guess I'm more tired than I realized."

When he slants a sly look at me, I know exactly what direction this conversation is going to veer in.

I can't help but mentally sigh.

It's a convo we seem to be having with more frequency.

And it's getting old.

"Does that mean you're too tired to hang out for a bit?"

I almost snort.

Apparently, *hanging out* is a euphemism for having sex.

"Umm..."

When I don't say anything more, annoyance flickers across his face.

I brace myself for a fight.

Instead, he stares out the windshield.

The strained silence doesn't sit well with me, and I twist my fingers together in my lap. "Sorry."

The fact that I feel the need to apologize irritates me. I shouldn't feel bad about not being ready to take that next step with him. So, I go with the most plausible excuse, which just so happens to be the truth.

"It's been a long day, and I'm really tired."

"Yup." His tone is flat.

That one succinct word leaves me fidgeting on the seat. Even though we're alone in the car, I drop my voice. "It's just that...I haven't gone to the clinic yet."

The annoyance that had flickered across his features moments ago now settles. "I thought you were going to take care of that last week?"

I shrug as a prickle of unease grows in the pit of my belly. I'm not sure why I'm dragging my feet. We've been together for two months. It couldn't be more perfect.

And yet...

"I didn't have time," I mumble.

That's not altogether true. I've had plenty of time.

After the first month, Ryan made it perfectly clear that he wanted to have a sexual relationship. When he grew pushy, I finally told him about my lack of experience.

That bought me a few more weeks.

But he's running out of patience. What he doesn't understand is that the more annoyed he gets, the less inclined I am to go through with it.

I wish he'd just chill out and let it happen naturally.

"When are you going to make the appointment?" His deep brown eyes lock on mine before he asks with a hint of acid, "Or are you not going to bother?"

"I will." When he raises a dubious brow, I blurt, "I'll call this week." I force a slight smile, hoping we can put this conversation to rest.

But no…

Apparently, he's not ready to let it go.

"Look, if this isn't something you want, just level with me. Don't string me along, telling me it's going to happen when in actuality, it never will."

Stringing him along?

He's acting like we've been together for years.

Decades even.

It's been two months, buddy.

Eight weeks, to be exact.

I didn't realize I was expected to fall onto my back and spread my legs for him right away. Foolish me thought we could take our time getting to know one another before deciding to become more intimate.

"Look," I say with a bit more bite. "I didn't have time this week. I'll call tomorrow and make the appointment. There's been a lot going on with the start of classes and moving into my apartment."

"I just want to make sure you're on board with this. If you're not ready for an adult relationship with this level of intimacy, you need to be straight with me. I don't want to push you into it. I'm not that kind of guy."

Adult relationship?

Really?

I arch a brow.

Like I'm a baby because I've never slept with a man before?

Is he seriously implying that having sex makes you a grown up?

That's the most ridiculous statement I've ever heard in my life. It's tempting to tell him exactly that, except I don't want to get into it with Ryan at eleven o'clock at night when I'm already wiped.

As far as him not wanting to appear pushy…

Ha!

I'm beginning to think that's exactly the kind of guy he is.

I suck in a deep, cleansing breath and attempt to settle all my riotous thoughts. Today was really nice, and I don't want to ruin it by getting into a wicked argument with Ryan over the fact that we haven't slept together.

"Look," I say with far more patience than I'm currently feeling. "I do want this. I'm just trying to make sure it's right."

As soon as the last sentence escapes from my lips, I realize it was the wrong thing to say.

"And you're not sure if it's right?" He pauses as his voice deepens. "With me?"

Grrr.

Any moment, I'm going to lose it.

I shake my head. "That's not what I meant. I want to make sure *I'm* ready for this. It has more to do with me than you."

If I'm being completely honest with myself, there's a tiny voice inside my head that wonders if I'm telling the truth.

Satisfied with my response, Ryan gives my hand a small squeeze before bringing my fingers to his lips and brushing a kiss against my knuckles. Under normal circumstances, that gesture would melt my heart, but I'm still peeved about this conversation.

"You know that I'm going to make it perfect for you, right?"

I force another smile. "I do."

I think he'll try to be, I don't know…*gentle.*

"I want your first time to be good."

Everything within me that had become strung tight gradually loosens with his soft words and the intimate look that fills his eyes.

For the first time since this conversation began, I feel like we're both on the same page. My exasperation melts away, and I'm reminded of what attracted me to Ryan in the first place.

Maybe he was just thrown off guard that I hadn't called the clinic and scheduled an appointment for birth control. You're damn straight I'm still going to make him wear a condom. I want to be as protected as I can. Maybe I don't have firsthand experience with sex, but I've heard plenty of horror stories while living in the dorms. Not only pregnancy scares, but STIs as well. In fact, I took a health class last year that pretty much terrified the crap out of me. The photographs were entirely too graphic.

If you're looking to be scared straight off sex, just take Sexual Health. Can't say that I didn't learn a lot that semester. Although, sometimes I have to wonder if maybe I didn't learn a little *too* much.

*I*t wasn't all that long ago that I was out every night, partying my ass off.

Even during the season.

Hell, *especially* during the season.

And yet, no matter how shitfaced I got the night before, I was still able to haul my ass out of bed every morning and show up to practice on time. I'd perform well, too. Sure, on the inside I was dragging, but I still looked better than half the dudes out there.

That was then, and this is now.

I no longer pick up random chicks and go home with them.

I don't have a table reserved at my favorite club.

And I've stopped trying to drown myself in alcohol.

It's a very quiet life I'm leading these days.

Know what the highlight of my week is now?

Thursday night dinner at Garrison's place.

I look forward to it all week long. I could pretend and tell myself that it's because I don't get home-cooked meals very often, but I think we all know that would be a lie.

Ever since I bought a house in the same development as Liam, I've been extended an open invitation. I can't say I don't enjoy it.

Gia's cooking is just one of the reasons. I legitimately enjoy hanging out with Liam, his wife, and their kids. It's a chaotic, happy mess most of the time with lots of laughter. It's a far cry from the stuffy dinners with my own family.

Those are to be endured and never enjoyed.

Even at the ripe old age of twenty-five, I still dread being summoned home like an errant child. Since I've been keeping my nose clean, it doesn't happen with nearly the same amount of frequency as it once did.

For whatever reason, my father and I have never seen eye to eye. There was a time when I desperately wanted his love and tried my damnedest to earn it by impressing him in school or out on the field, but that proved an impossible task. Once I finally came to the realization, I stopped seeking out his approval and just started doing what I wanted.

All right, fine…I'll admit it—I actually got off on pissing him off. Every time he lost his temper was a point scored in my column. It goes without saying that the four years I spent in college, plus the first three of my NFL career, were spent racking up a shitload of points.

It took me a long time to realize that in my father's eyes, there was only Joe, my older brother. His mini-me.

Joe can do no wrong.

As much as I wish I could hate Joe for feeling pitted against him my entire life, I don't. The issue lies with my father, not my brother. There are times when I suspect that Joe Sr. doesn't want us to get along. It irritates him that there's a bond between us. I think he'd prefer to forget I existed.

Most of the time, I long for that as well.

I get along with my mom, but she doesn't go against my father. No matter what he says or does, she stands quietly by his side. I spent a lot of years being pissed off that she didn't do more to protect me from his wrath or try harder to even things out between me and my brother.

But I'm over it.

All I feel now is pity that she's married to such an asshole.

The Garrison household is a far cry from how I was reared. And I love it. Revel in it. Secretly long to be a part of the madness. It has me believing that relationships, marriage, and families can be different from how I grew up.

Which brings us to Claire.

Even though she barely gives me the time of day, I enjoy being in the same room with her. I like listening to her talk about her week and the classes she's taking along with her student teaching placement. I could listen to the sound of her voice all night long and never grow tired of it.

I'll admit that I was hoping she might unbend if we spent more time together. Maybe even let my past douchey behavior be water under the bridge.

That hasn't happened.

Even though Liam and I live in the same subdivision, our houses are spread out. I'm a couple miles down the street from his place. Each plot of land is a couple of acres, so there's a lot of privacy. Liam and I aren't the only football players who live here. There are four other families who call this gated community home.

Instead of walking over, I take my Porsche.

I rap my knuckles against the front door and wait for someone to let me in. Already, I can hear the chaos unfolding inside. There's never a dull moment, that's for sure. That's also part of the charm. Even standing outside on the front porch, I hear the kids yelling. Laughing. Running around like crazy.

A few moments later, Ty opens the door. That kid is the spitting image of Liam. Dark hair with large, gray eyes framed by thick eyelashes. Although, he doesn't have his head shaved on the sides like his father. I'm expecting that'll come soon enough, because he seems to want to be just like his dad.

A delighted grin lights up his face when he sees me. Before I can blink, he's hurtling his solid body into my arms. The Superman cape he has on billows behind him.

From what I've heard, he won't take the damn thing off. He'll only part ways with it to go in the pool and even that's a battle. Gia told him at the barbecue that if he wore it in the water, it would end up in the washing machine and he wouldn't be able to wear it for a couple of hours. You should have seen the indecision flicker across his small face. It took a solid five minutes of internal debate, but he finally opted to part with it for the sixty minutes he was splashing around.

"Hey, Superman. Any problems with Lex Luthor?

"Nah." There's a serious expression on his face as he shakes his head. "Just Charlotte." Then he deadpans, "Mom says she's a real pain in the butt sometimes."

His words bring an easy grin to my face. Charlotte, at three, is a handful. And she does her damnedest to keep up with her older brother, which he alternately loves and hates. Sometimes, he likes having a cohort to get into trouble with, and other times he just wants to be sneaky and get into trouble all by himself.

I close the massive eight-foot front door and carry him in my arms to the spacious kitchen with its white cabinets, white marble countertops, and stainless-steel appliances where it sounds like everyone is gathered. Unlike my own home growing up, the Garrison kitchen is the hub of activity.

Kind of like a beehive.

Gia enjoys cooking, and it seems like the kids are usually munching away on something or other. I've noticed that it's mostly fresh fruits and vegetables. The Garrisons have a big garden out back, and the kids enjoy going out with baskets and picking whatever produce they're growing.

I like hanging around here because you can tell just how much they all love one another. Gia and Liam genuinely enjoy their growing family. Again, it's far different from the environment I was reared in. I spent more time with our housekeeper than anyone else. The woman is like a second mother to me...or maybe a first.

Just like always, my gaze is drawn to Claire as I walk into the brightly lit room. I'm guessing that's why it takes me a moment to notice that there's someone else in the kitchen besides the normal Garrison bunch.

What the hell...

This is supposed to be a family thing.

And, you know…me.

Who invited the interloper?

"Hey man, want something to drink?" Liam asks, interrupting my thoughts.

I glance at him. "Sure, water's fine."

He tosses me an ice-cold bottle from the fridge, and I catch it with one hand. Because Ty is still wrapped around my upper body like a barnacle, I'm unable to open the bottle.

"Here, buddy. Can you use some of that superhuman strength and pry off the lid?"

He grins before snatching the bottle out of my hand and practically ripping off the plastic cap.

"Thanks," I say with a laugh. "Better tone that down a bit or you'll end up hurting someone."

Ty flexes his arms before grunting like a couple of our teammates do when they're bench pressing a shit ton of weight.

Everyone laughs.

The kid has personality, that's for sure.

When he starts to squirm, I set him down and he shoots out of the room like his ass is on fire.

Gia watches him go with a speculative gleam in her eyes as she beelines for me. "He hasn't been that still all day. Hopefully, kindergarten will be good for him." When she's close enough, she reaches up on her tiptoes and presses a kiss against my cheek. I grin at Liam before wiggling my brows.

There are times when I like to poke the bear just for the fun of it.

Instead of getting all fired up, he rolls his eyes.

They're disgustingly in love. There's nothing Liam wouldn't do for Gia or his kids. Or his sister, for that matter. Family is everything to these people.

It's not like I'm jealous or anything, but sometimes I think it might be nice to come home to a family at the end of the day. People of my own. People who actually care about what happens to me. All this chaos and activity that is bursting at the seams is a far cry from my own quiet home.

Similar to Liam's house, mine is five thousand square feet. With the finished basement, it's somewhere in the vicinity of seventy-five hundred. When I'm there alone, which is all the damn time, especially since I'm no longer going out and burning time with women, parties, and hangers-on, it's so quiet that I can actually hear myself think.

I'm not sure what compelled me to purchase the place, but it's a nice retreat. Even if Green Bay ends up trading me at the end of the season, I wanted something more than the apartment I'd been renting downtown. I needed to get away from the clubs and bars that were a stone's throw away from my front door.

My gaze settles on Claire as the thought of a family churns through my brain. And just like always, she studiously avoids my gaze. I get the feeling she's trying to look anywhere *but* at me.

Jackwad is at her side.

Before I can greet her, he steps forward, thrusting out his hand in my direction. His eyes look like they'll pop out of his head any moment.

"Hey, man. Nice to see you again. I'm Ryan, Claire's boyfriend."

I hope Liam is right about this guy, and he won't be around for long. There's something about him that rubs me the wrong way. The fact that he's with Claire and more than likely trying to get in her pants is probably the reason.

For the next thirty minutes, he proceeds to yap my damn ear off, hitting me up with all sorts of invasive questions, regaling me with story after story of his glory days playing ball at Green Bay.

Seriously, dude?

Mentally, I've shaken my head so many times that I've lost count.

When he brings up some of my more noteworthy brawls along with an actress I was linked with last year, I decide I've had my fill of this guy and excuse myself to use the john. There's not much that drives me to drink nowadays, but a minute more in his company would have done the trick. I'm seriously contemplating the merits of finding Ty and hanging out in his room, playing with his superhero collection until dinner is ready.

The entire time he was firing off questions like he works for TMZ, Claire was in the kitchen, helping Gia prepare dinner. I'd catch little glimpses of her every now and then from where I'd strategically placed myself. Since Liam was entertaining the two older kids and keeping an eye on the baby, that, unfortunately, left me and Claire's boyfriend to fend for ourselves.

I huff out a relieved breath as I step into the hallway decorated with oversized photographs showcasing the Garrison clan. Since I'm in no rush to return to the family room, I take my time, looking at each one. I find a few of Claire taken years ago and can't help but study them. She looks exactly the same. Long, dark, shining hair, slender build, smile curving her lips upwards, and wide gray eyes that stare straight into the camera.

I only catch glimpses of that smile when she's talking with someone else.

The bathroom is located at the far end of the hallway. The farther I get from Claire's boyfriend, the more relaxed everything within me becomes. Not that I necessarily have to take a leak, but my plan is to hide out in there until I can come up with something else.

As I make a grab for the brushed nickel handle, it swings open. I'm not sure who's more startled, Claire or me. Although, I'm willing to bet it's Claire. She stifles a small yelp before jumping almost a foot. My hands settle on her shoulders to steady her. Even when she remains still, I don't relinquish my hold. In the three years I've known Claire, not once have I laid my hands on her. Some irrational part of my brain is actually irate that the guy she chose to date gets to do it any damn time he wants.

Once the surprise of our near run-in wears off, her face morphs into the cool mask of indifference she always wears in my presence. I've seen that look dozens of times. Now that I think about it, I have some very fond memories of that stony expression aimed in my direction.

When it becomes obvious that I'm not going to release her of my own volition, she snaps, "You can let go of me now."

Why I find her irritation amusing, I have no idea.

It's the reason one side of my mouth hitches at the starchiness weaving its way through her voice. "Just trying to be a gentleman and make sure you didn't fall."

"Yes, you're always the perfect gentleman." Her voice fills with mockery as she snorts. "Now let go of me."

I give her shoulders a gentle squeeze, my thumbs gliding over the silky soft skin left bare from the tank top she's wearing. Her eyes flare wide at the caress.

Unfortunately, there's no longer a reason for me to continue touching her. Even though it's the last thing I want, I set her free.

But I'm reluctant to let her run off just yet. The woman will barely give me the time of day. This is the longest conversation we've had in months.

As she tries to slide past me, the words shoot out of my mouth before I can rein them back in. "Is that guy really your boyfriend?"

She stops in her tracks as her gaze swings back to mine. "Excuse me?"

I'm tempted to call him jackwad, but I'm smart enough to know that will only piss her off more. I'll admit that I enjoy watching the way her eyes spark when she's angry, but I'm honestly not trying to rile her up. It just so happens to be a natural byproduct of my company.

I nod toward the family room where I assume he's patiently awaiting my return. "Are you seriously dating him?"

Annoyance flickers across her face as she crosses her arms over her chest and narrows her icy gray eyes. I probably shouldn't mention how much that turns me on. I'm going to be completely honest. There isn't much about Claire Garrison that doesn't get me going. Apparently, that's just a natural byproduct of her company.

"Yeah, I am. Why are you asking?"

"Because he seems more interested in the people you know than in you."

Is that an asshole thing to say?

Probably.

But it's the truth.

And I don't want to see Claire get hurt by a dude who's just out to use her. It happens all the damn time when you're famous. Or related to someone who's famous. People want to get close, and they'll use whoever they have to in order to do it.

"Every time I see him, he's talking with everyone *but* you."

She rears back as if I've slapped her. I didn't think it was possible for her tone to become frostier. "That's not true."

I raise a brow, because we both know it is. She just doesn't want to admit it.

And certainly not to me.

Unable to stop myself, I inch closer, invading her personal space. It's just enough to catch a subtle hint of the beachy scent that clings to her. Needless to say, it goes straight to my head.

Umm…my other head.

"Listen, you should be with someone who likes you for you and doesn't give a damn about who you're related to or the people you're friends with. *You* should be the most important person in the room. No one else."

When I'm around this girl, she's the only one I'm conscious of.

I can't imagine any other guy feeling differently.

Her hands get planted on her slim hips as her dark brows lower. "Not that it's any of your business, but he does like me. He just so happens to be a huge football fan. Last time I checked, that wasn't a crime. And honestly, it's none of your business who I go out with."

She's right. It isn't. But that kind of minute detail isn't going to stop me.

"I've seen this guy twice, and both times, he's been more interested in talking to your brother's teammates than spending any time with you. That's not how I'd treat a girlfriend."

With a scoff, she rolls her eyes. "Like you've ever had one of those."

She's got me there. I've been linked to a ton of women, but most of them have been long-distance relationships that had the lifespan of a gnat. They only lasted that long because we weren't in the same city. Most of the time, we weren't in the same state or time zone.

When I remain silent, she advances before ramming a finger into my chest.

"Exactly! So don't you dare try to dole out relationship advice. You have no idea what you're talking about."

My fingers lock around her upper arms before I haul her body to mine. I must be having some kind of psychotic break, because there's no way this will end well for me.

Claire's eyes flare so wide that I'm able to see all the varying flecks of gray that make up her irises. Her delicate scent surrounds me, cocooning me in familiarity. It makes the blood thrum almost violently through my veins. I want to suck in a giant breath of her. Or maybe snort her like a line of coke.

My gaze pins her in place. "What I know is this. If you were mine, there's not a damn person who could pull my attention away from you."

Hell, she's not even mine, and I have a hard time pulling my attention away from her. She eclipses everything and everyone.

She has from day one.

Time stills.

In that moment of silence, I can hear and feel the thundering of her heartbeat as our gazes stay locked. After a second or two, her eyes fall to my lips, and it takes everything I have inside not to throw her over my shoulder like a caveman and leave the house. I want to get her away from her douchey boyfriend before he touches her in the ways I've always fantasized about.

I have no idea how long we stare before she whispers, "I'm not yours, JT." Her voice is so low that it sounds as if it's been roughed up with sandpaper. It continues to gain strength as she adds, "I will *never* be yours."

That being said, she wrenches out of my arms before inhaling a shaky breath and racing down the hallway like the hounds of hell are nipping at her heels. She doesn't bother to glance back before turning the corner.

Long after she disappears from sight, I stand there with my fists clenched at my sides, because there's nothing I can do. I don't understand what it is about Claire that tugs something deep inside me. Over the years, I've tried to figure it out. Or, more accurately, snuff it out, because there's nothing more pathetic than pining after someone who wants nothing to do with you.

But I can't.

In all honesty, I don't want to.

CLAIRE

For the first time ever, dinner with my family feels like torture.

And it's all *his* fault.

I'm at the point of wanting to scream because his green eyes always seem to be directed my way. I can practically *feel* them licking over me, watching every single rise and fall of my chest. I have never been so aware of another human being as I am of JT Higgins.

It's driving me nuts.

What is it about him?

Why is he able to force such a reaction from me?

I should be able to ignore him like I've done for the past three years, but that's impossible.

At least before—when he'd been drinking, ho-ing around, and getting into fights every other weekend—he wasn't bothering me. When we'd see each other, he would proposition me, but it was easy to brush him off and ignore him. There were always so many distractions that he was never one hundred percent focused on me. He was like an unconscious person fading in and out of slumber.

That's no longer the case.

Actually, it hasn't been that way for six months.

Now when we're thrown together, his gaze stays pinned to mine. The sensation makes me feel like a nervous, fidgety mess. It ties my insides up into intricate little knots.

No matter how many times I attempt to brush him off, he never fails to try and strike up a conversation. It's maddening. I liked it better when he was drunk, and I could sidestep his attention and advances.

With Ryan seated next to me at the table, JT has positioned himself directly across from me. Gia and Liam are at the ends. They each have a child by them, and Max is down for a nap.

I really wish JT hadn't touched me earlier in the hallway. It's almost as if his tight grip has been imprinted onto my shoulders and arms as a constant reminder. And the way he grabbed me, hauling me close…

A shiver dances down my spine.

His touch hadn't been rough or punishing.

For a moment, I'd been terrified he might kiss me.

Or maybe I'd been scared that he wouldn't.

I don't think I've ever wanted to be kissed more by a man.

My fork stalls midway to my mouth as that thought ricochets through my brain.

Oh my god. How can I want that?

No.

I don't want JT to kiss me.

The guy is a total ass.

And yet, I can't deny the spark of electricity that ignited within me when I stared into his eyes. Or when he pulled me close to his muscular body. Need curls like a wisp of smoke at the bottom of my belly as I lift my gaze in confusion.

How can I want him to lay his hands on me when I can barely stand to be in the same room with the guy?

It doesn't make sense.

I should be feeling these little zings of attraction for Ryan. He's the one I'm going out with.

As soon as our eyes collide, his gaze holds mine captive. It's almost as if he's been sitting across from me, patiently biding his time. Air gets trapped in my throat as everything around us fades away.

What I've noticed over the past couple of months is that his watchfulness has only intensified. It's like a physical caress skating over my skin. Although, his attention has never been quite so...blatant. He's usually stealthier about it. Especially around Liam and Gia. But Ryan is talking to Liam, who's preoccupied with trying to get Ty to eat his dinner. And Gia is focused on Charlotte, who's making a mess of things.

Which leaves the two of us.

That's all it takes for my skin to prickle with awareness, and I shift under his intense scrutiny. Self-consciously, I push food around with my fork. Even though I was starving when Ryan and I arrived earlier this evening, I've completely lost my appetite. My only defense is to yank my attention away and focus on my plate.

I just want to get out of here. I need to get away from him and the strange feelings he's teased to the surface. I don't understand them. And I'm not sure I want to, either.

They feel dangerous.

A Pandora's Box I shouldn't open.

I hate that he's ruining something I look forward to all week. I love spending time with my family, and now I don't want to be here. I wish it were possible to ignore him. More than anything, I want everything to go back to the way it used to be.

I don't like this new and improved JT.

And I definitely don't like how physically attuned I am to him.

"When do you start student teaching?" he asks, breaking into the turmoil of my thoughts.

My gaze reluctantly lifts to his.

Even though no one else is paying attention, I can't sit here and ignore him. He must realize that. If we were alone, he'd get a one-word response. In front of my brother and sister-in-law, I'm forced to converse politely when all I want to do is bare my teeth and growl.

You know what?

I think he'd actually enjoy that.

"In a few weeks."

"And you'll be working at an elementary school?"

Jeez. Who the heck gave him the lowdown on my life?

Stupid question…

Liam couldn't be prouder that I'm making my dreams of becoming a teacher into a reality. He tells anyone who will listen. I'm pretty sure all the guys on the team know my GPA along with the courseload I'm taking.

I nod. My gaze reluctantly flickers to him. Every time it does, he captures it, holding it ensnared. He doesn't even pretend to look away. It's as if all the pretense between us has been stripped away.

That thought makes my mouth turn cottony, and I shift on the chair.

"Yes. I have a placement this fall at one of the local elementary schools. Next semester, I'll work at a different one."

I silently pray this will be the end of our polite discourse and we can go back to eating in stifling silence. It's not like I'm trying to keep the conversational ball rolling. I glance at Ryan, annoyed that he's not paying attention to what's going on.

He's completely oblivious.

In fact, he's peppering Liam with dozens of questions about playing pro ball as he throws out pointless football trivia facts. Even though my brother is trying to humor Ryan, his attention is focused on Ty and getting him to eat his dinner instead of playing with it.

JT's comment from earlier creeps back into my brain before echoing hollowly, which is ridiculous considering that Ryan's interest in Liam or any of the other guys on the team has never bothered me before.

So why am I reading more into it now?

Because JT, who doesn't know my boyfriend at all, threw out a few crappy comments?

Why am I listening to him?

It's like his words have taken root inside my mind and are now flourishing. When my gaze unconsciously settles on JT, a knowing smirk fills his eyes, and he arches a brow as if to say, *See? Exactly what I told you.*

Grrrr.

I don't think I've ever met anyone who has infuriated me more.

"Claire's wanted to be a teacher ever since I met her when she was fifteen. She was just a freshman in high school." Gia pauses for a moment before continuing. "Seems like it was just yesterday, and yet here we are, six years later." She shakes her head as a faraway look fills her eyes. "I don't know where the time has gone."

My sister-in-law glances at me as a smile plays around the edges of her lips. Something softens within me at the memory. Gia is the reason I was able to turn everything around for myself in high school. She spent a lot of her spare time tutoring me. The year after Liam was drafted to Green Bay, Gia stayed behind to teach second grade. Without her intervention, I wouldn't be on my way to graduating this May with a bachelor's degree in education.

JT's eyes settle on Gia as she helps Charlotte scoop up some vegetables with her spoon.

"Sounds like you've known Claire for a while. What was she like back then?"

"Claire has always—"

I straighten on my chair and blurt, "I don't think JT's interested in hearing about all that." Nor do I particularly want him to know anything more about me than he already does.

"Of course I'm interested." He flicks a lazy glance toward my boyfriend. "Aren't you, Ryan?"

Both of our gazes fall on my boyfriend, who's in the middle of telling Liam a very detailed story regarding his glory days at UW-Green Bay from the sounds of it. Something about running the ball into the end zone…blah, blah, blah.

A hot blush stings my cheeks as I elbow him in the ribs. Even though I'm trying to be discreet, the grin on JT's face doesn't go unnoticed.

An annoyed expression mars Ryan's face as he turns toward us. His brows are pinched together.

His gaze bounces between JT and mine. "Huh?"

JT clears his throat, sounding like he's on the verge of bursting into laughter.

I swear to god, if one damn chuckle escapes from him, there's a good possibility that I'll leap across the table and throttle him with my bare hands. I'm not even kidding right now.

It's also tempting to strangle Ryan as well.

Even though he doesn't realize it, all he's doing is proving the point JT made in the hallway earlier.

"Gia was just telling us about when Claire was fifteen."

Confusion clouds Ryan's eyes. "Oh, really?"

A second ticks by before he swings back to Liam and picks up the threads of his previous conversation.

My sister-in-law focuses on the blond man sitting across from me. "Yup, even then she wanted to be a teacher."

"Sounds like you've always known what you wanted to do. Not many people realize that at such a young age."

I shrug, not wanting to get drawn into an earnest conversation with him. I have no desire to get to know JT on a deeper level or view him in a different light.

"When she was a sophomore in high school, she'd get a ride to the elementary school where I worked and would help with the kids in my classroom. They loved her. Claire has always had a great deal of patience when dealing with children. She's a natural born teacher. She's worked so hard to get into college and the elementary education program. With the number of applicants, it's quite competitive. Not everyone gets accepted."

It's tempting to bury my face in my hands. Gia is practically gushing. I have no idea why she's telling JT all of this.

Does she actually think he cares about anyone other than himself?

Ha!

Not a chance.

At this point, I'm hoping Charlotte will cause some kind of ruckus so Gia will be forced to focus all her attention on the three-year-old.

That doesn't happen.

"What grade will you be teaching?" he asks, unwilling to let the conversation die.

"Student teaching," I correct quickly before softening my tone. "First grade. I want to work in lower elementary. Maybe even kindergarten. Once I have a few years under my belt, I'll apply for a master's program in reading intervention with the goal of becoming a reading specialist down the road."

We'll see how it goes.

He nods thoughtfully.

It's painful to acknowledge that JT is more focused on what I'm saying than Ryan. Who, by the way, is *still* talking about playing college ball. Irritation thrums through me.

"You must be pretty excited about getting into the classroom."

A wave of self-consciousness washes over me and I glance down at my plate.

"Come on, Claire," Gia encourages. "You've been looking forward to this since you started college."

That's an understatement.

I loved being in the classroom when I worked with Gia sophomore year in high school, and then I was able to help out during my senior year as a teaching assistant.

But still, is there a reason we have to discuss this with JT?

By the amused expression on his face, he knows the thoughts running rampant through my head.

"Yes," I finally admit. "I'm looking forward to getting back into the classroom. After I get acclimated, I'll be able to start creating my own lesson plans."

"How many classes are you taking this semester?" he asks.

"Just three."

His eyes never once relinquish their hold, and I get the strange feeling he sees more than I'm comfortable with. There's an entirely different level of intensity about him now. One I find unnerving. I'm unsure what to do with all the feelings he rouses within me. Especially when my boyfriend is seated beside me while it's happening.

"Sounds like it'll be an easy one."

"For the most part." Even though I agree, I know it won't be a cakewalk. One of the classes I'm taking is a statistics course, and I've heard the professor can be a real stickler. Since it's a requirement for graduation, he's not afraid to flunk people.

"Aren't you taking stats this semester?" Gia asks.

I flash her a slight smile. "Yup."

Her face scrunches. "I always hated stats."

A little sigh escapes from me. "I'm not looking forward to it either." Math has always been a struggle. I have a hard time wrapping my head around the concepts and breaking them down into understandable chunks that can be easily digested. I'm certainly no stranger to the math tutor lab on campus.

They know me by name.

"If you ever need help, all you have to do is ask," JT says, drawing my attention back to him.

My eyes widen.

There must be an incredulous expression on my face because his lips bow up into a smile. "I aced stats in college. Math is something I've always excelled at."

"That's shocking. I would have thought you'd be too busy partying to actually attend your classes." The words are out of my mouth before I can stop them.

"Claire!"

Amusement lights up his face. "Nope. Made it to all my classes and was still able to find the time to party." He winks. "I've always had excellent time management skills."

I wince at Gia's chiding tone.

She's right.

I shouldn't have voiced that comment out loud.

And normally, I wouldn't have. It's not who I am. All I can say is that this is the first real conversation JT and I have had that hasn't revolved around him hitting on me. Maybe I'm uncomfortable having such an honest discussion with him.

I don't know.

I just know that I'm feeling…

Crap. I don't even know what I'm feeling. A little bit confused, maybe. I don't like all the thoughts I've been having lately where he's concerned.

This conversation has been entirely too...

Pleasant.

There.

I said it.

For just a moment, we were having a friendly conversation. Maybe it's the unnerving way he's been focused so intently upon me. Especially when the guy who *should* be paying attention is still ignoring me while he talks to my brother about the team's prospects this season. Or maybe I'm intent on ruining the fledgling friendship springing up between us.

Even though I don't want to apologize, it's the right thing to do.

"Sorry," I mutter begrudgingly. "I didn't mean it like that."

I absolutely meant it that way.

By the laughter brimming in his green eyes, he understands it too.

It's not like we all haven't heard the stories about his party days and the hell he raised at the Big Ten university where he played ball. If memory serves me correctly, he was almost kicked out at one point. By the time JT was drafted to Green Bay, his bad-boy reputation preceded him. And the last three years have only solidified it. I have zero interest in getting tangled up with that.

Or him.

He leans forward, somehow managing to close some of the distance that separates us. Even though he's sitting across the table, I feel his nearness. It's as if the intensity of his green eyes is capable of swallowing me whole.

"There's nothing for you to apologize for. I fully admit to partying. I had a good time in college and yet I still managed to do well in my classes. Especially statistics. So, if you ever need help, the offer stands." His gaze remains focused on mine, burning into it. "I'm more than willing to give you a little one-on-one attention."

My eyes widen. I have the sneaking suspicion he's not talking about stats anymore.

"Thanks, but I'm sure the professor can help if I have any questions," I say stiffly.

He shrugs before relaxing against his chair. "Up to you."

The way his eyes continue to pierce mine along with the soft cadence of his voice sends a delicate shiver racing down my spine.

Ryan takes that moment to break free from his conversation with Liam to say, "Babe, if JT wants to give you a little personal tutoring, you should take him up on it."

JT's smile grows in response.

I huff out a breath.

Why does it feel like everyone is conspiring against me?

CLAIRE

"Just call if you need anything, all right?" Anxiety threads its way through Gia's normally mellow voice as she presses one last kiss against Max's chubby cheek before sweeping a hand over his downy head. "We'll both have our cell phones on the entire time, so don't worry about interrupting anything. And we're sticking close to home. We won't be more than twenty minutes away. We can always cut the evening short if we have to. It's not a big deal."

My brother, who stands behind his wife, meets my gaze before slowly shaking his head and mouthing, *"Do not call."*

I rein in a gurgle of laughter and smirk before shifting my gaze to Gia. She's floating around the foyer like a high-strung butterfly. My heart goes out to her. This is the first time since Max was born that Liam has been able to convince her to go out for a date night. The only way he managed to do that was by planning the evening himself. He surprised her with reservations at her favorite restaurant and then a night out on the town. It was something she couldn't say no to.

They haven't even left the house yet, and already she looks stressed. I think Gia would grasp onto any flimsy excuse to cancel their plans and stay home. It's not very often that she leaves Max with anyone, and when she does, it's only with Liam.

Or me.

And it's more like thirty minutes.

An hour at the most.

"I just pumped, so there's fresh milk in the fridge if Max gets hungry." She glances at her watch. "He shouldn't need to eat for another two hours. I'm hoping he'll sleep the entire time we're gone. I tried to keep him up this afternoon."

Not only is Gia starting to ramble with her nervousness, but she's also wringing her hands. Max is fast asleep in my arms. He'll probably be sacked out until his next feeding, so watching the kids this evening should be a piece of cake. I'm not anticipating any major problems. I've been helping out with them since Ty was born.

I'm an old pro at this.

"Don't worry," I say with a smile. "I'll call if I have any problems or questions."

When her blue eyes lift to mine, I see the deep concern etched within them.

I can't take offense. I know how much she trusts me. Just as I know this is difficult for her. In one of my child development classes, we talked about separation anxiety. Seems like it goes both ways.

For parents as well as kids.

"I'm going to take good care of them, Gia." I show her Max. "See? He's already sleeping. I'll lay him down, and then I'll play a few games with Ty and Charlotte. We'll eat dinner, watch a show or two, and then it'll be off to bed. Everything will be fine. Promise."

Both the older kids are running around with their superhero stuff. Naturally, Charlotte has her own Wonder Woman paraphernalia. They don't seem to realize their parents are on the verge of walking out the door. Those two are way more interested in whacking each other with foam swords to care about anything else.

Another five minutes slides by before Liam wraps his arms around his wife and steers her gently toward the front door. "Come on, babe. Our reservation is in thirty minutes."

She worries her lower lip. "Are you sure you'll be all right?"

"I'll be fine. And I'll call or text if there are any problems. No worries. Really."

With a nod, Gia grabs her purse from the credenza in the front hall. It takes another five minutes for Liam to hustle her out the door. Once their truck is rolling down the drive, I drag in a breath before smiling down at Max, who is still sleeping soundly in my arms.

I should probably lay him down in his crib so the kids don't wake him. Ty and Charlotte are laughing and shouting as they run around the first floor. If I'm lucky, they'll tire themselves out and go down a little easier.

Even though Max is completely sacked out, I whisper, "We're going to have a good time tonight, aren't we, little man?" I can't resist giving him a soft kiss on the forehead. Just as I do, I hear a thwack and then loud, noisy tears. Ty comes running into the foyer holding his head. He searches the front entryway with watery eyes.

"Where's Mama?"

"Mama and Daddy left for dinner. Remember? They won't be gone long."

As soon as he realizes that his parents are no longer here, he cries even harder. By the sound of his voice, I can tell he's getting himself all wound up.

"Why don't you tell me what happened."

Tears continue to run down his face. "Charlotte hit me on the head with her sword!"

When I don't immediately respond with outrage, he adds indignantly, "*On purpose!*"

Max squirms in my arms before letting out a loud howl. I jostle him around, trying to bounce him back to sleep.

"Let me take care of Max, and then I'll look at your head, okay buddy? I think you're all right. Then I'll talk to Charlotte. Maybe you guys shouldn't play with the swords anymore."

"She's not supposed to hit me on the head." Then he yells, "Mama says no whacking each other on the noggins!"

A smile twitches around the corners of my lips. "That sounds like a pretty good rule." In an attempt to distract him, I say, "Go tell Charlotte that I'd like to talk with her." It's only then that I realize she's conspicuously absent. It's not uncommon for Charlotte to go into hiding when she knows that she's in trouble, which probably means she hit him on purpose.

His tears dry up as he races from the room. "Charlotte! You're in big trouble with Aunt Claire! *Charlooooooooootte!*"

As Ty's loud bellows echo off the walls, Max cries even harder. I shift him around, holding him against my shoulder all the while trying to bounce his small body because he seems to like that the most. Unfortunately, it does nothing to soothe him. After about five minutes, Ty runs back into the kitchen where I'm trying to calm the baby.

"I can't find Charlotte," he says breathlessly.

Even though my heart hitches at the news, I nod.

She does this.

I'm not going to freak out.

At least, not yet.

There's no way she could have snuck out.

But still...I want to find her.

Ty and I walk through the entire house while Max screams in my arms. We move from one room to another, checking each one as we go. Ty gets down on the floor, looking under each bed. We peer in all of the closets. There are five bedrooms on the second floor along with a playroom.

We don't find her anywhere.

"Charlotte," I call out, anxiety threading its way through my voice. "You need to come out now. You're not in trouble, sweetie."

Ty's dark brows snap together. "Yes, she is! She hit me." He points to the spot on his head. "She almost broke my brain."

I huff out a laugh. "She didn't break your brain, buddy. You're perfectly fine."

Very seriously he says, "She *almost* did."

"And I will definitely talk to her about that. But we need to find her first." As we head downstairs, I ask, "Any other ideas where she could be?"

He ponders the question for a minute. "In her closet?"

"We looked there. Anywhere else?"

He shakes his head.

The last thing I want to do is call Gia or Liam.

If Gia finds out that we can't find Charlotte, she'll have Liam turning the truck around before she's even off the phone with me, and I don't want to ruin their evening. But it's been fifteen minutes, and I still can't find her. And Max hasn't settled down like I'd hoped he would.

The doorbell rings, and Ty races toward the front entryway.

"Don't open the door until we know who it is!" I shout, unable to give chase with Max in my arms. "Ty?"

Even if he heard me, it's doubtful he'll listen.

By the time I make it to the entryway, Ty already has the front door flung open and is chattering away, proudly showing off his owie to whomever is on the other side.

"And then she hit me on my brain!" he grumbles.

I skid to a halt and find JT standing at the door. His hands are in Ty's thick hair, sifting around for a wound. He must sense my presence because his eyes immediately lift to mine.

"Seems like you're going to live to see another day," he tells Ty.

Max continues to wail in my arms.

"Charlotte's in big trouble. We can't find her."

JT's brows jerk together at that little bit of unsolicited information before he sends me a

questioning look. "Charlotte's missing?"

I suck in a deep breath and attempt to downplay the situation. "Sometimes she hides if she thinks she's in trouble." Hopefully, I can shoo JT out the door. Things are crazy enough as it is around here. The last thing I need is to add him into the mix.

He nods toward Max. "Is he okay?"

"Yeah." I glance at the squalling infant before laying a gentle kiss on his head. I hate to admit that my nerves are starting to fray. The kids are usually so good. But Gia is always here, and she has a way of handling them. "I think he's just overtired. Gia kept him up so that he'd sleep when I got here."

Since JT hasn't budged, I try to hasten his departure by adding, "Liam and Gia aren't here. I'm babysitting." I step toward the door, ready to shut it in his face. "I'll be sure to let my brother know you stopped by."

With a frown, he eyes the crying baby who is now squirming in my arms. "Maybe I should stay. You look like you could use some help getting things back under control."

Even though it feels like all hell is breaking loose, I say with a bit of a snap, "Everything's fine. I can handle it on my own."

This man is the last person I want to accept assistance from. Didn't he get that the other night when he offered to help me with stats?

I don't like the way he makes me feel. I'd rather contend with the situation by myself than spend time alone with him.

Instead of taking the hint, JT raises a brow.

I'm starting to really hate it when he does that.

"How long has it been since you've seen Charlotte?"

My teeth sink into my lower lip.

Fine…Point taken.

Apparently, I don't have any other options at the moment.

I can either allow JT to help with the kids.

Or I can call Liam and Gia.

Conceding to him feels suspiciously like rubbing salt in an open wound.

And by the look in his eyes, he damn well knows it.

Grrrr.

JT

Claire might not want me here, but right now, she *needs* me.

And you know what?

I'm going to take full advantage of that situation.

"Why don't you take Max up to his room and try to get him to sleep while Ty and I look for Charlotte." As much as she hates the idea of me being helpful, I can see the relief that floods her gray eyes as I take control of the situation. "I'm sure by the time you get him down, we'll have found her."

Indecision flickers across her face before she capitulates. With a nod, she takes Max upstairs to his room.

I can't resist watching the sway of her hips as she walks up the curved staircase in the front entryway. Once she reaches the landing, she hesitates and spears me with a glance. It's one that reveals the inner turmoil that burns through her where I'm concerned. I picked up on the undercurrents of it the other night at dinner. Our eyes lock and hold for a beat or two before she disappears down the hallway on the second floor.

That one look arrows unexpectedly through the heart of me.

What is it about Claire Garrison?

I've never had a woman affect me this way.

47

Unable to dwell on my feelings for her, I glance at Ty, who stands at my side.

"All right, little man. Let's go find your sister."

It takes ten minutes before we find Charlotte curled up, sleeping behind the couch in the playroom. It was her slight snores that alerted us to the fact that she was there. I scoop up her small body and carry her downstairs. Within a few seconds, she wakes up in my arms. Her brows draw together as she blinks big blue eyes at me in confusion.

"Heard you've been a naughty girl," I say teasingly.

A tiny smile curves her lips as she buries her face against the hollow of my neck. Her warm breath feathers against me before I set her down carefully on the couch in the family room. Since I can still hear Max wailing from the second floor, I know Claire won't be down anytime soon.

It makes me doubly glad I stuck around to help.

"All right, guys. What should we do now?"

Charlotte lifts her head, jet black curls tumbling around her face, before pointing a tiny finger at the eighty-inch TV mounted to the wall above the stacked-stone fireplace. "Georgie!"

With a frown, I look to Ty for clarification.

Who the hell is Georgie?

"*Curious George,*" he says as if I should already know this.

As if *everyone* and their mother knows this.

"Okay." I grab the remote from the coffee table and flick on the TV. "Do you know what channel it's on?"

"Mama records them."

"That certainly makes things easier, doesn't it?"

I press 'Recordings' and a shitload of *Curious George* shows pop up. I click one, and within seconds, the cheerful theme music fills the family room.

Since it's right around five o'clock, I ask, "Did Aunt Claire feed you guys dinner?"

Charlotte seems physically incapable of ripping her gaze away from the television screen. She appears to be in some kind of monkey-induced coma even though her eyes are wide open.

I'm not going to lie, it's a little disturbing. Although, I do like that they're both quiet and staying put. It's doubtful I'd score any points with Claire if I lose one of them before she makes it downstairs again.

Ty shakes his head as I scratch mine, considering the possibilities.

I have no idea how long Claire will be upstairs with Max. I can still hear him howling angrily. As much as I want to help, I have zero experience with babies. Actually, I have zero experience with kids. I'm kind of flying by the seat of my pants here. My guess is that I should probably hold down the fort until reinforcements arrive.

I head to the fridge and open the bottom freezer door before rummaging around.

Hmmm.

What do kids like to eat?

Better question—*what do kids like to eat that I can actually prepare?*

I hit pay dirt and pull out a bag of organic frozen chicken fingers along with smiley fries.

Definite winner.

I walk back into the family room and hold up a bag in each hand. "Who wants chicken fingers and fries?"

They both cheer.

Chicken fingers and smiley fries it is.

I set the oven and dig through the cabinets until I find a cookie sheet to dump a quarter of each bag onto it. When the oven dings, I shove the silver pan inside and set the timer before heading back to the family room.

Interestingly enough, neither has moved a muscle since I turned on the show. I glance at the TV screen. There's a little monkey who looks to be causing mischief. And the narrator...damn, but he has a soothing voice.

"Good show?" I ask.

Neither answers.

They're completely riveted.

It's kind of crazy.

And a bit scary.

Not necessarily in that order.

I take a seat and watch the monkey wreak havoc wherever he goes as the man in the yellow hat frantically tries to clean up after him. It seems like only a few minutes have slipped by when the timer goes off.

With a frown, I wonder if I didn't set it right. I'm barely able to rip my attention away from the TV as I head into the kitchen to check out how the chicken and fries are coming along. I peek in the oven and am surprised to find that they're done.

Awesome.

I grab two oven mitts and pull the metal sheet from the oven before setting it on top of the stove. As I wait for it to cool, I grab two plates before divvying up the chicken and fries. I'm wondering if maybe we should eat at the kitchen table but…

Then we can't watch the rest of the show.

Actually, we're already on the second episode.

Don't tell anyone this, but I'm kind of liking this little monkey dude.

He's hilarious.

Making an executive decision, I carry their plates into the family room and set them down on the coffee table.

"Okay guys, we're going to have a little picnic dinner."

Charlotte and Ty's eyes light up as they pull themselves up to the table before digging in. Ten minutes later, they've finished eating and are back to sitting on the couch watching George. We've just wrapped up the third show.

When it finally ends, the pair look expectantly at me.

"Another one?" I ask.

They nod in unison.

I'm so into this monkey show that I don't notice when Claire makes it back downstairs. It's the sound of her voice that finally penetrates the George-induced haze that's fallen over me.

"You fed the kids?"

George is doing something crazy, and I find myself unable to rip my eyes away from his amusing monkey shenanigans.

"Um, yeah. I thought they might be hungry."

There's a moment of silence before she asks, "Are you actually watching *Curious George?*" Bemusement is riddled throughout her voice.

"I'm not going to lie, it's completely addictive," I admit with a sheepish smile.

She settles next to the kids on the couch.

They've yet to even glance at her.

"Yup, they love it."

"I can see why. That narrator's voice is like taking a Xanax."

She chuckles. "Pretty much. Why do you think Gia has so many of them recorded?"

It finally occurs to me that Claire—the same Claire Garrison who has made it completely obvious how much she hates my guts—is actually laughing in my presence.

All right, it might not be a full out laugh, but it's damn close. And it's because of something that came out of my mouth.

It takes a Herculean effort, but I tear my gaze away from the show to meet hers. Something prickles to life at the bottom of my gut at the smile that tilts her lips.

I clear my throat. "Gia's a smart woman. I'm going to have to find out when this show is on, so I can watch it."

Not only does the smile tremble on her lips, it blooms into a full blown one.

And I love it.

"JT Higgins watching *Curious George.*" She shakes her head. Her thick, mahogany-colored hair drifts around her shoulders. "Now that I would like to see."

Unconsciously, my body strains toward hers. The little monkey on the TV screen is now totally forgotten. "I can arrange that."

Those softly murmured words have the grin falling off her face.

In hindsight, I probably shouldn't have said that, but I can't help myself where Claire is concerned. Wariness fills her eyes. The guarded expression is one I've come to expect from her. I could really kick my own ass for putting it back on her face again.

She breaks eye contact, glancing at her niece and nephew before clearing her throat. Her voice becomes formal, as if we're nothing more than strangers. "Thanks for feeding them. It was really helpful."

Instead of continuing to move forward, I've sent us tumbling back.

"It wasn't a problem," I say, willing her to look my way again. There's something about having those liquid gray eyes focused on me that I enjoy.

The need to put her at ease again thrums through me. "Max is finally down?"

That's when I notice the exhaustion seep into her eyes. "Yeah. I think he's just overtired. Once he closed his eyes, he was out like a light. I'll have to wake him to eat in a little while, but hopefully, he'll go right back to sleep again until Gia and Liam return."

After a moment of silence, she says haltingly, almost as if it's difficult to wrap her lips around the words, "Thanks again for all your help."

"Ouch." I pretend to wince, unable to stop myself from teasing her. "That sounded painful."

Even though her eyes narrow, a tiny smile simmers around her lips. "You have no idea."

"Oh, I can imagine. Normally, you can barely tolerate being in the same room with me."

Heat ignites in her cheeks as she glances away.

"That's not true," she mumbles.

I hoot with laughter. "Come on, Claire. You can be honest. We both know I'm one of your least favorite people."

She picks at an invisible thread on her jeans before spearing me with her gorgeous gray depths. "Fine, I'll admit it. You're not exactly one of my favorite people." The look she sends me is rife with challenge. "Happy now?"

Am I happy that she's admitted to disliking me?

No, not really. It only confirms what I've suspected for years.

Instead of answering her question, I say, "This is probably the first full-on conversation we've ever had."

She falls silent before shrugging. "Every time we ran into each other, you acted like a jerk. I guess we never had much to talk about."

"You're right. I was a jerk."

Surprise flashes across her face before her brows slant together as if she's turning something over in her head.

When she remains silent, I prod, "Go ahead. Just say it."

She tucks her feet beneath her. The position makes her look younger than she is.

"Why were you always…" Her voice trails off as if she's unsure how to phrase what she wants to ask.

I see the question filling her inquisitive eyes.

"Asking you to come home with me?"

Claire glances sharply at her niece and nephew to make sure they're fully engaged in the show before jerking her head in a tight nod.

I draw in a breath and give her question some consideration before folding my hands behind my head and stretching out. Even though I might look relaxed, I'm not. My muscles are coiled tight.

"I've always been attracted to you. I guess I went about trying to get your attention the wrong way."

A heavy silence falls over us as she steadily holds my gaze. Nerves hum in the pit of my gut. I'm a twenty-five-year-old man, and I've never told a woman that I liked her or was attracted to her.

I don't want to sound like a jackass, but I never had to. Ever since I hit puberty, females have gravitated to me. I've never felt the urge to tie myself down to a specific one. Back in high school, I was too busy trying to piss my father off. Plus, what was the point in getting attached when I was leaving in a few years?

Maybe I was unwilling to open myself up to anyone else hurting me. I got enough of that from my parents.

In college, I was focused on making my way to the pros, having a good time, and finally being free of my father. I didn't slack off at school. Even though Claire has been operating under the assumption that all I did was party, I graduated from college with a three-point-seven grade point average.

There was never time for relationships, and I didn't have any

interest. Then, I returned to Green Bay and back to my parents'
realm.

If I'd thought that I partied a lot in college, it was nothing
compared to what it was like after the move. There were too many
people rolling out the VIP treatment and too many beautiful women
throwing themselves at me.

Claire is the first woman I've found myself interested in. And that
attraction hasn't waned in the three years I've known her. If anything,
it's only intensified.

Our eyes hold as something shifts in the air. It doesn't take long
for the tension to become palpable.

"Auntie Claire, will you read me a story?" Ty asks.

I catch her swift intake of breath, as if she's relieved at the timely
interruption. Instead of responding to what I've just admitted, her
gaze cuts away from mine and settles on her nephew. "Of course. Why
don't you run upstairs and pick out a few books."

He jumps off the couch and takes off. It doesn't take long for his
feet to pound up the back staircase before thumping down again with
a thick stack of books he can barely hold in his arms. He curls up on
her lap and hands her the first one. As she opens the book, Charlotte
migrates to her other side.

Now that they've lost interest in the show, I click off the TV. For
the next thirty minutes, Claire reads story after story. I sit in the chair
across from them, mesmerized by the way she uses her voice to insert
inflection and suspense into each book.

Barely can I take my eyes off her.

She's really great with Charlotte and Ty. It's obvious how much
they love her.

By the time she plows her way through the stack of books, it's
almost eight o'clock. Claire ruffles their hair before telling them it's
time to head upstairs, brush their teeth, and go to bed. Just as they all
rise to their feet, Max squawks through the baby monitor.

"Why don't you take care of Max, and I'll get these two settled in
bed?"

The grateful smile she flashes arrows clean through me as she beelines to the kitchen and pulls a bottle from the fridge to warm.

I clap my hands together as my gaze bounces between the pair. "All right you two, let's get moving."

They race up the back staircase to their rooms. Once they've brushed their teeth and I'm shown their pearly whites to inspect, I hustle their little butts into bed. They cajole me into reading one more story, as if they haven't heard enough, and then I tuck them in. As I'm about to head back downstairs to wait for Claire, Charlotte reappears in the hallway.

"I have to go potty."

"Umm, okay."

She scrambles to the bathroom. After a moment or two, she's back again before giving me an adorable smile and asking if I'll tuck her in.

How am I supposed to say no to a face like that?

The answer is that I can't. So, I follow her into the room and tuck her back into bed.

This girl is going to be real trouble when she's older. I say goodnight again. Just as I head to the staircase, Ty steps into the hallway.

"I'm thirsty. Can I have a drink of water?"

With a nod, we head to the bathroom, and I fill up a small glass with about two inches of water. Giving him more than that seems like a bad idea. Afterward, I walk him back to his room and tuck him in all over again.

This time, I silently wait in the hall for a few minutes to make sure neither of them are going to pop out of bed. Just when I think it's safe to head downstairs, Charlotte makes another reappearance.

"I need water, too."

When I give her a hard look, she bats her big blue eyes. They may not be the same color as Claire's, but they still remind me of her. It doesn't take long for me to fold like a cheap house of cards.

"All right," I grumble. "But this is it. No more getting out of bed. Got it, short stack?"

She flashes me a grin.

Once she's re-settled, I wait another five minutes before creeping down the staircase and collapsing on an overstuffed chair. These kids are exhausting. Not that I've been thinking about having children anytime soon, but the last twenty minutes have me seriously contemplating the merits of a vasectomy.

No lie.

As the silence settles around me, I hear the soft strains of Claire singing. It takes a moment to realize that it's coming from the baby monitor in the kitchen. Everything within me stills as I lean back and close my eyes, listening to the melody float through the device. Once her voice trails off, I hear a door open and close on the second floor before she pads down the stairs.

I've been asking myself for three years what it is about her that gets to me. As of yet, I haven't been able to come up with an answer. I just know there's something about Claire Garrison that has ensnared me. When I'm around her, all I want to be is closer. I want her to look at me with something other than disgust and disdain in her wide gray eyes.

Today is the first time that's happened in the three years I've known her. As that thought rolls around in my head, another occurs to me.

I don't want tonight to end.

I don't want to leave and see her again only to have everything shift back to the way it's always been between us.

Just as she reaches the last tread, our gazes catch, and she halts in her tracks. "I wasn't sure if you were going to stick around or not."

JT

*D*id she seriously think I was just going to slink off into the night?

No way.

She should know me better than that.

I shrug, wanting to dispel some of the tension that has gathered in the atmosphere. "Just wanted to make sure everything was okay."

She nods before her feet start moving again. Almost guardedly, her eyes watch mine as she perches on the edge of the couch across the room. She weaves her fingers together in front of her as if not quite sure what to do with them.

"Thanks again for all your help."

I shrug. "Like I said before, it wasn't a problem. Actually, I enjoyed it."

She glances away before shifting on the couch. "I'm sure you have plans. If you want to take off, that's cool. I think all three of them are down for the night."

"Nope," I say quickly. "I don't have anything going on." I clear my throat, hoping this doesn't turn into some kind of epic fail. "I was thinking we could watch a movie." Before she can respond, I tack on, "That way, if Max gets up again and there's an issue with Charlotte or

Ty, I'll be here to give you a hand." A smile curls around the edges of my lips. "I don't know how Gia does it all day long by herself. Those three are definitely a handful."

Surprise fills Claire's eyes as they slice back to mine as her mouth hitches. "I think it's better now that Ty's in school. Once Max is a little older, it won't be so bad."

I arch a brow.

Is she forgetting that we couldn't find Charlotte for a solid twenty-five minutes?

Or that Max was wailing earlier for almost an hour?

Easier my ass...

Those three should come with a warning label or something, so you know exactly what you're getting into. They may look angelic, but they'll definitely give you a run for your money.

"If your brother has his way, there'll be another Garrison joining the ranks in about a year and a half."

When Claire bursts out laughing, I can't help but grin in response.

I really love when she smiles.

Especially at me.

Admittedly, it's not very often.

"Yeah, he mentioned that to me, too. He loves having a big family. I think he'd have as many kids as Gia's willing to give him."

I like Claire when she's like this. Smiling and laughing. Eyes sparkling with humor. Relaxed with her guard lowered. I don't want to do anything that will ruin the moment. This has to be the first time she's not straight up dismissing me.

Or pretending I don't exist.

It doesn't take long for her face to sober, and a shield falls over her eyes as uncertainty flickers across her expression. "You don't have to stick around. I'm sure this whole domesticated thing is a huge bore."

"Have I looked bored at all this evening?"

Of course, I'm going to attribute that to the hooligans now sacked out upstairs. Tonight has been oddly enjoyable. Trust me, I'm equally surprised by the realization.

I've spent the last seven years going out, being surrounded by groupies, fans, and so-called friends. Hanging out in nightclubs and at rowdy parties. Even before I turned twenty-one, I had no problem getting in wherever I wanted. VIP rooms with models and actresses hanging on my every word. The fights that would inevitably break out. Dudes who just wanted to goad me into throwing a punch so they could have their fifteen minutes of fame by loading a video onto the internet before threatening to sue me for pretty much nothing. The paparazzi looking for me to do something crazy or illegal so they could sell their pictures to the highest bidder. Not to mention the hangovers and waking up with random women in my bed the next morning.

That lifestyle might have been a blast in the beginning, but it isn't all it's cracked up to be. It gets old fast. Not to mention expensive. It's like you're always trying to up the ante to get the same kind of rush. It doesn't take long to realize that even though there are all these people around you, you're still alone.

Isolated.

The GM hauling my ass into his office at the end of last season was probably the best thing that could have happened to me. It forced me to take a hard look at what I'd been doing and finally get my shit together or risk losing everything I'd spent years working for.

I've been walking the straight and narrow since last February.

I haven't had a drop of liquor since then. And I've never been one to mess around with drugs. Not even steroids. I've never touched the shit. I believe in getting big the old-fashioned way—by making gains in the weight room. Plus, working out has always been an outlet for me.

I haven't stepped foot in a club since the playoffs last year.

And the women?

I haven't been with one in months. Being hung up on one specific girl kind of ruins all the others for you.

When she remains silent, I add, "I could really use a movie night. You know, just chill out for a while."

There's a contemplative look on her face. It's obvious that she's conflicted. We've never spent any time alone together. And without the kids and their chaos acting as a buffer, it's just the two of us.

There's nothing more for me to do than sit on the edge of my seat and wait for her to make a decision.

Is she going to kick my ass out or let me stay?

I'm sweating bullets over here.

"I guess," she murmurs as if she's still not convinced this is a good idea. "If you really want to."

My muscles loosen. "I do." The words shoot out of my mouth before I can rein them in. Obviously needing to dial it down a bit and act more chill about the situation, I add as if us hanging out is an everyday occurrence, "It'll be fun."

Claire levels me with a dubious expression.

Can't exactly say I blame her for it.

She picks up the remote from the coffee table and tosses it to me. My gaze never releases hers as I catch it with one hand. With a smirk, she rolls her eyes. That move seems to break the escalating tension between us.

"Why don't you pick out the movie and I'll make a bowl of popcorn." She hops up from the couch and heads into the kitchen.

I nod and turn on the TV, pressing 'Demand' to see what new movies have been released.

Hmmm.

This is going to be tricky.

Can't go with anything that has a lot of nudity because I don't want to make Claire feel uncomfortable. So, we'll definitely forego any adult movies this evening. And I'm not going to pick anything too gruesome, since I have no idea how squeamish she is.

Now...I could go with a chick flick, but I'm not sure if that seems too date-night. I don't want her to think that I think this is a date, even though—depending on how this evening turns out—that's *exactly* what I plan to consider it.

That leaves a good, old-fashioned psychological thriller.

Yup, I think that fits the bill rather nicely.

I rattle off the name of something that looks brand spanking new.

"Is it out already?" she asks from the kitchen. "I've been dying to see that. I didn't get a chance when it was in the theater."

I almost pump a fist in the air but somehow manage to restrain myself.

Houston, we have liftoff.

I repeat—we have liftoff.

Claire carries two large bowls of popcorn as she returns to the family room. Handing one to me, she sets hers down on the coffee table before heading back into the kitchen.

"What do you want to drink?"

"Water's fine."

Now that I'm not drinking alcohol, I'm more conscious about what I put into my body. I'm not as fanatical as some of the dudes on my team who are into the whole *my body is a temple and I treat it thusly*, but I am trying to be more conscious about what I stuff in my piehole.

That's a start, right?

But I'll make an exception tonight for popcorn.

Returning for a second time, she hands me a bottle of water before picking up her bowl and settling on the couch.

I don't think I've ever seen her look so comfortable in my presence, which is precisely why I keep my ass firmly glued to the chair I'm sitting on and don't try setting myself up over there. Even though I would much rather be sitting next to her, that's not going to happen.

Clearly, we need to ease into this relationship.

And I can do that.

I can take this slowly.

I had no idea when I headed over here this evening to discuss some team bullshit with Liam that Claire would be watching the kids. We're talking total jackpot score. Even better, her boyfriend is conspicuously absent.

Double jackpot.

Once she's settled, I hit play.

We're both quiet as the movie unfolds. Although, I have to admit that my attention is distracted throughout the entire film. Claire, on the other hand, is completely immersed.

I give myself another pat on the back for choosing the movie. It was a good pick on my part.

When Max squawks mid-way through, I hit pause while she runs up and checks on him. Luckily, he settles back down within moments, and we're able to get through the flick. By the time the credits roll, I could tell you the general plot, but the finer details are lost on me because I was too distracted to get into it.

As I click off the TV, her cell rings. She picks it up and glances at the screen before her gaze jerks to mine. Then, she leaps off the couch and beelines to the kitchen. I can tell by the tone of her voice exactly who's on the other end. It takes less than three minutes for her to wrap up their convo.

How do I know this?

For starters, I keep glancing at my phone, checking the time. I'm also doing my damnedest to eavesdrop on their conversation. The only thing I can be completely sure of is that she didn't say 'I love you' before disconnecting, which is a huge relief.

This is something I can work with.

My gaze cuts to hers as she returns to the family room. After a silent moment, it becomes obvious that she isn't going to mention the call.

As much as I'd love to play this cool, the question flies out of my mouth. "Was that the boyfriend?"

Too late do I realize the course of our evening has been irreversibly derailed by those four words. An invisible shield, one I've become all too familiar with over the last three years, slams into place.

I could seriously kick my own ass for opening my big trap.

"Yeah, he was hoping I'd be done babysitting by now."

The logical part of my brain understands that I should let the conversation drop, but I can't.

Holding the questions back feels impossible.

"Did you mention that you've had company?"

Something flares in her eyes before she glances away. She presses her lips together and doesn't say a word, which tells me everything I need to know. I'm fairly confident that if she had mentioned I was here, he'd already be on his way over so he could continue yapping my damn ear off.

"I'll take that as a no," I say.

She crosses her arms tightly against her chest before glaring. "You helped out with the kids. That's it."

I point to the TV. "We just watched a movie together."

Fuck.

I seriously don't know when to shut my damn mouth.

Color floods her face. It's just another sign that I've totally messed this night up.

"You stopped by to see Liam and then stayed to help with the kids. We watched a movie and hung out." Her voice flattens. "It was nothing more than that."

"You're right," I concede. "It was nothing more."

Contrary to what it looks like, I'm not trying to start an argument. The time we've spent together tonight is more than what we've spent collectively in the three years I've known her. So, I'm not looking to undo all the painstaking progress I've made this evening.

That being said, I have a few points to make about the tool she's dating.

"You realize that you can do better than him, right?"

Surprise flickers across her face before her expression morphs into anger. "Excuse me? You don't even know Ryan."

"Trust me," I say with a snort. "I've seen more than enough to know exactly the type of guy he is." Since I haven't dug a deep enough grave for myself, I tack on, "All the guy does is talk about himself."

"He's just nervous around you guys. He was trying too hard to impress you, that's all," she says through gritted teeth.

What I can't tell is if she believes the excuses she's feeding me or not. "You know what? He shouldn't be worried about impressing anyone other than *you*."

Silence descends as she scowls before giving her head a little shake as if to clear it. "My relationship is none of your business." She tosses a hand up in the air and adds, "I certainly don't involve myself in yours."

"I'm not involved in any relationships."

"Fine." She sucks in a deep breath as she continues to glare from across the room. There's a frigidness to both her eyes and voice. "You won't hear anything from me regarding whoever it is you're currently sleeping with."

"I'm not sleeping with anyone, Claire." My gaze stays pinned to hers as I lean forward, wanting to somehow get closer. "In fact, I haven't slept with anyone in months."

"Why are you telling me this?" she whispers.

I shrug, but there's nothing casual about the gesture. "Just want you to know."

It's as if every muscle has gone on high alert. She looks like a star-tled animal whose fight or flight instinct has kicked in a little too late.

"Why?"

"Because there's only one woman I'm interested in sleeping with, and half the time, I think she hates me," I say honestly, tired of holding back the truth.

As soon as the last word falls from my lips, it feels as if all the oxygen has been sucked from the room.

The silence that engulfs us turns even more stifling before she whispers in a strangled voice, "It's way more than half the time."

My lips bow up at the corners. "Yeah, I figured. I was just hoping you'd be too polite to point it out."

The anger of moments ago drains, leaving confusion in its place. "You shouldn't be telling me any of this. I have a boyfriend."

"He's not right for you."

"And you are?" she asks with a scoff. "Is that what you're trying to tell me? The guy who's *never* been in a relationship? The one who quickly moves on to the next warm, willing body?"

In the past?

Yup, that's *exactly* how I operated.

I've never wanted the complication of a relationship to deal with, but there's something about Claire. No woman has ever been stuck in my head. And certainly not for three damn years. The funny thing is, I knew right from the start that she was unlike anyone else I'd met. I also knew I wanted to get closer to her. I spent all this time trying to do exactly that. Only now do I realize that I kept going about it the wrong way. Even though I knew she was different, I kept approaching her as if she wasn't.

Instead of answering her questions, because there's nothing I can say that she'll believe, I change the subject. "Have you slept with him yet?"

Her eyes flare as her mouth tumbles open. It wouldn't surprise me one bit if she threw my ass right out of the house.

But she doesn't.

In fact, she doesn't move a single muscle. She just stares at me in shock.

I realize that she's embarrassed by the question.

"That's none of your business," she finally snaps.

That response doesn't stop me from digging deeper.

My grave, that is.

"Have you ever slept with *anyone* before?"

After listening to what Liam had to say on the subject, although granted he doesn't know everything about his sister's personal life, I'm willing to bet that she's still a virgin. At this point, I want—no, I *need*—to hear her say the words.

A dull blush scalds her cheekbones as she clenches her teeth.

She really does look beautiful all flushed and angry. Then again, Claire always looks beautiful.

"I'm not answering that."

Guilt pricks at me for pushing so hard. "It's nothing to be ashamed of."

"I'm not," she bites out. "It's just none of your business whether I have or not."

With a tilt of my head, I study her. "Is he pushing you to have sex with him?"

I swear to fucking god that I'll beat the shit out of the little punk if that turns out to be the case.

Hands bunched, she leaps off the couch. Her body is whipcord tight as she shakes with anger. Even though I'm the one who's upset her with my questions, the urge to take her into my arms and soothe her thrums through me.

"I refuse to have this conversation with you." She jerks her chin toward the front entrance of the house. "You should leave."

I rise to my feet and stalk toward her. She's probably right. I should walk my ass right out the door so I can salvage a few remnants of this evening.

But I can't stop myself from advancing.

Even more than that, I don't want to.

For the first time in three years, it feels like everything between us is finally out in the open. And there's no way I'm going to walk away from that.

Or from her.

CLAIRE

It only takes a few steps until he's standing in front of me.

Until there's no more than a foot of space to separate us. Even from here, I feel the thick waves of tension that radiate off him. The barely suppressed power harnessed within him.

I hate it.

Hate how much he's able to affect me without ever touching me.

It's been this way from the very beginning.

From the first moment he captured my fingers in his larger ones and shook my hand, his eyes piercing mine, staring unabashedly until my skin flushed with heat and color. Even though I've spent years trying to tamp it down, the feelings continue to simmer beneath the surface as if they're just waiting for a chance to break free.

All it takes is one look flicked in my direction to breathe new life into it.

It's the reason I've always gone to great lengths to avoid being near him.

There's something about JT that pulls at me, even though it's the last thing I want.

The man is ridiculously tall.

Taller than most.

He sticks out in a crowd. I never have any trouble unconsciously seeking him out when we're thrown together for an event. Plus, he's usually surrounded by females.

They adore him.

When he stands this close, invading my personal space, I have to raise my chin just a bit to hold his eyes as they drill into me.

The sheer breadth of his shoulders is impressive. He gives new meaning to the words "well-defined" and "sculpted, sinewy muscle". All those hard slabs of strength rippling and tensing. My belly flutters just thinking about it.

And don't get me started on the tousled blond waves…

Have I been tempted to sift my fingers through the silky-soft strands a time or two?

Yup.

Would I actually do it?

No way. I'm much too afraid of where it would lead.

I think every woman in America has probably had a fantasy of JT Higgins somersault through their heads.

But that's all it is.

That's all it will *ever* be.

I'm admiring something pretty.

A gorgeous specimen.

A handsome face.

Amazing pectorals and biceps.

Thickly corded thigh muscles and tight glutes.

I have zero intention of doing anything about the persistent thoughts that have been invading my brain with more frequency.

To get involved with JT would be the very definition of insane. He's a womanizer. A heartbreaker.

I've been around long enough to know that JT Higgins will never change.

Why should he?

Plus, the man rubs me the wrong way.

He has right from the start.

He thinks he's god's gift to the female species and I don't have time for that.

So, when he tells me that he hasn't slept with someone in months and that he wants *me*, of course my heartbeat stutters and hitches at the idea. What woman wouldn't want to hear those words fall from his full, sexy lips?

The real question is, *do I believe him?*

That would be a negative, Ghost Rider.

For him to saunter in here tonight, lower my defenses by helping out with the kids, and be so damn cute about it before feeding me a line of bullshit really pisses me off.

His deep voice breaks into the chaotic whirl of my thoughts.

"You never answered my question," he says.

I draw in a deep breath before slowly forcing it out again, all the while trying to get a firm handle on my emotions.

"Actually, you asked several, and I told you that I wasn't going to answer any of them."

His hand rises to settle beneath my chin. The gentleness of his touch is something of a surprise. You would expect someone with such large hands and who uses them to crush their opponents on a weekly basis to be much rougher. Maybe a little unaware of their own power and strength.

But he's not.

His touch is possessive yet tender. And I hate the way it makes my heart hammer with new awareness. I hate that my first impulse is to close my eyes before sinking into his touch. I should be pulling away and distancing myself, not thinking about what it would be like to get closer.

"My guess is that you're still a virgin. I don't like the idea that he might be pressuring you to do something you're not ready for."

When I open my mouth to protest, he cuts me off.

"I'm not trying to embarrass you. I think you should be proud of the fact that you've waited. That you want it to be with the right person."

I can't help but snort, because it doesn't feel like an amazing achievement. More like a hindrance. One I'm ready to relinquish.

"And when did you lose your virginity?" I ask. "Hmmm?" I'm willing to bet it was a while ago. Maybe when he was sixteen or seventeen?

Or god forbid, younger.

For a long moment, he remains silent. His eyes pin mine in place until it's impossible to breathe. "I wish I'd waited for someone special, but I didn't. There's been a long string of nobody specials in my life."

Even though his words have something delicate fluttering to life within me, I squash it down before muttering, "So what you're really saying is that all you've done is sleep around, and yet you're now trying to tell me not to have sex with someone I've been going out with for two months?"

His answer is swift and to the point. A growl fills his voice and vibrates through his chest.

"That's *exactly* what I'm telling you. He doesn't deserve something so special."

"It's not special," I snap.

He sobers. "It's more precious than you know."

Frustration bubbles up inside me that I've been dragged unwillingly into a discussion regarding my sex life. "It's not your decision to make, JT. It's mine."

"True." His eyes darken before dropping to my lips. "But I can give you something to think about, can't I?"

Before I can figure out what that means, his mouth settles over mine. I press my lips firmly together, knowing that I'll be lost if I give in to him. He pulls away as his deep chuckle hits my ears before his mouth is back, exploring with a renewed energy.

When that doesn't get him what he wants, he nips and licks at my flesh until he's devouring it. Devouring me until I can't stand a single moment more. Until I open for him so that his tongue can slip inside my mouth to mingle with my own.

His other hand snakes around me so he can cradle the back of my head in his palm, and I'm anchored to him. Any moment, he'll plunder my mouth. I wait for it, prepared to fight him, but it never happens.

Instead, it's all slow and sensual strokes of his velvety soft tongue against mine. Every once in a while, he tilts his head, shifting our positions. I have no idea how long we stand pressed together, our lips teasing and savoring one another.

It takes me a while to realize that my arms are entwined around his neck, and my breasts are flattened against his muscular chest.

He licks at my mouth again before drawing away and searching my eyes. "Unless he can put that look on your face, he has no business being with you."

Just as he's about to step away, he mutters something under his breath and his lips crash back down on mine.

This kiss is everything the first one wasn't.

This one is forceful and intense.

It's exactly how I imagined JT would kiss. It feels as if I'm being plundered in the best way possible.

There is no pretending that I don't want it.

Because I do.

I don't think I've ever wanted anything more.

His lips, teeth and tongue ravage me until every thought whirling through my head vanishes and I'm lost in a sea of churning desire. When he finally rips himself away for a second time, my trembling fingers drift to my swollen lips as my gaze rises to his.

"Here's a bit of unsolicited advice—when you finally give yourself to someone, make sure they're worthy of you. And unless they can put that look on your face, don't even bother with them."

When I remain silent, he says in a more conversational tone, "I'll show myself out now."

The front door opens and then closes softly behind him. For a long moment, I stand rooted in place as everything that happened swirls madly through my head. It's only when Max makes a few noises through the baby monitor in the kitchen that the spell JT wove around me dissipates and I release a shaky breath.

CLAIRE

I don't bother to check out the black menu board written in chalk behind the counter, since I drop in this coffee shop most mornings and order the same thing each time.

"I'll have a latte with a shot of vanilla, please."

"Make that two, thanks," a deep voice says.

Recognition slams into me as I spin around, surprised to find JT. Before I can do or say anything, he hands a twenty to the barista.

"Keep the change."

She scrutinizes his face before her eyes widen almost comically. Even with a ball cap pulled low over his forehead, his piercing green eyes are impossible to conceal. Not to mention his trademark blond hair.

Plus, the guy is ridiculously massive. Broad in the shoulders and taller than everyone around him. One glance would make you suspect that he was a professional athlete of some sort. It's his sheer size, along with the way he carries himself.

Excitement grows in her voice as she presses closer to the counter as if she's contemplating a crawl across the surface in order to reach him.

"Aren't you JT Higgins? *Ohmygod.*" Her words are all smushed together, barely distinguishable. "*Itotallyloveyou! Youremyabsolutefavoriteplayer!*"

Amused by the situation, I watch the exchange unfold. It's a surprise when he shakes his head in denial. I thought for sure he'd eat this kind of thing up.

The man is a total attention whore, right?

"Sorry, darling. Not me." He gives her a little wink to soften the blow. "But I get that all the time."

Her eyes narrow as if she's trying to decide if he's telling the truth.

"You're really not him?" she asks, voice filled with disappointment.

An apologetic expression settles on his face.

Sort of.

"Nope."

"Oh." Her shoulders fall as she deflates before our very eyes. Without another word, she turns to the next customer in line and dismisses us.

JT slips an arm around my waist and steers me off to the side, away from the long line of customers, some of whom heard the brief exchange and are now eyeing him with piqued interest. He tugs the brim of his hat a bit lower as if that will make a difference.

His gaze stays pinned to mine. The heat of it never fails to set my nerves on edge, making me ridiculously aware of him.

It's disconcerting.

"What are you doing here?" I ask, pulse racing.

I haven't seen him since Saturday night, and quite frankly, I'd rather not think about that humiliating conversation ever again.

Or the kiss we shared.

If I'm being honest with myself, I haven't been able to get either one out of my head. My plan had been to avoid him indefinitely.

"I was in the area," he says with a shrug.

I raise a brow. "Really?"

This particular coffee shop is about midway between my apartment and campus. I stop here every day before heading to school, and not once have I run into JT. It's nowhere near his house or the stadium where he practices.

He flashes a smile and something unwanted pings at the bottom of my belly. I quickly tamp it down.

"Sure."

When our order comes up, JT grabs both drinks before nodding toward a small table buried in the back corner.

"Do you have a few minutes to talk?"

I glance at my cell phone. Class starts in about forty-five minutes.

"Yeah, but not much." After what happened Saturday night, I can only imagine what he wants to discuss.

As we settle across from one another at a small table, his long legs brush mine. Every time he touches me, a little zing of electricity sizzles through my body, leaving me to feel fidgety. Tension builds in the air around us.

Unsure what to do with my hands, I pick up my coffee and blow on it before taking a small sip. It's scalding hot. Just the way I like it. As I take another swallow, everything loosens within me.

Like always, his eyes are solely focused on me as if I'm all he sees. It makes me feel even more aware of him of him than I already am. I shift on my chair as memories of his mouth sliding over mine careen unwantedly through my head. Unconsciously, my gaze falls to his lips.

How did I go this long without realizing how sexy they were?

All the kisses I've experienced…none have been like that.

Say what you want about the man, but he definitely knows what he's doing in that department.

When a deep, growling noise rumbles up from JT's chest, my gaze snaps to his in question. He strains forward as if trying to close the distance between us.

"You keep eyeing me up like that and I'm going to throw you right over my shoulder. Anything I have to say at this point will be moot. Understand?"

Even though it's on the tip of my tongue to deny the accusation, I don't.

I know *exactly* how I was looking at him and what was running through my brain.

I drop my gaze to my coffee and clear my throat, more ill at ease than before.

He needs to spit out whatever he came here to say so we can both be on our way. The less time I spend with JT, the better off I'll be.

There's this weird, amped-up attraction flowing between us, and I don't like it. Not only do I not understand it, I don't want to feel it.

I have a boyfriend.

Not to mention that I don't even like JT. Apparently, my body doesn't care about things like that.

Instead of addressing the comment, I ask instead, "What did you want to talk about?"

"Eyes on me."

I jerk in my seat as my gaze slices to his in question before fluttering away again. "Excuse me?"

My mouth turns cottony as the low notes of his voice reverberate at the very bottom of my belly, strumming something deep within. Something that leaves everything inside me clamoring.

Even though I'm loath to do it, I can't help but acknowledge that no man has ever affected me this way.

It's maddening.

"I want your eyes on me when we're talking," he says again.

A hint of color blooms in my cheeks as my gaze reluctantly settles on his.

"Better." The word is nothing more than a grunt.

Shifting uneasily, I repeat myself. "What do you want to talk about?"

I used to avoid him because I thought he was an asshole. Now, I wonder if I spent so much time eluding him because of the attraction that has always hummed beneath the surface.

It's thick and heavy.

Only now do I realize how undeniable it is.

It scares the hell out of me.

"Have you slept with him yet?" he asks in a clipped tone.

Oh my god…*seriously?*

My mouth falls open before I slam it shut again.

Through clenched teeth I hiss, "Please tell me you didn't come all the way down here so we could discuss *that* again." It's almost a relief when my temper ignites, dousing the attraction smoldering in the air between us. "You need to get it through your thick skull that whether or not I'm sleeping with *my boyfriend* is none of your damn business."

He sweeps his tongue across his teeth as he contemplates me. "That's where you're wrong. I'm making it my business."

Grrr!

His audacity makes me want to scream.

You know what?

I'm not doing this with him.

As I shoot to my feet, his hand snakes out and wraps around my wrist, halting any further movement. My icy gaze snaps to his. "Let go of me. We're done."

The intensity of his gaze pins me in place. "Just hear me out." His voice dips, the deep timbre of it reverberating throughout my body. "Please?"

For reasons I'm unable to fathom, I'm powerless to move a muscle. I hate the strange hold he has over me.

"I've already told you that it's none of your business." Even as I snap out the response, I sink onto the chair. The voice inside my head is screaming for me to run, to get as far away from him as possible, and yet, I don't budge.

"I realize that you don't have much experience when it comes to men."

My brows soar across my forehead. *"Excuse me?"*

It's doubtful I could feel more mortified than I do at this moment. I just want to sink through the floor and disappear.

His smoldering green-eyed gaze holds mine captive. The fact that I'm mesmerized by him is infuriating.

When I remain silent, he asks gently, "Am I wrong?"

I press my lips tightly together, torn between flat-out lying and agreeing with the statement. I'm startled to realize that his fingers are covering mine when he gives them a squeeze. My gaze drops to our clasped hands as something unwanted ripples through me again.

"Just tell me if I'm wrong," he whispers.

The softly imploring way he says the words has the fight draining away. With a sigh, my shoulders collapse as I mutter, "You're not wrong."

This whole conversation leaves me cringing. I'm starting to suspect that JT Higgins enjoys humiliating me.

"You should be with someone who's willing to make you his first priority. Who's going to make sure your first time is special." He tilts his head. "Do you really think Ryan will do that?"

"I wouldn't be with him if I didn't feel that way," I counter.

Even though I force out the words with conviction, deep down, I'm none too sure. Everything JT threw at me Saturday night has been rolling around in the back of my head like marbles. I've spent more time than I'm comfortable with comparing the kiss JT and I shared to the ones I've experienced with my boyfriend.

Unfortunately, there is no comparison.

If I'd hoped that response would dissuade him from delving head-long into this unwanted conversation, or maybe shake the confidence radiating off him in suffocating waves, it doesn't.

Not even a little.

His lips tug into a slow smile that simmers around the edges as his teeth flash.

I wish to god I didn't find him so attractive.

"Come on, Claire. We both know you're lying. That guy is a complete tool."

I roll my eyes at his choice of insult. "He is not a *tool*."

His brows rise. "Yeah, he is. If you were my sister, I wouldn't allow you to date him."

I straighten in my seat. The idea of someone trying to tell me who I can and cannot date rankles me, and I fully welcome the anger bubbling up like a geyser. It's so much better than the attraction that rushes through my veins.

"I'm not your sister," I fire back.

"No, you definitely aren't. What I feel for you isn't at all sisterly."

"What is it that you want, JT? Why are you here?"

Even as the questions shoot out of my mouth, I have the feeling I already know the answers.

JT

I reach across the table and slip my fingers beneath her chin until her gray depths are focused solely on me. Until I have her complete and undivided attention. I've been going round and round in my head about this. No matter how many times I tell myself to let it go, to move on and forget about her, I can't.

I've tried.

"Let me be the one," I murmur.

That statement is met with a deafening silence. One that blankets us until she's finally able to choke out a response.

"What?"

It would be almost comical if I weren't dead serious. Unable to help myself, I press against the table that separates us. "I want to be the one, Claire. Let me be your first. I'll make it good for you. You know I will."

By the stunned look in her eyes, I've taken her by surprise. For almost one full minute, she stares at me in shock. Finally, as if waking from a trance, she shakes her head almost violently. My fingers remain under her chin to hold her in place.

I won't allow her to physically distance herself from me.

I like touching her.

I like being this close.

Normally, she doesn't allow me into her personal space.

Now that I'm here, I want more of it.

"No," she croaks.

"Why not? It's obvious we have chemistry." There's so much electricity sparking between us. There's no way she doesn't feel it.

When her tongue darts out to lick at her lips, my gaze dips to the movement.

Her mouth is in the perfect shape of a cupid's bow.

There's so damn much I want to do to her. So many different ways I want to spread her out and explore her delectable little body. That thought alone has my cock stirring with anticipation. I shift on the chair to release the growing pressure in my jeans.

I've never wanted a woman the way I want Claire Garrison. We're talking three years' worth of pent-up longing.

"That's not a reason to sleep with someone," she hisses.

Even though she sounds annoyed, there's something else buried deep within her trembling voice.

"Actually, it's an excellent reason. In fact, it's one of the best damn reasons I've ever heard."

"I have a boyfriend," she reminds.

But it's weak.

And we both know it.

"Cut him loose. He's not worth your time."

Her spine stiffens. "I'm not going to break up with someone I've been seeing so I can sleep with you instead."

"He doesn't deserve you."

She jerks out of my hand. "And you want to sleep with me because I'm a virgin." Her words are low and shaky.

Heated.

"That's not true. From the very first moment I laid eyes on you, I wanted you. I think you know that."

"There's a difference between wanting to be with someone and simply wanting to sleep with them." Anger continues to swirl and roil through her voice. "You're no better than what you're accusing Ryan of. All you want to do is use me."

She lurches out of her seat for a second time. "I'm not interested in sleeping with you, JT. I'm not interested in doing *anything* with you."

It's only a matter of moments before she flies out the door.

"Give me your phone."

She laughs as if I'm crazy.

And who knows, maybe I am.

"You're the last person I want to have my number."

I turn to the girl studying alone at the table next to us. "Can I borrow a piece of paper and a pencil?"

Her brows draw together as she huffs out a breath before glancing up from the computer screen she's focused on. The irritation melts away as soon as her gaze locks on mine.

"Oh. Um, sure."

She rips a piece of paper from her notebook before handing it to me along with a pen. I refocus my attention on Claire, thankful she hasn't stormed away. She's in the process of gathering up her purse and steaming cup of coffee from the table.

The last thing I want to do is push her any further. Quickly, I scribble down my number before thrusting out the paper.

"No, thank you," she says with a snort.

When it becomes clear that she won't willingly take the sheet, I fold it up and shove it into the front pocket of her jeans. She grits her teeth and narrows her eyes.

"I don't want to see you again, JT," she snaps straightening her shoulders. "Don't contact me. Don't talk to me. And stop coming to dinner on Thursday nights. I won't tell Liam about this because, for some bizarre reason, he seems to like you. But if you continue to bother me, I'll have no choice in the matter."

I'll admit, this isn't how I imagined this conversation unfolding. After Saturday night and the way she'd responded to my kiss, I thought she might be more receptive to the offer.

Clearly, that's not the case.

If I actually thought the dude she was dating was with her for the right reasons, I might consider stepping—

Nah.

I want Claire Garrison.

And just like I claimed, I've wanted her since the first moment I laid eyes on her.

Unwilling to let her walk away, I rise to my feet, ready to follow her outside onto the sidewalk.

Fire leaps to life in her eyes as she raises her voice so that it cuts through the buzzing noise of the small coffee shop. "JT Higgins is right here, folks, and he wants to sign autographs and snap a few pics!"

For a second, that announcement is met with silence. Almost like the calm before the storm as heads snap in our direction.

"Bye, JT." With a smirk, she gives me a little wave with her fingers and disappears out the glass door and onto the street.

"I knew it! I just knew that was JT Higgins!"

All hell breaks loose as every person in the shop converges on me.

CLAIRE

The nerve of that guy!

I can't believe he tried to convince me to break up with Ryan just so I can sleep with him instead! It's not exactly like he wants me for himself.

He just wants to…

To pop my cherry.

I almost flinch as that disturbing thought circles through my head.

Men are pigs.

Maybe it's just JT who's the pig.

I'll make it good for you.

I almost snort. I don't doubt that. After experiencing his kisses firsthand, I wholeheartedly believe that JT is well versed at sex.

And pleasure.

But still…

There's no way I can sleep with the guy.

More than that, I don't want to.

I might not have much experience, but I know enough to realize that men and women are very different. Especially where sex is concerned. Men can pick up a random woman at a club, sleep with her, and never think about her again.

Women…well, most don't operate that way. There usually has to be some kind of emotional connection. For us, it's not just a biological function. An itch that needs to be scratched.

I'm not saying *all* women think that way, but enough of them do.

How many times has one of my friends cried on my shoulder because she hooked up with some dude at a party who then didn't give her the time of day when they bumped into each other on campus?

Too many to count.

And I know myself. I can't sleep with someone and then move on the next day without so much as a second thought. I always pictured that my first time would be with someone I cared about. Someone who returned the sentiment. I'm not delusional enough to think that I'm going to marry the first guy I sleep with, but I'd like there to be some kind of affection between us.

Something meaningful.

The feelings I have for JT are *definitely* not like that.

"He really said that to you?"

Holly, my roommate, looks just as stunned, if not amused, as I'm feeling.

"Yup, he really did."

It's mind boggling.

This isn't just me overreacting because I'm inexperienced, right?

Holly, who has a lot more knowledge when it comes to men, shakes her head. "So, what are you going to do?"

What am I going to do?

Nothing. That's what I'm going to do.

"I started off by telling him that I never wanted to see him again, and then I ended it by siccing a bunch of crazed fans on him. I'm fairly confident that drove home the point in regard to where I stand on the issue."

She raises a dark brow. "Do you really think so? This is JT Higgins we're talking about. He doesn't strike me as a guy who's easily deterred."

Holly has tagged along with me to a few parties over the years and met JT. She's also drooled over him. She's probably even thrown herself at him a time or two. The girl is a flirt.

"You want my honest opinion?" Her gaze locks on mine. "I'd be surprised if he lets it go."

My shoulders collapse. She's probably right about that, but still…

All it would take is one little comment to my brother about JT's harassment, and the guy would be in traction for the rest of the season. That's not really something I want to do. I'm perfectly capable of handling my own issues. I don't need my big brother swooping in and solving my problems. It's the reason I never mentioned all the times JT hit on me.

I'm trying to get Liam to ease up and give me some much-needed space. That won't happen if I tell him what's been going on. My plan is to continue ignoring him just like I've always done. Sooner or later, he'll get the hint and move on.

"Once I sleep with Ryan, JT will lose interest."

That's my hope.

I just wish he'd never kissed me. I hate that it's always there, rattling around in the back of my brain. Now, I'm constantly comparing Ryan to JT. And every time I do, Ryan somehow comes up lacking.

My roommate doesn't look nearly as confident about that statement. "I don't know, Claire." She glances down at the toenails she's painting. Her brows are furrowed in deep concentration. "Kind of seems like he has a thing for you."

The words aren't even out of her mouth before I shake my head in denial.

"I think what you meant to say is that the guy has a weakness for sleeping with anything that has a vagina."

With a grin, she glances up from her handiwork. "Well, I can't deny that, but still…" She pauses before sending me a sly look from beneath her lashes. "I've always thought there was a chance you two might get together."

I can only stare in horror.

Holly has never mentioned anything of the sort to me.

"What?" I sputter out the rest. "Are you being serious?"

"Yeah, I am. He's hot and wants you. There are times when I think all that loathing you feel for him is just longing you've channeled in a different direction."

My jaw drops. It's only recently that I've started to suspect the very same thing myself. But I've certainly never voiced that realization to Holly. Her intuition is a little freaky.

"Maybe you just need to go for it."

"Are you forgetting that I have a boyfriend?"

"I'm not forgetting. Just wondering if he's really the one you want to be with." She shoots me a searching look. When I fail to respond, she continues. "It's okay if he's not. You two haven't been together all that long."

I can't believe she's questioning me about this.

Why is she practically telling me to sleep with JT?

Has she lost her mind?

"Ryan's the only one I want," I reiterate.

She shrugs before her gaze drops to her nails. "I just don't want you to think that you have to sleep with him if you're having doubts. This isn't something you're locked into," she adds softly.

I stand in the middle of her room where I've been pacing, unsure how to respond. Why does it feel like Holly is trying to talk me out of having sex with Ryan?

Is that what's going on here?

Or am I misreading the situation?

Why would she think I'm having doubts?

Or that I feel locked in?

Of course I can change my mind at any time.

I know that.

Sure...Ryan can be pushy, but ultimately, the decision is mine.

"I want to sleep with Ryan," I tell her. "In fact, I was planning to do it this weekend."

She studies me for a long moment before nodding. "If you're sure that's what you want, then good."

"I am." I huff out an irritated breath.

Honestly, I'm tired of thinking about this all the time. Overthinking it, actually. I'm ready for this.

I flop onto her desk chair and stare up at the ceiling. "In fact, Ryan invited me to a party at his fraternity house Friday night. So, the plan is to do it Saturday."

There's a big part of me that just wants to get it out of the way so I can move on with my life. Maybe it's not the best reason for wanting to have sex, but so what?

I'm tired of waiting.

"Ryan must be thrilled."

For the first time since I brought up the topic, it finally feels like this conversation is back on track.

"He doesn't know," I admit. And that's because I just decided this about sixty seconds ago.

Screw JT.

Poor choice of words.

Obviously, I will *not* be screwing JT.

When she remains silent, I say, "We can go out to dinner on Saturday and then come back here. It'll be a surprise." It sounds like as good a plan as any.

Her eyes light up. "We should get you something sexy to wear."

I groan. That seems so...I don't know.

Unnecessary.

"No. I don't need anything like that."

"Yeah, you do." She puts the finishing touches on her fingernails and waves her hands back and forth before blowing on them. "Just give me a minute to let these dry, and then we'll run over to the mall. I bet we can find something Ryan will want to tear off you with his teeth."

"Please, don't make me go."

"You're going," she says with a laugh. "And if it doesn't get used with Ryan, you can definitely wear it for JT."

My eyes widen. As I open my mouth to blast her, she dissolves into a fit of giggles. "Just kidding! Come on, it'll be fun."

Doubtful.

Trying on sexy little scraps of lingerie doesn't sound fun at all.

In fact, it sounds downright painful.

CLAIRE

"Hey, babe!" Ryan grabs my hand before leaning in and planting a kiss on my lips. It's really nothing more than a quick brush of his mouth across mine. "Glad you could make it." He looks happy and in his element. "This place is crazy, right?"

He's not kidding.

Their fraternity house is packed with people wearing togas. It's totally cliché, but the first Delta Sig party of the year is always a toga party. Apparently, they think it harks back to their origins or some nonsense like that.

Ryan has a white linen sheet draped across his body that shows off his light summer tan and muscles rather nicely. I can't say that he doesn't look good.

He might not be built like JT but—

I almost wince as that unfiltered thought as it pops into my head.

JT Higgins is the last person I should be thinking about.

Especially when I'm with Ryan.

"Where's your costume?" he asks with a frown. "You were supposed to dress up."

"Sorry, I didn't have time to pull a costume together."

I'm sure if I told him about my plans for tomorrow night, he wouldn't say another word about me not draping my body in bed linens. But I don't mention it because I want it to be a surprise. Even now, nervous excitement courses through me at what tomorrow will bring.

Holly dragged me to the lingerie shop in the mall, and I bought not one but two wispy, ridiculous scraps of material that reveal a lot more than they conceal.

Which, Holly informed me, is the point.

Not that I'll admit it to my roommate, but trying on the skimpy garments did make me feel pretty sexy. The first one is a practically see-through pale pink confection that hugs my slender curves and has garters and a matching thong. The other one, because Holly insisted that I needed more than one, is a tiny babydoll. It has silky black cups that conceal my breasts and sheer material that falls in gauzy waves to my upper thighs.

I hold up my arms and glance down at the simple outfit I picked out for tonight. "I'm pretty sure the ancient Greeks wore T-shirts and jeans."

He raises a skeptical brow before pulling me close and nipping at my neck. "I have a sheet or two upstairs." He wiggles his brows. "How about I assist you with changing into something a little more appropriate?"

"Nah, I'm good." It's doubtful we would make it back down to the party if I allowed that to happen.

Ryan has been ratcheting up the pressure for the last week. He's tired of waiting. It's the reason why I have big plans for us tomorrow. Plans I know he'll enjoy.

"Are you sure?" Heat ignites in his eyes.

"Yup, pretty sure," I say with a grin.

"Hi, Ryan."

Holly, on the other hand, refused to leave the apartment until she was perfectly outfitted in something she picked up from the costume shop at the mall. She looks stunning. One shoulder has been left bare, and there's a braided gold rope cinched around her waist. Even though her long, chestnut colored hair has been pulled up on both sides, it cascades over one shoulder. A woven golden band sits on her head like a crown. Gold eye shadow and bronzer applied to her high cheekbones accent her face. Strappy gold sandals that lace their way up her calves complete the look.

She's a vision in gold and white.

Ryan does a double take before his gaze slowly runs down the length of my roommate.

It appears that a lot of people decided to throw a sheet around themselves and voilà, instant costume. Not Holly. That girl never half-asses anything.

The three of us have been friends since freshman year, and he's never paid her any more attention than he does other girls. For just a second or two, it makes me wish I'd bothered to dress up instead of being content to throw on a T-shirt and jeans.

Once he drags his attention away from my roommate, it resettles on me. "How about a beer?"

I glance at Holly with a raised brow. Although, I know what the answer will be before she responds. Holly enjoys cutting loose. Her social life has always been more active than mine.

"Sure, we'll have one."

Tonight, I'm going to take a page out of my roommate's book. I don't go out very much, and with classes kicking into high gear along with my student teaching placement, I don't see that changing anytime soon.

That being said, I don't plan on consuming my weight in beer. After my mom took off, Dad struggled with alcohol. It took him a long time to get sober. Because of that, I've always steered clear. I witnessed how much it controlled him and the bad choices he made while intoxicated.

Ryan takes off and returns a few minutes later with red plastic cups for both of us. Holly flashes him a smile before tossing back half the drink. I take a small sip, trying not to wince as the cold liquid trickles down my throat.

An hour later, Holly is immersed in a game of beer pong. Two of Ryan's fraternity brothers are vying for her attention. Ryan remains steadfast at my side. My hand is clasped tightly in his as he drags me from room to room, greeting and talking with people along the way.

After we carve out a small space in the hallway, he leans closer and whispers, "I have a present for you."

"You do?" A smile lights up my face. "Really?"

A matching grin curves his lips, making him look boyishly handsome. "Yeah, it's upstairs. Want to see what it is?"

I nod.

With our hands firmly clasped, we make our way toward the front of the house where the staircase is located. The Delta Sig house is massive. There has to be at least ten bedrooms upstairs and a few more in the basement. Ryan is a senior and has his own room.

A pledge stands guard at the bottom of the curving staircase. He scrambles to remove the rope barring the entrance before allowing us to the second floor. As we climb up the stairs, the noise of the party gradually fades.

All right, maybe it doesn't disappear completely, but it's no longer ringing in my ears.

Ryan's room is at the far end of the hallway. He takes out a brass key and unlocks the door before pushing it open and allowing me to enter first. Once I'm over the threshold, he follows me in and closes the thick wood behind him. Even though he's nonchalant about it, I notice him twist the lock before leaning against the door. His lips slink up into a smile before he pushes away from the wall and saunters past me to the desk on the other side of the room. He pulls open the middle drawer and grabs something before closing his fist around it. As he swings around to face me, he shoves both hands behind his back.

"I saw this and thought of you." He holds his arm out in front of him before slowly opening his hand. Something shiny and metallic catches my eyes as it drops from his fingers before catching and dangling in the air between us.

Gaze pinned to the gift, I close the distance between us before reaching out and gently picking up the silver pendant in the shape of a

C that hangs on a delicate-looking chain. Sparkly gems frame the letter.

"Thank you," I whisper, voice full of awe as my surprised gaze slices to his. "It's beautiful. You didn't have to buy me anything."

"I wanted to. I really like you, Claire. I hope you know that." His smile brightens. "Turn around, and I'll put it on."

A smile blooms across my face as I give him my back before gathering up the long strands of my hair. His fingers brush against the nape of my neck as he sets the *C* gently against my chest before clasping the lock. It takes him a few attempts to get it. Just as I'm about to release my hair, he presses his lips against the column of my exposed throat. The gesture sends goose bumps skittering down my spine.

"It looks good on you," he whispers thickly, placing another lingering kiss against my flesh.

My eyelids feather closed as he licks and nips his way along my shoulder. His arms slip around me as he tugs me closer. That's when I feel his thick erection pressing against my lower back.

"I want you so much, baby."

I gulp, wanting that too.

His hands slide from my hips up my sides until they're cupping my breasts. The unexpected movement has my breath catching at the back of my throat. When I don't protest, he gently kneads them. A couple seconds later, they're gliding down my belly before slipping under my T-shirt and drifting back to my chest. It doesn't take long for his fingers to delve into the silky material of my bra so he can palm my naked flesh.

He growls in my ear as he continues to fondle me.

Even though I'm unsure about letting him go much further, what he's doing feels good. His lips drift along my neck as his fingers stroke my breasts. Every once in a while, he plucks at my nipples. As his lips work their way upward, trailing across my cheek, I turn my head until his mouth can settle over mine. He nibbles at me before his tongue plunges inside.

I don't realize we've moved until he breaks the contact and my back hits the mattress as he falls on top of me. Barely do I have time to gasp for breath and his tongue is delving inside my mouth again. His hips rock against mine as his erection grinds into my pelvis.

A few more minutes pass before he rips away long enough to mutter, "I want you so much, Claire. I'm tired of waiting. Aren't you?"

He doesn't give me a chance to respond before his lips crash back onto mine. Only this time, they're more demanding. Ryan can be a bit pushy, but I've never felt like I was being overpowered. I'm not sure I feel that way now, but I want him to chill out. Everything is starting to feel frenzied. There's a part of me that's afraid I won't be able to stop him if this continues much longer. I want to have some control over the situation and right now, it feels like it's slipping through my fingers.

Panic slices through the thick arousal clouding my brain. When his fingers settle on the button of my jeans, flicking it open and tugging down the zipper, I know I need to say something. Before I can stop him, his hand slips inside my underwear. As his fingers touch me, I twist my head so we're no longer kissing.

"Ryan, you need to slow down."

Instead of answering, his lips seek out mine and I turn my face away.

The weight on top of me suddenly feels heavy.

Too heavy.

I shove at his chest as a fresh burst of panic explodes inside me. I want him to get the hell off me and give me some room. I can't breathe with his bigger body pinning mine to the mattress.

It feels like we both got a little carried away and need to take a moment to rein it back in again. I'm not about to lose my virginity at a frat house. It's not like I'm expecting to be whisked away for a romantic weekend at a quaint bed and breakfast in the country where there's champagne, candlelight, and a roaring fire. But it sure as hell isn't going to be at a crazy toga party where there are hundreds of drunk people downstairs.

His fingers bite into my cheeks as he twists my face toward him. Even with his eyelids at half-mast, I can see how turned on he is.

"What's the problem, Claire?" His voice is deep and low, strained at the edges.

I inhale a shaky breath, needing to calm the anxiety crashing through my body. I wish I could say that it's lust and longing rushing through me, making it impossible to think, but it's not.

I feel trapped.

Like an animal.

And I can't breathe.

Instead of giving me some much-needed space, he doesn't budge. Already I can tell by the expression on his face along with the tone of his voice that he doesn't want to stop messing around.

"There isn't a problem," I lie, unable to keep the thin waver from my voice.

The edges of his lips slide upwards as he stares down at me. Our gazes stay locked as he lowers his mouth to mine, kissing me gently before pulling back again.

"Good. I'm tired of holding back with you." He thrusts his hips so that his hard cock rubs against the V between my legs. "Doesn't that feel good? Don't you want me inside you?"

Alarm bells trill inside my head. "Yes," I gulp. "But not tonight."

He rocks against me as his lips drop back to mine. When I twist my head to the side, his mouth lands on my cheek instead and his warm breath feathers against me as he licks and sucks at my skin.

"You're so beautiful, Claire. I've wanted you since freshman year. Three years I've been after you. I'm tired of waiting." He lifts his face until his eyes can bore into mine. "I'll make it good for you, babe. I promise. You just have to trust me."

That's all it takes for my fight or flight response to kick in. I push against his chest, attempting to dislodge him, but he doesn't budge. Ryan might not be a mountain of muscle, but he's still strong.

Much stronger than I am.

"I can't breathe, Ryan," I gasp. "Get off me."

"You just need to relax, baby," he says, attempting to soothe me with gentle words. "I'm not going to hurt you."

It has the opposite effect.

He's not listening. It hits me that I'm trapped. He can do whatever he wants and there's no way for me to stop him. Full-fledged panic sets in and a scream gathers in my throat.

"Please, Ryan," I plead. "Get off me. I need a few minutes to think."

"Shhh. What you need to do is relax. You should have had a couple more drinks. It would have helped loosen you up. You're making this more difficult than it has to be."

His hand delves back inside the front of my jeans. A second later, his finger pushes inside me.

A smile breaks out across his face as he chuckles. It's low and deep, full of triumph.

"See?" He thrusts back inside me again. "You're already wet." He presses another kiss against my mouth. "I knew you wanted this. You're just nervous because you're still a virgin. But I promise, I'll be careful. You just have to calm down and let it happen."

No, no, no!

I don't want this at all. Unsure what to do, I squeeze my eyelids tightly shut. He's much too heavy to budge from on top of me. And I'm confused, not to mention mortified, because he's right.

I *am* wet.

He didn't have any problem sliding his finger inside me. But I've asked him to stop, and he refuses to listen. Maybe, in the beginning, I wanted his kisses. And I enjoyed the way he was touching my breasts, but I don't want to have sex with him. It doesn't matter if my body is telling a different story. I just want to get the hell out of here. Tears fill my eyes as Ryan continues to rhythmically thrust his finger inside me.

"You're so fucking tight, baby. God, but I can't wait to bury my cock deep inside you."

Even though I want to scream, I slow my breathing and try to come up with a way to get him off me. When I finally come up with a plan, I lay there for another moment and force myself to relax into the mattress. It's so tempting to claw at him. Instead, I stop trying to dislodge him and slide my arms around his neck.

Ryan immediately notices the change in my behavior.

"See?" The arrogant note filling his voice sets my teeth on edge. "That feels good, baby, doesn't it? You want more of that?"

"Yes," I whisper with a nod.

"Widen your legs. I need to stretch you a little bit more. I'm pretty big. I don't want to hurt you any more than I have to."

Right...

I've touched his penis. Several times, in fact. And I didn't find him to be gargantuan or anything like that.

I force my legs farther apart as he thrusts two fingers inside me before scissoring them, slowly moving them in and out. There's a bit of a burn, but it's not totally unpleasant.

"I can't wait to taste your pussy on my lips."

Unsure how to respond, I remain silent. Luckily, he doesn't seem to notice or care about my lack of enthusiasm.

After a few more minutes slip by, I ask, "Do you have a condom?"

His movements still as he pulls away enough to stare down at me with lust-filled eyes. "Yeah, in my desk drawer. I'll get it."

And just like that, he's off me.

As soon as his heavy weight disappears, I suck in a gulp of air before quickly zipping up my jeans and rolling from the bed in one swift motion. Ryan slams the drawer shut before glancing over his shoulder with a condom clutched tightly in his hand. Confusion mars his expression as to why I'm no longer sprawled out on the bed. He was probably hoping that I'd shimmied out of all my clothes.

Asshole.

"Claire?" His eyes narrow as if only now realizing he's been tricked.

I tear the necklace from my throat and hurtle it at him. Even when it whizzes past his head, his gaze never deviates from mine.

"I told you to stop," I accuse. "And you wouldn't."

He drags a hand through his disheveled hair as irritation flickers across his face. "Are you being serious right now?"

I jerk my head in response.

"How long do you expect me to wait? I've been more than patient with you, Claire." His eyes harden into icy chips as he folds his arms across his chest. "It's not like you're fifteen, for fuck's sake. You need to grow up. This behavior shows just how immature you still are."

My eyes widen and I take a step toward him before slamming a finger into my chest. "*I* decide when I'm ready to have sex. Not you. *Me.*"

"I'm tired of waiting," he says with a roll of his eyes. "And I'm really tired of jacking off in the shower."

His lack of regret is almost disturbing.

"I don't want to see you again."

"Fine." He shrugs as if he couldn't care less.

And maybe he doesn't.

Since there doesn't seem to be anything else to say, I spin toward the door and unlock it before disappearing into the hallway. My feet pound down the carpeted staircase as the need to leave this house and distance myself from Ryan thrums through me. Halfway down, I stop and survey the thick crowd. Most are dressed in sheets or costumes similar to Holly. In the dim lighting, everyone looks the same.

When I pull my phone from the pocket of my jeans, a slip of paper falls out with it. I reach down and scoop it up.

Ugh.

JT's number.

He shoved it into my pocket before I left the coffee shop the other day. Even though I should just wad it up and toss it into the crowd, I don't. Instead, I shove it back in my pocket before opening up the home screen of my cell and firing off a quick text to Holly. After the guy manning the staircase lets me through, I push and shove my way through the sea of students, craning my neck to search for my roommate.

When a couple minutes tick by without a response, I call. After four rings, it goes to voicemail. I disconnect and try again. No answer.

She has to be around here somewhere. The Delta Sig house is a sprawling old building, and it looks like the party has spilled out into the backyard.

At this point, I just want to get out of here. And I sure as hell don't want to run into Ryan. I'm liable to deck that asshole if I do.

But I can't just take off. Holly drove us here, and our apartment is at least two miles away. I can't walk home alone at this time of night.

If I call Liam, he'll grill me relentlessly, and I don't want him to find out what happened with Ryan. That means I can't call Gia either, because she won't keep something like this from her husband. Not that I blame her, but it doesn't help solve my current predicament.

I blow out a breath as frustration churns inside me.

Who does that leave?

My friend Angie?

Maybe she can—

Oh, wait. She left yesterday to visit her boyfriend at UW-Madison.

Shit.

I glance around, searching the face of every person in the vicinity. At this point, I'll take anyone who looks remotely familiar.

But there's no one. I'm stuck.

My shoulders collapse as I tip my head back and stare blindly up at the ceiling. Even though I don't want to, I pull out the wadded-up piece of paper from my pocket. JT is the last person I want to call, but I'm fresh out of options. I cringe and force myself to tap in the numbers before waiting for the line to ring.

I'm sure he's out. Or he won't recognize my number.

"'Lo?"

My eyes widen, and for a moment, my mind blanks as the breath stalls in my lungs.

"Hello?" he says again.

With a shake of my head, I clear my throat. "JT?"

"Claire?" As soon as he recognizes my voice, his tone changes. Every drop of laziness disappears.

I release a steady breath before getting straight to the point. "Can you pick me up?"

I expect him to fire off some questions.

That doesn't happen.

"Text me the address. I'll be there as soon as I can."

Even though he can't see me, I nod as relief floods through every cell of my body and weakens my knees.

When I fail to respond, he snaps, "*Claire?*"

"Yeah, sorry. I'll text it right now."

"Are you okay?" he asks in concern. "Are you safe?"

Again, I nod before glancing around the party that continues to rage. "I'm fine. I just need a ride home."

"I'm getting in the car right now."

"All right. I'll wait outside."

I text the address as soon as I disconnect. Just as I fire off the message, fingers wrap around my arm and spin me around.

I don't think I've ever felt this jacked up in my life. Not even the first time I walked onto the field in Green Bay did I have a pit the size of a lemon sitting at the bottom of my gut.

I have no idea what's going on.

Claire wouldn't have called unless there was no other choice in the matter. I had to be dead last on her phone-a-friend list. Maybe I should have asked a few more questions when I had her on the line, but all I could think about was jumping in the car and getting to her as quickly as possible.

With the way I'm driving, it takes about ten minutes to reach the college. I glance at the GPS on the phone. I should be turning onto the street she gave me in a minute or so. There are two more turns before I slow my Porsche to a crawl and search the people I pass on the sidewalk. Clearly, there's a party in progress. Or maybe five. Drunken students spill out onto the lawns and walk in large groups.

I keep my eyes peeled for the address. I'm willing to bet that it's the massive white house with the Greek letters prominently displayed above the porch. It seems like most of the students are pouring out of there.

My gaze slowly sweeps the area, but I don't see Claire anywhere.

I'm about to reach for my cell when I catch a glimpse of long, dark hair. My brows slam together, because her boyfriend has his hands on her. I don't bother parking the sports car along the side of the street. I hit the hazards and kill the engine before slamming out of the car and barreling toward them.

It pisses me off to watch him manhandle her. I ball my hands as fury burns through my veins. Clearly, something happened between them. As soon as I'm close enough, I rip his hands off her body and pull her close. It takes everything I have inside not to throw a punch.

Instead, I keep the urge contained.

It's not easy.

"What the fuck, dude?"

As soon as his gaze lands on me, his expression changes. This must be the first time he doesn't look overjoyed to see me. His gaze narrows before slicing to Claire.

"You called him?" The question is more of a grumble.

She straightens her shoulders and lifts her chin. "Yeah, I need a ride home."

"I told you already I'd drive you," he grits through clenched teeth.

His hands flex impotently at his sides. I can tell by the look on his face that he wants to grab her again but won't because I'm here. And he sure as hell isn't going to try and get in my face. Although, I would dearly love it if he did.

I smile thinly at the thought.

"I don't want to be alone with you right now," she says.

My eyes narrow at the reason behind those words. The guy must have pulled some real crap for Claire to react this way.

For her to call *me*.

"Claire…" He gives me a bit of side eye before whining. "Come on. I already apologized. Can't you let it go?"

"No." She abruptly dismisses him before shifting her gaze to me. "Can we get out of here, please?"

She doesn't need to ask twice.

"Absolutely."

I wrap my arms around her just in case this asshole gets it in his mind to stop her. He'll have to go through me to do it. I have no idea what happened, but I'm going to damn well find out as soon as I have her tucked safely inside my vehicle.

"I'll call you tomorrow, Claire," he shouts after her.

"Don't bother." She tosses the words coldly over her shoulder. "I told you we were over, and I meant it."

His lips flatten as he glares, but he's smart enough not to open his yap. I lead Claire to my car and open the passenger door before assisting her inside. Then, I jog around the sleek hood and slide in beside her. Within seconds, the engine is roaring to life and we're shooting off down the tree-lined streets near campus.

With her next to me, everything strung tight inside me gradually loosens. I glance at her, but she remains quiet as she stares out the windshield.

Unable to take the stifling silence another moment, I clear my throat. "Are you all right?"

Even though I'm unsure where we're headed, I just keep driving. I want to get her as far away from here as possible. As far away from that knucklehead in case she changes her mind. Although, Claire doesn't strike me as the kind of girl to flip-flop on a decision.

The moment stretches between us until she finally turns her head just enough to meet my gaze. "I'm fine."

The urge to pull over and tug her into my arms thrums through me. I want to comfort her, but it's doubtful that would go over well, so I keep my hands to myself.

"Did something happened with," I pause, unable to remember his name, "your boyfriend?" Referring to him as "jackwad" would probably aggravate her. And I don't want to do that.

"He's not my boyfriend anymore."

Yup, that has most definitely been noted.

"Did he hurt you?" My voice is dangerously low. Rough. If that's what happened, I'll turn this car around right now and break both his goddamn legs.

Her gaze slices to mine before she shakes her head. "No."

"Are you sure?" For some reason, I don't believe her. There's an odd look filling her eyes that I'm having a hard time deciphering.

"Yeah, I'm sure."

Even though she's been tight-lipped, I continue to dig. "Did you have an argument?"

"No."

Before I can drill her with another question, a heavy sigh falls from her lips. "Look, I really appreciate you picking me up, but I don't want to talk about this right now." Exhaustion creeps into her eyes. "Do you mind if we just drive?"

Fine. I'll stop pushing, but at some point, she's going to tell me what went down.

After a couple of miles, I realize we're heading back to my place. Or Liam's. Since we live in the same sub. Maybe I should drop her off there. I don't want to take her back to her apartment. Who knows if that jackass will show up at two o'clock in the morning all wasted and wanting to work things out. If Claire were mine, there's no way I'd let her go without one hell of a fight.

As we roll up to the gate, I give the guard a nod before he silently waves us through.

"Should I drop you off at your brother's house?" Maybe she wants to talk with Gia. I still don't understand why she didn't call them in the first place.

She draws her lower lip between her teeth before chewing it. "You should probably take me back to my apartment." Her fingers rise to her temples as if there's a headache brewing behind them. "Sorry, I wasn't thinking."

A thought takes root inside my brain before I toss the suggestion out to her. "You want to hang out at my place for a bit?" There's a pause. "We could watch a movie."

There's a moment of silence. "Are you sure you don't mind?"

"Nah, I wasn't doing anything."

She snorts.

It's the cutest sound imaginable.

"That's twice now that you haven't been doing anything on a

weekend. Have I somehow become trapped in a parallel universe? One where nothing makes sense?"

I shoot her a smirk. "I told you, I'm trying to lay low. No more parties, drinking, women, fights, or bad press. Welcome to the new JT Higgins."

A noise that sounds suspiciously like disbelief escapes from her. "You must be extremely bored. Aren't those all your favorite vices?"

She's not wrong about my checkered past.

"I don't miss it," I say with a chuckle.

Without those distractions to take up my time, I've discovered that I don't have anything better to do than work out, which is why I'm in the best damn shape of my life. I'm lifting at least two hours a day and running on the trails through the woods out back. I also swim in my pool. Plus, it's kind of lonely at my house, so I find myself showing up at Liam's door more often than not, which allows me to see Claire.

I hit the garage door opener and slow roll my Porsche inside. We exit the vehicle at the same time and walk through the door that leads into the mudroom. Claire toes off her shoes before heading into the spacious kitchen. I flick on a light and watch as her eyes travel around the room with interest.

I don't realize I'm holding my breath, waiting for her reaction, until she says, "It's nice."

The floor plan is similar to Liam's, but there are a few subtle differences. With the finished basement, I have about seventy-five hundred square feet. It's a lot of house for one person. I wasn't thinking about that when I bought the place.

Honestly, it was the heated pool in the back and the amount of land that sold me on the property. I needed my own space. And I love to swim. Now, I can do it any damn time I want. And it's private. There's no one to bother me when I'm trying to get a workout in.

"Are you hungry? Want something to drink?" I ask.

"Sure, I'll take a water."

I beeline to the massive fridge. The face is cabinetry and blends with the rest of the dark cherry wood in the kitchen. I pull two bottles from the shelf before handing one to her.

"Thanks."

There's still a subdued air to her as she twists off the cap and takes a long swig.

I can't help but silently watch her. I'm not used to seeing Claire like this. Either she's ignoring me or shooting daggers with her eyes. She's usually perfectly put together. Not just clothes-wise, but her entire person. The way she conducts herself. She seems to know exactly what she wants out of life and how she's going to achieve it.

She also sees straight through my bullshit.

The girl isn't bowled over by my careless smiles or status as a professional athlete. Maybe that's because her brother is one as well. Although, it's doubtful that's the reason. Claire doesn't seem overly impressed with that kind of status. She's not into hanging out with the wives or girlfriends. And I've never seen her flirt with a player.

Tonight, though, she seems different.

Vulnerable.

Unsure of herself.

Maybe even a little lost.

It pisses me off that her boyfriend did something to shake her confidence. And it bothers me that she won't tell me what happened.

Even though I don't want her to leave, I need to do what's best for Claire. "Are you sure you don't want to go to Liam's house?" I shift before tacking on, "Maybe you should talk to Gia."

I glance at the clock on the microwave, only to realize that it's after eleven. Everyone is probably sacked out.

She stiffens. "Do you want me to leave?"

"No!" Unsure what to say or how to proceed in this type of situation, I drag my hand through my hair. "That's not what I meant." More than anything, I want her to stay. "It's just that I can tell something's wrong, and you won't tell me what it is. I'm just trying to make sure you're okay. That's it."

Claire breaks eye contact before padding over to the French doors that line the wall and overlook the pool. When she stays rooted in place, I gravitate to her side.

"I was going to sleep with him tomorrow. I had it all planned out."

My heart clenches at the soft admittance.

Not once does she glance my way. She only continues staring out into the night. Like Liam's yard, mine butts up to the nature preserve. There's a forest in the back, and to a small extent on the sides, to give me extra privacy from the neighboring estates.

She rubs her forehead with one hand and continues quietly as if muttering to herself. "He said he had a gift for me, so we went up to his room." Her gaze flickers to mine. "He lives at the fraternity house where you picked me up. They were having a big party."

I suddenly recall that there were people wearing ridiculous looking sheets and costumes. It didn't register before because I was so focused on Claire.

Even though I want to ask what happened next, I remain silent. I have the feeling she'll tell me on her own. I also have the feeling I won't like what she has to say.

"He gave me a necklace." There's another lengthy pause. "No one's ever given me anything before."

How can that be?

Whoever this girl is with should shower her with trinkets every damn day of her life. Claire is special. I felt it from the very beginning. Hell, I hadn't even met her. I'd only caught sight of her from across a crowded room and couldn't take my eyes off her.

Then, I realized she was only eighteen.

And the younger sister of a teammate.

"He put it around my neck and then started to kiss me."

Her voice snaps me back to the present. Her eyes are once again focused on the pool. There's something mesmerizing about the water and the way it sways gently under the moonlight that spills across it.

"Before I realized it, we were on the bed. What he was doing felt good. I can't say that it didn't."

Her brows draw together. It's not a full-out frown. Almost as if she's having a hard time understanding the thoughts running rampant through her own head.

"When he unbuttoned my jeans and started to touch me, I knew I wanted him to stop. Or, at least, slow down."

My hands clench at my sides. I want to reach out and pull her to me. Instead, I remain still, unsure if she wants to be touched. An uncontrollable urge to jump in my car and zip back to the fraternity house roars through my blood. I want to rip the place apart until I find that little prick and beat the piss out of him.

"I told Ryan that I wanted to stop. When he wouldn't, I tried pushing him away, but he was too strong." She shakes her head. "He kept telling me to calm down. That I was just nervous because it was my first time."

I've never wanted to slam my fist through something more than I do at this moment. But I can't do that. I need to take care of Claire and make sure she's all right.

"You didn't do anything wrong. You know that, right?"

Her shoulders stiffen as her gaze latches onto mine. "Yeah. I asked him to stop, and he didn't." Her voice grows stronger. "What happened is on him, not me, and I realize that."

The tension filling me drains away. It would be so much worse if she blamed herself for him being an asshole.

"Did he…" My words trail off. I'm not quite sure how to ask if she was raped.

And that's exactly what it would be.

Rape.

Even if she went willingly upstairs. Even if she was okay with what was going on in the beginning. When she told him to stop, he should have pulled back and given her space.

He didn't.

Instead, he forced himself on her.

"No. I pretended to be into what he was doing and told him to get a condom. When he rolled away, I jumped off the bed and ripped off the necklace before throwing it at him. Then, I told him we were through."

Another heavy silence falls over us.

Thank god she stayed calm and was able to think her way out of the situation. That's not always easy to do.

"When I couldn't find Holly, I called you."

The realization of what almost happened to her crashes over me, leaving a sick pit at the bottom of my gut. The urge to tug her into my arms pounds through me. I just want to wrap her up in my strength and never let go.

But I don't.

Nothing has changed between us.

"You did the right thing."

Her brows knit as confusion flashes across her face. "I didn't expect him to do that."

"That's understandable. You trusted him."

"Yeah," she says with a heavy sigh. "I did."

"Not all guys are like that."

She levels me with a hard look. "Really? How are you different? All you seem to care about is sweettalking someone into bed as quickly as possible."

When she puts it like that, my past behavior sounds pretty lousy. Maybe I have been guilty of hustling women into bed. Actually, there's no doubt about it. I've done more than my fair share of hustling. The only thing I can say is that women have been throwing themselves at me since before I can even remember.

Half the time, I'm the one being hustled.

But still…

"The difference is that when someone tells me no, I stop right there." I step a bit closer and slide my fingers beneath her chin, lifting it until her gaze locks on mine. "I would never force a woman into bed. When you said no, I backed off."

Her tongue darts out to moisten her lips. "Every time we saw each other, you'd hit on me."

"That's called persistence." The corners of my mouth quirk. "Nothing wrong with that. And who knows? You might have changed your mind."

Some of the heaviness fades from her expression as she gives me a slight smile.

"You were annoying."

"Yup, definitely guilty of that." I flick the tip of her nose with my finger. "But nothing more."

Since she seems to be feeling better, I say, "How about we check if there are any good movies on demand. We can decide what you want to do afterwards."

She nods. Even though I don't want to break the physical connection, I allow my hand to drift from her face.

Within ten minutes, we're both settled on the couch.

Believe it or not, Claire is right next to me.

I sat down first, wanting her to have a choice about where to take a seat. After everything she's been through, the last thing I want to do is make her feel uncomfortable. We decide on a rom com that was recently released. It's funny and lighthearted. Exactly what we need. As we share a bowl of popcorn, tension slowly ebbs from her as she continues to relax.

What happened with her asshole of an ex seems to be forgotten.

At least for the moment.

When the credits finally roll, I turn to Claire, surprised to find her curled up, sleeping soundly. I hadn't even realized that she dozed off. I click off the TV and ponder my options. By now, it's well past one o'clock in the morning. There's no way I can just dump her at Liam and Gia's house at this hour. And I don't want to take her back to her apartment.

Decision made, I scoop her into my arms and carry her up the staircase. Not once does she stir. As I reach the second-floor landing, I swing to the left and walk past the first two guest rooms before putting her in the one closest to mine.

I lay her on top of the comforter before padding to the closet and pulling out a blanket to drape over her sleeping form. After she's tucked in, I loiter in the darkness. I can't deny that I like seeing her in my bed.

Well, my guest bed.

But close enough.

I leave the door slightly ajar and head to my suite. It might be after one o'clock in the morning, but I have all this pent-up energy careening through my system, and don't know why.

All right, yes I do.

Claire Garrison is sleeping forty feet from me.

Even though she's safe, I can't stop thinking about what that asshole tried to do. He gave her a piece of jewelry in an attempt to soften her up before trying to fuck her.

My hands tighten until the knuckles turn bone white.

It's tempting to throw on workout clothes and head down to the gym in my basement, but I don't think I'm up for a lift. Maybe a swim instead.

A couple dozen laps will help settle everything that rampages within me, and then maybe I'll be able to fall into a dreamless sleep.

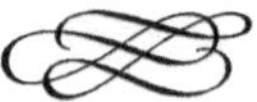

I wake with a start.

Even in the thick darkness that surrounds me, I know I'm not in my own bed. Everything feels different. And I'm not at my brother's place either.

So, where am I?

I sit up and realize I'm still wearing my T-shirt and jeans from this evening. Air rushes from my lungs as I scrub a hand over my face and attempt to jostle my sluggish brain into action before I totally freak out.

Holly and I went to a toga party at Ryan's fraternity. As soon as that thought pops into my brain, everything with Ryan rushes in to fill the void.

What an asshole.

Unable to come up with another way home, I called JT.

He took me back to his place and we watched a movie. I must have fallen asleep, and he carried me up to bed. I glance over at the other side of the mattress and find it empty. In fact, the bed is still made and I'm on top of the comforter.

My heartbeat slows as I relax against the pillows, willing myself to go back to sleep. There's no point in waking JT. I'll stay here for the night, and he can drop me off tomorrow morning. I spend the next ten minutes tossing and turning, attempting to find sleep again, but it remains elusive.

My mind is spinning.

As much as I don't want to dwell on what happened tonight, my thoughts continue to circle back to Ryan and what he tried to pull. I think I was in shock afterward and operating on autopilot. All I knew was that I had to get away from him. There wasn't time to get emotional.

But now, when I think about it...the entire situation just pisses me off. I want to go back to his house and punch him in the face.

A few times.

That's when I realize I won't be falling asleep anytime soon. I'm too jacked up to even close my eyes. Decision made, I throw off the blanket and pad to the open door before glancing into the hallway.

Everything is dark and silent.

JT's house appears to be the same configuration as Liam's, so his bedroom should be the one to the right. Since his door isn't closed, I tiptoe over before peeking my head inside. I have no idea if he's still awake.

I just need to talk.

The curtains haven't been drawn and it allows silvery moonlight to filter in through the windows. My gaze falls to the king-sized bed, only to find it empty. It looks untouched.

My brows draw together.

Is he downstairs watching TV?

Similar to my brother's house, there's dual staircases. I head down the back one that leads to the kitchen rather than the entryway of the house. There's a small light over the sink that illuminates the room enough to see that it's empty. The TV in the family room is off, and everything around me is silent. Undisturbed. It's kind of weird roaming around someone else's house in the middle of the night.

Where is JT? I can't imagine he would leave me here by myself.

That thought has a prickle of unease slithering down my spine.

I know he was angry about what happened with Ryan.

It's strange. I've known JT for three years. I can't say I ever liked him. His obnoxious behavior was such a turn-off. He was always drinking or wrapped up in a different woman every time I saw him.

And the fights...

He was definitely the bad boy of football.

Tarnishing the Green Bay name.

Not to mention his family one as well.

And then, at the end of last season, he did a complete one-eighty and cleaned up his act. Even though I've continued to keep my distance, I can't deny that I'm attracted to him.

What woman wouldn't be?

He's gorgeous with thick, messy blond hair, unusual light green eyes, and muscles galore. He seems even more ripped now than he was before. It's like he's channeling every last drop of energy into his workout regimen.

But this past week, when he helped me out with babysitting, and now tonight...

This is the first time I'm starting to think that maybe he's not the guy I originally assumed he was. I'm not sure who the real JT is, but part of me wants to figure it out.

As I'm about to head to the basement, movement from outside on the darkened patio catches my eye and my heart skips a beat. I force my feet into movement and creep toward the French doors that line the back wall of the kitchen. The lights from the pool are still illuminated.

It's only when I'm in front of the doors, scanning the darkness, that I realize someone is swimming laps. My muscles loosen as I realize that JT didn't leave me here alone.

I grab the handle and open the door before heading out onto the stamped concrete patio. It's early September and the days are still full of sunshine, but it's not unusual for the temperature to drop down to the low sixties or high fifties at night. Goose bumps break out across my flesh as a light breeze wafts over me.

The water must be freezing.

I step toward the edge of the pool as JT surfaces. Even though he looks surprised to see me, he doesn't say a word. Instead, he rests his thickly corded arms against the tiled ledge and sets his chin on stacked hands.

I squat in front of him so that we're closer to eye level. "You always swim in the middle of the night?"

He shrugs as his gaze stays locked on mine and his lips tip into a slow grin. I'm almost surprised by the burst of arousal at the bottom of my belly. Have I ever had all that charm aimed at me before? Over the years, I've become a pro at shutting him down and ignoring his advances.

"That's the beauty of owning your own pool. You can swim anytime you want." Before I can ask any further questions, he says, "I figured you'd be sacked out until morning. It seemed like you were pretty tired."

My gaze flickers away before being drawn back to him. "I woke up and didn't know where I was." There's a pause. "When I couldn't find you, I thought maybe you'd left."

The easy smile disappears as his attention stays focused on me. "I wouldn't have done that after what happened."

In that moment, something indescribable passes between us. There's a sizzle and then a snap of energy.

I shake away the strange sensation and clear my throat, "You must be cold."

He seems to understand my need to change the subject and his voice remains light. "Nope. Heated pool."

"Oh." I trail my fingers through the water. The temperature must be somewhere in the mid-eighties. It feels a lot warmer than the cool night air that swirls around us.

"Want to join me?"

My wide gaze cuts to his. "I don't have a suit."

"Keep your underwear on." One dark blond brow slinks upward when I remain silent. "I saw the bikini you wore at the barbecue. It can't be any worse than that."

Heat slams into my cheeks as I stiffen. "There was nothing wrong with my suit."

A potent concoction of humor and heat ignite in his eyes. "Didn't say there was."

Under normal circumstances, I would never consider stripping off my clothes and getting into a pool with JT but...

Our relationship has shifted.

Before I can overthink my decision, I rise to my feet and draw in a deep breath, banishing any nerves that try to hurtle to the surface. My fingers settle on the hem of my T-shirt and whip it over my head before allowing the cottony material to slide from my fingertips.

JT's gaze stays locked on mine as I unbutton the jeans and drag down the zipper before shimmying my way out of the thick material until it puddles around my ankles. And then I'm in nothing more than pink and black polka dot panties and a matching bra. Not once do his eyes deviate from mine. I don't know why that calms everything inside me, but it does. I step closer to the pool and drop down, settling on the cerulean-colored tile ledge before lowering my legs into the water.

That feels so good.

The chilly night air makes the water feel like heaven. Not wanting to waste another moment, I slide feet first into the water, ducking down until the liquid covers my shoulders.

"Want to swim to the other side?" he asks.

"Sure."

Without another word, we take off toward the deep end of the pool. Somehow, the water is able to wash away all the heaviness from earlier.

What's strange is that being alone with JT like this should feel awkward, and yet it doesn't.

We paddle around for a while before I recline on my back and stare up at the stars. It's as if the velvety night sky is littered with thousands of them.

I can understand why he would enjoy coming out here late at night.

It's peaceful.

"You're not thinking about getting back together with him, are you?"

Startled by the sound of his deep voice cutting into my thoughts, my gaze slices to his as he watches me intently from ten feet away. Not once has he crowded me or tried to get in my space. Actually, he didn't do it when he stopped by Gia and Liam's house the other night, either. Other than the kiss we shared before he left, he never touched me. I've dwelled on that kiss way more than I should have this past week. I'm embarrassed to admit how many times I've had to shove it from my brain.

I shake away those thoughts. "No."

I have no intention of talking to Ryan again. As far as I'm concerned, we're finished.

"Good. You deserve better than him. I tried to tell you that before."

I roll my eyes. The last thing I want to hear is *I told you so.*

Especially from JT.

"What does it matter to you who I date?" The question shoots out of my mouth before I can stop it.

There's a moment of silence as he searches my gaze in the darkness. "I like you, Claire. And I don't want to see you get hurt."

Warmth blooms inside me before reverberating to the tips of my fingers and toes. It occurs to me that I've spent more time conversing with JT in the last week or so than I have the entire time we've known one another. Stranger than that, it's been enjoyable.

"Because I'm Liam's sister?"

"No. what I feel for you has nothing to do with your brother."

My belly trembles at his honesty.

"I'm glad that you seem to be in a better place now," I murmur.

I like this version of JT a lot better than the one I originally met.

"Your brother has everything to do with that," he admits. "Liam's the only one who stepped up and offered to help pry my head out of my ass."

That doesn't surprise me.

"He's a really good guy." The very best. I might have been dealt a crappy hand in the parent department, but my brothers more than make up for it. I don't know what I'd do without their love and support.

He nods. "Damn right he is."

My tongue darts out to moisten my lips. "You're not going to tell him about what happened, are you?"

A hard glint enters his eyes before he shakes his head. "As long as you're not getting back together with him, then there's no point in upsetting Liam. We both know that he'd want to kick Ryan's ass." Anger flashes across his expression. "I'm tempted to beat the piss out of him myself."

"I swear, nothing happened," I reiterate.

As he swims closer, his gaze stays locked on mine. "Not for his lack of trying." His voice deepens, turning harsh. "If he had his way, tonight would have ended much differently." There's a beat of silence as he allows those words to sink in. "You realize that, right?"

That's the most frightening part of all.

I jerk my head into a nod. "Yeah."

Even though I'd asked him to stop, Ryan wasn't about to be deterred. Thank god I was able to stay calm and pretend to be into it until I was able to get away.

Otherwise, JT is right…tonight would have ended much differently.

"You have to be careful," he adds gruffly.

But that's the thing—I didn't think I needed to be cautious with Ryan. We were going out. I'd been planning to sleep with him the next day.

If he hadn't pulled that shit in the bedroom, I would have gone through with it. A little shiver skates down my spine. I'm not happy about how the night played out, but I'm glad I saw his true colors before I went through with it.

But the fact remains that I'm still a twenty-one-year-old virgin. And going out to a bar and finding a random dude to take home for the night isn't an option. I always imagined that when the time came, I'd have a boyfriend.

Someone who cared about me.

"I'm really tired of being a virgin," I grumble.

Heat flashes in his eyes.

Silence falls over us as our gazes cling under the moonlight.

"Then let me be the one."

He takes a few lazy strokes toward me.

"I'll make it good for you, Claire. We can take things as slow as you want. I'm not going to rush or force you into something you aren't comfortable with."

My teeth sink into my lower lip before drawing the corner into my mouth.

How is it possible that only a few short days ago, I told him I'd never sleep with him?

In fact, I told him that I never wanted to see him again.

And now, by some strange twist of fate, I'm considering his offer.

Wait a minute…is that what I'm doing?

Am I seriously considering having sex with JT?

I think I am.

Is there a reason why I shouldn't?

It's not like sleeping together will change anything between us. We're not dating. And I certainly don't have any burning desire to be JT Higgins' girlfriend.

I choke back a snort.

We all know that JT Higgins doesn't *do* girlfriends.

It would be more of an arrangement.

I turn the idea over in my brain.

He's been with his fair share of women. JT can probably make my first time really good. And there wouldn't be any feelings to get tangled up in. I could get it over with and then move on with my life.

The thought holds a certain appeal.

My gaze resettles on him as I ask, "It would just be straight-up sex, right?"

JT

"Of course." The lie rolls easily off my tongue.

The last thing I'm going to do is scare her away with the truth.

Air gets clogged in my lungs as indecision flickers in her gray depths.

When the need to be closer pounds through me, I swim toward her.

Honestly, I'm blown away that she's even considering my offer. The last time I saw her, she said she never wanted to see me again and threatened to tell her brother.

With a nod, she presses her lips together as if weighing the merits of us having sex.

A more shocking turn of events I could never have imagined.

"You can trust me, Claire. I won't hurt you."

She releases a pent-up breath. "I didn't think Ryan would hurt me either."

"I'm not Ryan," I cut in swiftly. "I would never force a woman to do anything. That's not who I am."

I continue to inch closer. When she doesn't immediately back away, I lean forward and cautiously capture her lips with my own. My hand slides to the nape of her neck to tug her forward.

The kiss is gentle.

If she wanted to retreat, she could easily do so.

Once I've had my fill of her mouth, I lick and nip a trail down the slender column of her throat before pulling away and meeting her heavy-lidded gaze.

"I've wanted you for three long years, but I won't force you into anything." I press my lips against her bare collarbone. I have to stop myself from dragging the silky cups of her bra away from her high, tight breasts and worshipping them in the same manner. When a small whimper leaves her mouth, I do it again. "The decision has to be yours."

"JT..."

The way she moans my name has my cock turning to stone. I drop another kiss along her warm flesh. I'd adore every damn inch of her body if she'd let me.

"Okay," she whispers.

Thank fuck.

That's the only thought that pounds through my head. I don't think I've ever wanted anyone more than I want Claire.

"Good."

When I press my lips against the shallow valley between her breasts, her fingers thread through my hair as if to hold me in place.

"I think we should probably head inside now. It's late."

Her breath hitches.

"To sleep," I clarify, gaze locked on hers. "We're going to sleep. Nothing more. We're not going to start anything tonight, okay? I want to give you more time to think it over, and then we'll talk."

She's absolutely gorgeous with silvery moonlight spilling over her and the backdrop of stars dotting the velvety night sky overhead.

"It's your choice. You can change your mind at any time."

Relief washes over her expression and some of the tension drains. "Okay."

I trail behind her as she swims to the other side and hauls herself out of the pool. Her arms band around her middle as the wind picks up.

I point toward a teak cabinet near the back of the house as she shivers. "The towels are in there. Would you mind grabbing one for me, too?"

She scampers to the cabinet and wraps herself in an oversized plush towel. With another in hand, she returns to the side of the pool and gives me a silent look of inquiry, since I haven't budged.

When she quirks a brow, I haul myself out of the water.

Guess she should see what she's getting into, right?

Her gasp is audible as I straighten.

She clutches the towel tightly as her gaze licks over my naked body.

Neither of us utters a word. I stand perfectly still, allowing her to eat me up with her wide gray eyes. I've had an erection the entire time we've been swimming, and the cool night air stirring around us has done nothing to diminish it.

I didn't think it was possible to get harder, but that's exactly what happens.

My gaze stays riveted to hers. I want to see every flicker of emotion that crosses her face.

I've always been in excellent shape. Partying until the wee hours of the morning and getting loaded never affected me. My workout schedule was enough to keep me in peak condition. Now that I no longer drink or hit the clubs and have dedicated myself to a disciplined regimen along with feeding my body a healthy mix of complex carbs and proteins, I'm in the best damn shape of my life.

Every sinewy muscle is cut and ripped.

Perfectly honed.

If the admiration in her eyes is anything to go by, then my newfound commitment has paid off.

When her gaze finally rises to mine, she whispers, "How is it possible that you're even more beautiful than I imagined?"

And…my cock just stiffened up even more.

It's so damn tempting to scoop her up and carry her to my

bedroom. I want to remove the sexy bra and panties, dry her off, and lay her out on the bed so I can enjoy every single inch of her body before showing her exactly how pleasurable sex can be.

"Can I have the towel?" My voice is low, scraped raw with pent-up need.

Her attention drops to my cock again. I can't help but smirk when she continues to stare before finally passing me the plush material. I take my sweet damn time, allowing her to look her fill as I dry off before wrapping the towel around my waist.

If I'd thought she would react this way to my nudity, I would have taken off my clothes years ago.

I hold out my hand. "Ready to go inside?"

She gives her head a little shake as if to clear it as her fingers flutter to mine. My grip tightens around her as if she might just try to escape. Now that I finally have her, there's no way I'll let her go.

Whether she realizes it or not, Claire Garrison is mine.

Her asshole of an ex opened the door for me to saunter right on through and finally seize what I've spent years pining for. I'll be damned if I throw this opportunity away.

We stop in the kitchen and make a light snack. A roast beef and cheddar sandwich on whole wheat bread that we split. Before she found me outside, I'd been in the pool for about forty-five minutes trying to swim off this pissed-off, restless feeling brewing inside me. Even though pushing myself through a good thirty laps burned away the worst of it, the feeling is still there, gnawing away at the bottom of my belly. The only thing that consoles me is the knowledge that Claire is with me now, where I can keep her safe. Her ex is never going to get his hands on her again.

After devouring the shared sandwich, we head up the back staircase. By now, it's after three in the morning. Our steps slow as we reach the door to the guest bedroom. I linger over the threshold as she stares expectantly.

I know what she's waiting for, and it's not about to happen.

Not tonight.

"Are you coming in?" she whispers.

I shake my head.

I'm trying to be a gentleman.

It's a first for me.

But Claire is different, and what happens between us matters.

"I told you earlier that I want you to think it over for a few days." Unable to resist, I tug her fingers, towing her toward me until I can wrap my arms around her and press a gentle kiss against her lips.

Do I want to deepen it?

Hell yeah.

But I don't.

"I told you that I want to do this. I want you to be my first." She tries to pull me inside the room, but I don't budge. I'm probably double her weight.

"I want that, too. But we don't have to rush into anything. The last thing I want is for you to regret what we do together. And a lot has happened tonight…" My voice trails off as Ryan's face morphs in my head and my resolve to treat her carefully strengthens. "You need to take a little time to process it." I kiss the tip of her nose. "Trust me, I won't change my mind anytime soon. But if you do, that's cool."

Air slides from her lips like a slow leak as her shoulders fall. Just when I think she might argue, she nods instead. "All right. I'll take some time to think about it." Her eyes narrow as she tilts her head. "But I won't change my mind."

"I hope you don't," I say honestly. "I just want you to be sure."

She rises onto her tiptoes and presses her lips to mine.

As much as I want to remain unaffected, I'm not.

The moment her lips drift over mine, I open to her tentative exploration. How is it possible that I've screwed more women than I can remember, and yet it's this one with practically no experience who drives me out of my damn mind?

When her tongue slips inside my mouth, it's game over.

A growl of need rumbles up from my chest as my arms snake around her body and haul her close until her softness is aligned with all my hard lines and my cock is pressed insistently against the apex of her thighs.

When a whimper escapes from her, I scoop her into my arms and carry her to the bed. Her legs wrap around my waist, locking me against her.

How many times have I imagined her long, lean legs squeezing me tight?

Too many to count.

Once I reach the bed, I lay her gently on top of the covers. The fluffy towel is still wrapped around her chest. My gaze stays locked on hers as I carefully unwrap the material like a much-anticipated Christmas gift.

That's exactly the way this feels.

Like it's every single Christmas and birthday gift I've ever received all rolled up into one amazing moment. The pink and black polka dot panties and matching bra set are slowly revealed. They're still damp from our midnight dip in the pool.

My gaze sweeps down the length of her before I slip my hands around her ribcage and carefully unfasten the hooks in the back. Her breath catches as I gently tug the silky material away from her body. I expect her to try and cover her breasts with her arms, but that's not what happens. She remains still and allows me to look my fill in the same way I did for her twenty minutes earlier.

Her breasts are high and tight with rosy little nipples that beg for my attention. Even though I shouldn't, because playing with her body is a slippery slope, I find myself unable to resist the lure.

I lean down and tongue the one closest to me before sucking it deep into my mouth. With a groan, her back bows off the mattress as if trying to get closer. My free hand settles over the other breast, plucking and tugging at the stiffened bud before palming the softness.

The incoherent sound that falls from her lips is music to my ears. Her fingers slide through my hair, pressing me closer and holding me tightly to her chest.

I kiss the other breast before licking a hot trail to the middle of her ribcage and then across her belly until arriving at the elastic band of her panties. My fingers hook into the damp fabric as I glance up, needing to see the consent in her eyes.

Claire has allowed herself to be more open and vulnerable with me than ever before. I won't do anything to jeopardize the tentative relationship being forged between us.

She jerks her head into a nod. "Please."

How can I resist the arousal burning brightly in her gray eyes?

I've never seen this kind of expression on her face.

Turned on.

Needy.

More than anything, I love that I'm the one who put it there.

My gaze fastens onto hers as I slide the material from her slender hips before slipping it down her legs.

And then she's completely bared to my sight.

She remains still, not moving a muscle, scarcely daring to breathe as my gaze slides from her breasts to the hollow of her belly and then lower to her core.

"You're so fucking perfect," I mutter.

I don't think I've ever seen a more beautiful woman in my life, and I've seen my fair share over the years. Hundreds of them. And yet, it's this one who turns me on more than anything or anyone else ever has.

"Are we going to have sex?" A faint tremble weaves its way through her voice.

I want to.

God, but I want to.

The thought of being inside her tight heat is almost more than I can bear.

My gaze fastens onto her pussy. It's so pink and delicate. Gorgeous. The need to explore her body rushes through me. I want to pull her lips apart and find her clit before licking and nibbling at it. I want to scrape my teeth against it until she's moaning and writhing beneath me, spreading her legs as far as they'll go.

Regret floods through every cell of my body as I shake my head. "No. I meant it when I said that you need to take a few days and think it over."

Her brows draw together as the haze filling her eyes clears. "I don't want to think about it. I've already made my decision."

"I don't want you to look back on this night and feel that I've taken advantage of you."

Claire blows out a steady breath. "You haven't."

"That's right," I agree. "I haven't, and I don't plan to. Not tonight."

A smile springs to my lips when a growl erupts from her.

I love that she wants this so badly.

That she wants *me*.

It's the balm I've desperately needed for all the years she spent shutting me down. Before I can say anything else, her legs slowly fall open and my gaze drops to her pussy that's now spread wide for me to admire. A tortured groan rumbles up from deep within my chest as I feast on every single delicate inch.

"Claire, what the hell are you doing?" I can't rip my eyes away from the gorgeous sight she makes spread out on the mattress.

"What does it look like? I'm trying to tempt you into doing what I want." Even though there's nothing funny about this, she says with a soft snort, "You have to see the irony of the situation, right?"

It would be impossible not to.

"I've…" Her hesitant voice trails off.

When her teeth sink into her lower lip, I whisper, "Tell me."

She clears her throat and forces out the rest. "Ryan and I never did *that*."

Once the meaning of those words sink in, my gaze snaps to hers in surprise.

I knew they hadn't had sex, but I figured they must have messed around. There are so many other delicious ways to give and receive pleasure without actually engaging in intercourse. Why wouldn't you explore them?

"He didn't go down on you?" I'm trying to rein in my shock, but it's not easy. "Like, ever?"

My fingertips graze her sensitive flesh. Every inch is silky smooth and open to my touch.

"He wanted to. I just…" She shakes her head. "I'm not sure why I always pumped the brakes, it just never felt right. I guess doing *that* feels more intimate than having sex."

I never really thought about oral sex like that, but I guess she's right about the intimacy level.

My heart clenches before beating into overdrive. "But you want me to?"

Her gaze stays locked on mine as she nods. The trust shining within her eyes both surprises and humbles me.

"I do."

How am I supposed to walk away when I know that she's never been touched by another man? And that she wants me to be the first?

The answer is that I can't.

Claire is my kryptonite. And for her to ask something of me that I've spent years fantasizing about, something she's never asked another man to do, is my complete undoing.

Only meaning to give her a few kisses, I settle carefully between her spread legs before leaning down and pressing my mouth to her heated flesh. She's just as velvety smooth as I always imagined, with just a hint of wetness coating her lips. Her fragrance teases my senses.

So fucking sweet.

Unable to help myself, I do it again, and a soft sigh escapes from her as she spreads her legs wider, granting me even more access to her honeyed center.

Fuck.

Being this close to her is torture.

When I nuzzle her again for a third time, she arches, pushing against my mouth.

"Please," she whispers.

Because I've wanted her forever and I've imagined this moment a hundred times before, that's all it takes to break me. My tongue dips inside her slick heat before I lap her slit with the flat of my tongue. I do this over and over until she's writhing beneath me before nibbling at her clit. Her moans fill the room as I gorge myself on her pussy.

She's so damn responsive to my every lick and stroke.

"I just want to eat you up all night long until you scream my name," I mutter against her softness.

"Please, JT," she whimpers. "Please don't stop."

I'm not sure if I'll ever be able to stop. I can't imagine a day when I'll be sated.

I know she's so damn close to coming unhinged, and I want to give her that experience. I want to hear her scream because of the pleasure I've given her.

I love the feel of her fingers tunneling through my hair, locking me in place as I nibble and lick at her. She's so damn perfect. The way she moves her hips, spreading her thighs wide, as she attempts to hold me close. Not in my wildest dreams did I imagine a moment where she would be stretched out naked before me and I'd take my sweet damn time loving her with my mouth.

Her muscles grow impossibly tight right before she screams out my name.

It's the best fucking sound in the world.

Her hips gyrate as I pin her firmly to the mattress.

When she thinks back to this moment, I want her to remember every single drop of pleasure I showered upon her body.

Once she melts into the bed, I press one final kiss upon her swollen pussy before straightening. I lift my hand and wipe my mouth with my thumb and forefinger. One taste of her will never be enough.

There's a dazed look in her eyes as a contented smile curves her lips. "That was…"

Her voice trails off as if she's unable to think of a suitable adjective to describe the rush of sensation she just experienced.

"Fucking amazing?" I supply in place of her silence.

Laughter falls from her lips. It's a low chuckle that does funny things to my insides.

"Yeah, that's a good way to describe it. Fucking amazing."

My lips lift into a grin.

I've never seen Claire like this before…

All mussed up.

Loose.

Arms and legs akimbo.

She looks as though she could sink into the mattress with utter contentment.

And the look in her eyes…
I love it.
Want more of it.
Want more of *her*.
Shit.
I haven't even fucked this girl yet, and already I can't get enough.

CLAIRE

It's slowly that I surface from slumber, almost in gentle waves before I stretch my arms above my head. Unlike when I woke up in the middle of the night, I know exactly where I am.

JT's house.

In one of his guest rooms.

I wanted him to spend the night with me, but he refused.

Talk about a role reversal. The guy who has been trying to hustle me into bed for the last three years refused to have sex with me. I couldn't even cajole him into spending the night in the same room.

It's like he's grown a conscience.

Or morals.

But still…what he did was pretty freaking fantastic.

I never imagined that a guy going down on me would feel so good.

All right, better than good.

Amazing.

Completely and utterly amazing. It was like I could reach out and run my fingertips through the stars twinkling in the dark, velvety sky.

It's only when I throw off the covers that I realize I'm naked.

My clothes are still on the patio where I shed them last night. I glance around for my bra and panties, but I don't see them. I wrap the blanket around my shoulders before rising from the bed and padding to the door. It takes less than fifteen seconds to reach JT's bedroom. It's still early. The sun is barely peeking over the eastern horizon with its pink and purple hues.

JT's door is cracked open just an inch or two. As soon as I'm over the threshold, my gaze falls on him. The sheet is crumpled at his waist, leaving the broad expanse of his chest and abs exposed.

I always knew he had a nice body.

Why wouldn't he?

The man works out for a living. His livelihood depends on him being conditioned within an inch of his life. But I never imagined him being so impossibly hard and muscular. As if every part of him has been chiseled from granite.

He makes Ryan look like a soft, barely developed teenager.

JT is just so big and bulky. Every sinewy muscle is cut before being stretched taut across bone. I want to run my fingers over every delicious inch.

Hell, I want to lick my way across his body.

From head to toe.

It never occurred to me that when he climbed out of the pool last night, he'd be naked. Heat floods my cheeks at the way I'd stared unabashedly at his cock. I never expected him to be so stunning.

I might not have much to compare it to, but that doesn't mean I'm totally ignorant.

He's huge.

Long and thick.

His light snores snap be back to the present, and I clutch the blanket more tightly as I creep closer. It's so tempting to crawl onto the bed and snuggle up beside him. My teeth sink into my lower lip as I contemplate what to do.

Screw it.

I've spent the past six years walking the straight and narrow. I focused all of my attention and energy on school so I could achieve my goals and make my family proud. I've sacrificed potential relationships along the way, and I refuse to do it any longer.

This isn't something I expected to happen.

Especially with JT Higgins.

Up until a week ago, I could barely stand to be in the same room with the guy.

And yet...here we are.

If I have any say in the matter, he'll be the one who takes my virginity. After last night, and the way he made my body come alive, there aren't any doubts in my mind about going through with it. I release the edge of the blanket wrapped around me and let it slither to the floor before cautiously climbing onto the mattress.

JT is lying on his back. One thickly corded arm is thrown over his eyes. Even in slumber, his chest ripples with chiseled musculature and definition. A smattering of blond hair covers it. Everything about him is masculine. It's not difficult to understand why women fall all over themselves trying to gain and hold his attention.

His deep breathing never falters as I settle next to him.

I have no idea how he's going to react when he wakes up and finds me in his bed. He was so adamant about keeping his distance. I would be lying if I didn't admit that I'm touched by his stance.

Especially after last night.

I can appreciate that he wants me to take my time and think it over. He wants me to do what's right for myself. The thing is, I'm going into this with my eyes wide open. I'm not delusional enough to think this will turn into a relationship.

But you know what?

If the pleasure he was able to give me last night is any indication, then JT is exactly what I need.

And I'll enjoy it for what it is.

Sex.

Pure and simple.

When you think about it with that mindset, it's surprisingly cut and dry. No messy emotions, expectations or complications to get in the way. It's a physical act. And JT obviously knows what he's doing. He'll make it a good experience.

He asked that I think it over, and I have.

JT is the perfect man to take my virginity.

There's zero chance I'll get emotionally involved, because I know exactly what to expect from him.

Which is very little.

He'll probably lose interest once the deed is done, and then we can both move on with our lives. The more I consider it, the more sense it makes.

As I settle in next to him, my gaze roams freely over his body.

The only downside to this arrangement is that I can't imagine another man ever living up to him. JT Higgins is stunning. I never thought I'd be a girl who was into super athletic men, but all those muscles are impossibly sexy.

I wasn't kidding about wanting to run my fingers and tongue over him. His shoulders are broad and sculpted. Hair swirls across his chest before arrowing down his rock-solid abdominals and disappearing beneath the sheet.

I nibble at my lower lip, staring at the part of him hidden by the cottony material.

I certainly got an eyeful last night.

He just stood there and allowed me to look my fill like it wasn't a big deal.

My five-minute perusal wasn't nearly long enough. I could have stared for hours. It took everything I had inside not to reach out and stroke my fingers across his flesh. He was impossibly hard. Beneath his thick erection were heavy-looking balls.

My hand closes over the edge of the sheet before carefully pulling it from his body, revealing more of his sun-kissed flesh. It seems to take forever to uncover the part of him I'm most fascinated with.

I edge closer to get a better look.

Even though his cock is soft, it's still impressively sized. It lies across the taut skin of his lower abdomen. JT makes a noise and my gaze flies to his face. His eyelids are still feathered shut. That's when I notice the thick sweep of his lashes against his cheeks. Most women would kill for lashes like that.

My attention drops to his chest. His breathing is still deep and even.

Good. I'm not ready for him to wake just yet.

I'm still busy taking him in. With him sleeping, I can stare at him without embarrassment.

When my attention wanders back to his cock, I find it standing to attention. My heartbeat thumps painfully against my ribcage as I flick a glance at his face. His eyes are heavy-lidded and there's a sleepy smile curving his full, generous mouth.

Exactly when did I start thinking that his lips were full and generous?

I'm going to hazard a guess and say that it was probably around the same time I became preoccupied with his cock.

"Good morning," he says as if finding me in his bed is completely normal.

One side of my mouth hitches in response at being caught ogling his goods. "Morning."

He lifts a brow. "Find something interesting?"

I shrug. "Maybe."

Before I realize what's happening, he lunges. I shriek as he rolls on top of me. Unconsciously, I spread my legs to accommodate his girth. When his thick erection presses against my pussy, a sigh of pleasure escapes from me as I arch against him, only wanting to get closer.

He immediately pulls away so that his cock doesn't slip inside.

"Was that really necessary?" I complain.

Wait a minute…am I actually whining?

Practically on the verge of begging for sex?

How the heck did this happen?

Has the earth fallen completely off its axis?

Nothing makes sense anymore.

"I want you," I tell him. "I haven't changed my mind, and I'm not going to."

With a groan, he swears harshly under his breath before saying in a much firmer tone, "I was serious about you needing to take a few days to think it over without the haze of sex and naked cocks clouding your judgment."

"Stop playing so hard to get. It's unlike you."

He grins before thrusting his hips against me. Sensation ricochets throughout my entire body.

"I'm trying to be a good guy here. And you're making that difficult."

I kind of hate how much I like this playful and sweet side of him.

He balances the bulk of his weight on his elbows as one hand rises to stroke my cheek.

"The last thing I want is for you to look back and decide that what we did was a mistake. I've wanted you for three years, Claire. No matter how much time you take, *me* wanting *you* won't change."

What he's saying makes sense. There's no reason for us to rush headfirst into something.

"Okay." As soon as the response escapes from my mouth, he grinds his erection against me, and my eyes nearly roll back in my head.

"Does that mean we can do *other* things?" I ask.

He arches a brow. "Other things such as…"

Heat floods my cheeks as I grumble, "Are you really going to make me say it?"

A devilish grin lifts the corners of his mouth. "I would dearly love to hear you say the words, sweetheart."

I draw in a steady breath before blurting, "I want you to eat my pussy."

He groans and smacks a kiss against my lips. "I thought you'd never ask."

With that, he slides down my body, raining soft kisses along the way until finally settling between my legs. I sigh when he spreads them wide and his warm breath feathers against me.

JT

ave I mentioned just how much I hate being summoned home by my parents?

It doesn't happen often, but when it does, my whole day gets turned to shit. It's the reason I avoid them as much as possible. My father is a real blowhard who is impossible to please. I should probably clarify that statement. There's nothing *I* can do to please him. My older brother, on the other hand, can do no wrong.

He's the golden child to my black sheep.

Joe is two years older and plays for Minnesota. He was drafted in the first-round pick and is a rising star in the NFL. I know my parents were hoping he would go to Green Bay. I don't think they gave a damn where I ended up.

Since my father played in Green Bay and later became involved in the organization, they've always kept a house here. Their place makes mine look like a shithole.

Ponder that for a moment.

My family comes from old money. Generations of it. I have no idea how the first Higgins made his fortune. Might have been railroads or banking. My father has yammered on about it over the years, but I couldn't tell you what he said. I have the habit of tuning him out whenever he talks.

Call it a coping mechanism.

Since I haven't heard from them in a while, it was only a matter of time. One of the upsides to staying out of the press is not being on the receiving end of a phone call from my father, reminding me of what a total disappointment I am. He'll also add how my mother is too ashamed to show her face at the Junior League and Historical Society meetings she presides over.

Now, I only receive a call when I'm told in no uncertain terms to hightail my ass home.

For what exactly?

I have no idea.

But I'm sure it won't end well for me.

It never does.

My father and I end up in a shouting match over something ridiculously unimportant. My mother will sit and stare at us, all the while wringing her perfectly manicured hands. I'll get fed up with it and storm out until the next time I'm summoned home.

It's an ugly cycle.

I suppose that would be one good thing about getting traded.

No more of that redundant bullshit.

As much as I hate going there, at least I can check in and see what Bess has been up to. We don't get a chance to see each other that often, especially during the season. Every once in a while, I'm able to cajole her into meeting me for lunch.

Even the thought of spending an entire afternoon in my father's austere company is mentally exhausting. Ironically enough, I seem to be the only one who rubs him the wrong way. I can't think of one damn thing we agree on other than the fact that we can't agree on anything.

I roll my Porsche up to the wrought iron gate at the bottom of the drive before punching in the security code and driving through. There's about a mile-long winding road that leads to a massive stone structure. Tall oaks and willow trees are scattered throughout the well-manicured property. There's a circular drive where I park before heading up steps to the front door and hitting the bell. I might have grown up in this house, but it's never felt like home. Shoulders hunched, muscles tensed, I shove my hands into the pockets of my khakis. It only takes a moment before the heavy mahogany door is thrown open.

"Jameson!"

I flash a devilish grin before wrapping my arms around Bess' stout body and pulling her in for a hug. She squeals as I lift her off her feet. While midair, she swats at me. Bess might pretend to hate when I do that, but I know otherwise.

She secretly loves it.

I set her back down again and ask, "How you doing, Bess? Long time, no see."

"Maybe if you'd come home occasionally for a visit, I'd be able to see my darling boy a bit more often." Her wrinkled hand rises to pat my cheek affectionately.

Bess was like a mother to me growing up. If she hadn't been here, taking care of us, life would have been unbearable. I've tried several times to entice her into moving to my house, but she refuses to leave my parents.

She must be a glutton for punishment.

"Been busy. Hard to find the time." It's not a total lie. But it's not the truth either, and we both know it.

Her hands settle on her wide hips as she tilts her head. "Even to see old Bess, huh?"

"If you'd take me up on my offer to move in with me, then we could see each other every day. I barely get a home-cooked meal anymore. I'm living on take-out." That's not altogether true, either. I have a meal service that preps healthy food. But I know the thought of me subsiding on restaurant food might change her mind.

Eyes narrowed, her gaze slides over me.

A disbelieving noise escapes from her. "I think you're lying. You look better than ever. The last thing you need is an old woman bustling around your house." She points a finger in my direction. "You need to settle down and find yourself a wife. A woman who will take good care of you."

As if on cue, an image of Claire pops into my brain.

A grin splits her face. "Ahhh, I see you've finally met someone."

My mouth tumbles open before I have the good sense to snap it shut again. The change in my relationship with Claire is much too new to dissect. I've always suspected that Bess might be part witch. Or gypsy. When I was a kid, she always knew what mischief I was intent upon. Sometimes even before I got the notion in my head.

When I press my lips together, refusing to comment, she chuckles.

"You come see me in the kitchen after you've greeted your parents properly and I'll get it out of you." She nods as if it's already been decided. "One way or another."

I rock back on my heels. "Would one of those ways include snickerdoodle cookies?"

She smiles smugly. "It very well could."

It's the click of high heels against marble that has me turning. The scent of Chanel precedes my mother's arrival in the entryway.

She gifts me with a slight smile before her gaze settles on the older woman. "Is dinner set for three o'clock?"

"Yes, ma'am."

"Good." My mother inclines her head ever so slightly. "Thank you, Bess."

Bess gives me a cheeky wink before bustling off to the kitchen. Her sensible, rubber-soled shoes don't make a sound as she moves through the long corridor before disappearing from sight.

Once we're alone, my mother turns her full attention to me. Her light green eyes travel slowly over my body as if she's inspecting a parcel for damage before they slide back to my face. Even though it feels awkward, I wrap my arms around her. Before I can fully sink into the embrace, she steps away, distancing herself.

And that, my friends, is precisely what a cozy embrace looks like in the Higgins household. Honestly, it's a wonder I'm not more fucked up than I am.

"You're looking well, Jameson."

I incline my head before returning the compliment. "As are you, Mother."

It's true. Rather amazingly, the woman never seems to age. She always looks the same. There's not a single blonde hair out of place or wrinkle bracketing her eyes or mouth. Even though it's Saturday afternoon, she's dressed as if heading out to a society function instead of a simple family dinner at home. My great-grandmother's pearls are clasped around her slender neck, and her makeup is impeccable.

"Your father is waiting in the library."

God forbid he actually gets off his ass to greet me himself.

I say nothing to that. In fact, I have to hold back the grunt that desperately tries to escape from my lips.

I do a few quick mental calculations. It's around two o'clock in the afternoon. Apparently, dinner will be served at three, which means that I'm probably stuck hanging around until at least four. Maybe even five.

Unless, of course, my father and I get into a heated exchange. Then, all bets are off. Even thinking about spending the next two to three hours of my life trapped here has me tugging at the starched collar of the pressed button-down shirt I'm wearing, because it feels like I'm being choked to death. I would much rather sit in the kitchen with Bess and enjoy the snickerdoodle cookies she bakes for me.

Mom links her arm through mine and leads me down the echoing corridor until we reach the wood-paneled library. There's a large window that overlooks the back lawn and gardens. Too bad the view is more idyllic than the people in this house.

I grind to a halt when I realize that my father isn't alone. My brother Joe is sitting on the sofa at the far side of the room. He looks perfectly at ease, lounging against the antique leather with his ankle casually resting on his knee. His dark hair is swept across his fore-head. He's the spitting image of my father. If you glimpsed a photo-graph of Dad when he was Joe's age, you'd be hard-pressed to tell them apart.

I wasn't aware that my brother was home for a visit. Although, I suppose it makes sense considering that Minnesota is on a bye week.

With a smile tugging at the corners of his mouth, Joe rises to his feet and meets me halfway across the room before clapping me heartily on the shoulder. Out of the three of them, he's the only one who looks genuinely pleased by my presence.

"Glad you could make it, man," he says.

"I didn't even know you were in town."

"Just got in yesterday. Can only stay a few days, then I'm heading back to Minneapolis."

Maybe this dinner won't be so bad after all.

Usually, my father is a lot more jovial and forgiving when my brother is around to soften him up. One would think I'd resent Joe for being the light of my father's life, but it's the opposite.

My brother is an expert at drawing attention away from me.

And I'm all for that.

While Dad has always set high expectations, Joe exceeds them enough for the pair of us. I, on the other hand, always fall short. Or, if I do manage to achieve something, it's still not good enough for Joe Higgins Senior. He can find a flaw or problem with whatever I accomplish.

No matter how minuscule.

Once I realized the pattern of his behavior, I gave up trying to please him.

Do you have any idea how freeing that was?

"Thought I'd come see the game tomorrow." He waves a hand toward our parents. "Actually, we're all planning on being there."

That knowledge sinks to the bottom of my gut like a heavy stone.

Great.

I hate when my parents are at the stadium for games. It'll be stuck in my head. Which is ridiculous, I know. I'm not a fucking child and yet, these damn people have a way of making me feel like a sulky, fourteen-year-old punk who will never live up to the illustrious Higgins name and all it represents.

Even though my gut now churns, I keep a smile plastered across my face. There's no point in trying to talk them out of their decision. I'm sure they'll be using one of the boxes. My family might live in

Green Bay, but they only make it to a few games a year. Most notably, the ones where my team is pitted against Joe's.

We're like the Manning brothers in that regard.

Trust me, the broadcasters thoroughly enjoy playing up the rivalry.

Except, my parents are only rooting for one of us.

And it isn't me.

This day just keeps getting better and better.

The only thing I can say is that it started out a hell of a lot nicer than it'll be ending.

There's no better way to wake up than with Claire Garrison warming my bed.

Actually, it was more like waking up to Claire staring at my cock like it was the most fascinating thing in the world. Said appendage twitches at the memory.

"Would you like a drink, dear?" Mom asks.

Before I have a chance to decline the offer, my father snaps, "He'll take a water, Margaret. Have you forgotten there's a game tomorrow? Jameson needs to be clearheaded. He shouldn't be drinking any alcohol during the season."

Mom bites down on her lower lip before nodding in agreement. "Of course, you're right. How could I have forgotten? I'll have Bess bring a bottle of water."

I glare at my father before gritting out, "You know what? I'll take that drink instead. Make it a scotch on the rocks."

Dad's jaw locks as his eyes narrow.

For a moment, Mom stands rooted in place, unsure what to do. I shouldn't have allowed her to get in the middle of our pissing match.

My intention had been to turn down the drink and ask for something else instead.

Until he piped up and took the decision out of my hands.

I'm a twenty-five-year-old man, for fuck's sake.

I'll make my own damn decisions.

I almost snort.

I'm a twenty-five-year-old man who is now going to pour himself a double in an effort to goad his father into reacting. It's like I'm looking at this farce from high above and shaking my head at how my dad continuously pulls my strings like I'm nothing more than a marionette.

With my hands stuffed in my pockets, I saunter to the minibar that lines one of the mahogany-covered walls. "Never mind, I'll get it myself."

Even though my back is turned toward him, I can almost hear my father gnashing his teeth.

"Do you really think you should be drinking the day before a game, Jameson?"

Just like I anticipated, the man is practically frothing at the mouth.

Hell, this must be a new record for us. I usually make it through at least twenty minutes of polite small talk before we're at each other's throats.

Even though I'd only planned to hold the liquor without consuming it, his growled-out question has me lifting the heavy crystal tumbler to my lips and taking a healthy swallow.

"Yup."

The rest of the afternoon only slides downhill from there.

CLAIRE

Something's wrong.

JT isn't playing like he normally does. There's an aggressiveness that I'm not used to seeing from him on the field. It's like he's on the verge of exploding. One of the assistant coaches has pulled him aside twice. On the sidelines, he seems sullen and angry.

Pacing back and forth like a caged animal.

When he dropped me off early yesterday afternoon, it seemed like everything was good. Better than good. The way he kissed me after pulling up in front of my apartment building was enough to curl my toes. If I could have, I would've crawled onto his lap. Actually, I did try crawling onto his lap, but it's difficult in the Porsche he drives.

Normally, I attend every home game with Gia and the kids. We sit in a private box, so the children can run around without disturbing anyone. Ty alternates between watching his father on the field and playing with his iPad. There are other wives or girlfriends who bring their kids as well. So, it's fun for everyone. Kind of like a playdate. Over the last three years, I've gotten to know quite a few of the ladies.

They're a nice group.

Down to earth.

It's not that I expected JT to acknowledge me in any kind of way, but…

All right, maybe I did. He's never been shy about staring at me. But he hasn't glanced this way once. It's like he doesn't even know I'm here.

Ugh.

I really need to remember that this relationship is strictly sex. We're not dating or going out. I'm not his girlfriend.

I can't allow myself to go there or I'll end up with bruised feelings.

This is JT Higgins we're talking about.

Mr. I've slept with more women than I can possibly remember.

Mr. I'll throw a punch at a club any damn time I want, thank you very much.

Mr. I can drink like a fish and still dominate on the field the next day.

Mr. Nothing fazes me, so bring it on.

I scrub a hand over my face at my own stupidity for allowing this to happen.

And it only took one night!

Sheesh.

I know better. It's one of the reasons I spent the last three years holding him at a safe distance. Deep down, I've always felt the sexual energy humming between us. It was all too easy to ignore when he was acting like a total ass.

If I could stop this train in its proverbial tracks, I'd do it in a heart-beat. Unfortunately, last night pushed us way past the point of no return.

For better or worse, JT and I are a done deal.

We're going to happen.

He's going to be the one.

The thought of him breaking my heart leaves me cringing.

Uncomfortable with the thoughts circling through my head, I push them to the back of my mind and refocus my attention on what's playing out on the field.

Unfortunately, JT doesn't fare any better during the rest of the game.

Even from the private box, I can feel the pent-up anger rolling off him in thick, suffocating waves. He's dodged his way through the other team's offensive line, and Green Bay has been able to rack up yards, but he normally plays with more finesse.

If he keeps going like this, he'll end up being carried out of the stadium on a stretcher. I sit on the edge of my seat, my foot tapping, unable to take my eyes off him. It's actually a relief when the game ends with Green Bay bringing home another win.

Gia rearranges Max in her arms as she leans toward me. "I wonder what's going on with JT."

With a shrug, I keep my mouth firmly zipped and pretend this is like any other game and I don't care about what's going on with JT Higgins. It's not like I can tell Gia about the plans we have to sleep together. Although part of me does wish I could sit down with her and discuss how everything has changed between us. Gia and I have always been close. Like sisters. She's usually the first person I turn to when I need to hash something out.

But I can't do that with this.

I can't tell her about my brother's teammate.

I'm sure she'd think it was a mistake. And I'm not altogether certain I would disagree.

When I remain silent, Gia asks, "Is everything okay?"

I force my lips into a smile and lie through my teeth. "I'm just thinking about my classes."

"Your student teacher placement starts next week, too, right?"

"Yup." It's what I've been focused on since I was twelve years old. It may not seem like much, but it's a dream come true, and I've worked hard to make it happen.

She reaches out to squeeze my hand. "You're going to be great."

"Thank you."

Now that the game is over, fans are exiting the stadium en masse. There are several sports reporters interviewing players on the side-lines, doing their best to get soundbites.

I scan the field, but I don't see JT. He's probably already in the locker room.

Now that the game is over, there's a private meet and greet at the stadium. One of the restaurants on the concourse has been reserved for the event. I have some work to finish up before class tomorrow, so I don't plan on staying long. Since Liam is the QB, he usually has a press conference after each game along with the head coach and a few other key players. He'll be one of the last guys to arrive at the party.

I nibble my lower lip and wonder if I should skip the get-together. It's just so weird the way everything felt so great when JT dropped me off yesterday, and now, for reasons I can't explain, it feels like I should keep my distance.

I haven't even spoken with JT and yet—

"You ready to head down?" Gia asks, interrupting my thoughts.

"Umm, I was thinking of taking off instead," I hedge.

Her dark brows slide together in confusion. "What?"

Those all-seeing blue eyes of hers immediately scour my face for insight as to what I'm attempting to hide.

"Yeah." I clear my throat because I'm a terrible liar. "I have a ton of stuff to finish up. I should probably get it started."

"How about you grab a quick bite to eat and then you can sneak out," she suggests.

My shoulders collapse. Honestly, I was hoping to avoid JT until I have a better understanding of what's going on between us.

"Yeah, sure," I finally mutter. "But I can only stay for about thirty minutes, then I have to go."

She looks pleased to have secured my acquiescence so easily. In a way, Gia is kind of like a mother figure to me, and I have a hard time saying no to her. Especially when I haven't been forthcoming in the first place.

Guilt.

It'll get you every time.

Fifteen minutes slip by before we gather up the children and make our way to the concourse. As we walk into the restaurant, Gia stops to greet several people. Since I've been hanging around for the past three years, I know them as well. I've become quite adept at making small talk regarding the season, team, and prospects.

My gaze scans the vicinity until it lands on JT and a group of people I don't recognize.

After a few moments, I find myself asking Gia, "Do you know who's with JT?"

I've been covertly watching them for the past couple of minutes, and I can't place them. There's an older couple along with a dark-haired man. Upon closer inspection, it seems obvious that the two men are related. They're practically carbon copies of one another.

I narrow my gaze and try to place the younger man.

He looks strangely familiar, and by his build, my guess is that he plays football. He has that look about him. Like pumping iron is his life's work. Although, I know he's not with this organization.

He's also extremely good-looking. I would have remembered if he was with Green Bay.

I'm still staring, trying to figure out who they are, when the younger man's deep brown eyes collide with mine. A small smirk immediately quirks his lips. My face heats as I rip my gaze away and pretend that I didn't just get caught checking out some random dude.

"That's his family."

Whatever I was expecting her to say, that wasn't it.

My brows shoot up in response.

I've heard a lot about them. Not from JT, of course. But anyone who's well versed in Green Bay history knows that his father spent the majority of his career playing and coaching in this town. That must mean that the younger, dark-haired man would be none other than—

"Hello, ladies. I don't believe we've had the pleasure of being introduced."

Joe Higgins.

JT's older brother. The one who plays for Minnesota. The same one who has taken the league by storm. He's made quite a name for himself and, unlike his brother, none of it has been through bad press. Joe is the golden boy of the NFL. He has numerous multi-million-dollar endorsement deals, from sexy underwear to toothpaste. His name and face are plastered everywhere right now. I should have immediately recognized him. But I guess when JT is around, I have trouble seeing anyone else.

Thank goodness Gia is still standing next to me with all three kids. Max is squirming in her arms, Charlotte is decked out in a fancy, over-the-top tulle skirt, and Ty looks like a mini Liam with his Garrison jersey and eye black smudged on his chubby cheeks.

Even though Joe's attention stays focused on me, my sister-in-law is the one to clear her throat. "Gia Garrison. Nice to finally meet you."

His dark gaze swings to hers and takes in the kids. His smile broadens. Just as he opens his mouth, Liam slides an arm around Gia before hauling her and Max close.

Whatever Joe had been about to say gets cut off when Liam growls, "This is my wife, Higgins. If you value your life, you'll stay far away from her. In fact, don't even bother to look in her direction."

The other man doesn't take offense.

He chuckles before taking Gia's hand and shaking Liam's. "Great to see you, man. Been a while."

"Not nearly long enough," Liam grumbles. "Don't we play each other in three weeks? That's good enough for me."

When my brother says nothing more, Joe's gaze slides back to mine. "And you would be?"

"This is my sister, Claire," Liam grumbles. "I probably don't need to say this but, I will—stay away from her as well."

His voice deepens, turning no-nonsense, as if he's issuing an actual warning.

Not put off by my brother's rude behavior, Joe grins good-naturedly. "Nice to meet you."

I extend my hand for him to take and he keeps a light hold on my fingers until I find myself tugging them free. A smile graces his lips the entire time.

I'll say this about Joe Higgins—he's handsome. What's strange is that he looks nothing like his brother. Where Joe has short, dark hair and deep espresso-hued eyes, JT has long, golden blond hair and vivid, light green ones. Both men are muscular, over six feet tall, and broad in the shoulders.

Trapped in those thoughts, my gaze wanders to JT. Air gets clogged at the back of my throat when I find his attention focused on me.

Joe tosses a look over his shoulder before his gaze swings back to mine with interest. "So that's the way of things, huh?"

I flick a glance at Liam to see if he's picked up on Joe's comment, but he's wrapped up in his family.

"No," I say quickly.

"Good." He steps a bit closer before whispering, "He'll break your heart, darling. And I'd really hate to see that happen."

Everything in me stiffens. Probably because those exact same thoughts were circling around in my brain while watching JT on the field this afternoon.

And I don't want that to happen.

I lift my chin. "We're just friends."

He flashes an easy smile, revealing bright, white teeth. "I think we both know that my brother doesn't have female friends."

"Maybe it would be more appropriate to say that we're more like acquaintances," I fire back.

He steps closer, invading my personal space. "Can I get you a drink or something?"

I have the feeling he's more interested in the *something* else.

I shake my head before taking a step in retreat. My quick scramble backward seems to amuse him.

"If you'll excuse me..." My voice trails off as I dart toward the restrooms.

I don't have to go, but I needed an excuse to get away from him. It felt like Joe was hitting on me, and under normal circumstances, I would have been flattered.

But not right now.

Not when I'm conflicted about his brother, and certainly not with JT watching us from across the crowded room. It was difficult not to squirm under the liquid intensity of his stare.

I splash a little cold water on my face and decide that I should get moving. I'll say a quick goodbye to Liam, Gia, and the kids before ducking out.

With an escape plan in mind, I exit the bathroom and head down the short hallway that leads to the restaurant. There have to be at least two hundred people filling the space. Everyone is milling around, laughing and making small talk.

Just as I beeline for my brother and sister-in-law, I catch JT and his father from the corner of my eye. I can't help but grind to a halt and stare openly. They look as if they're in the middle of an argument. JT looks pissed. His father is turned away from me, so I'm not able to see the expression on his face.

I have no idea what propels me to change directions, but that's exactly what I find myself doing. It only takes a few moments before I'm closing in on them. Just as I'm about to approach, JT's eyes cut to mine. It's only then that his expression changes. His green gaze widens ever so slightly.

The lines of his face tighten and a muscle tics in his cheek. Even though he doesn't say a word, I get the feeling he wants me to leave them alone. He might not appreciate it, but he looks like he's in need of rescue, and that's exactly what I'm going to do.

As soon as I'm close enough, I wrap my arm around JT's waist and reach up on my toes to press a quick kiss against his cheek. There's just a bit of scruff covering his jaw. It's a look I've always found sexy.

It's even more so on JT.

Whatever his father had been in the middle of saying gets cut off as I paste a bright, friendly smile on my face. His dark gaze bounces between the pair of us as if he doesn't know what to make of me.

When neither of them acknowledges my presence, I thrust out my hand in his father's direction. "Hi, it's nice to meet you. I'm Claire Garrison."

His eyes narrow as he turns my name over in his head. I can almost see the wheels in his brain turning, wondering if I'm someone worth knowing or just some random hanger-on he can easily dismiss.

I don't know this man, but already I don't like him.

"Garrison, you say?"

"Yes, sir. Liam is my brother."

That's all it takes for the anger brewing in his eyes like storm clouds to clear. Now, it's all sunshine and rainbows. He reaches out and wraps his larger hand around mine before pumping it heartily as if we're old friends.

"Joe Higgins. Nice to meet you."

Even though I've only been standing with these two men for a matter of moments, I feel the thick, suffocating tension that sits between them. It makes me doubly glad that I decided to interrupt whatever was going on. I'm almost surprised when JT's muscular arm slides around me and hauls me closer.

The older man takes a swallow of his drink as he eyes me speculatively. "And what is it that you do, Claire?"

"I'm a student at UW- Green Bay and will be graduating this spring with a degree in elementary education."

His eyes remain hooded as he studies us, as if trying to figure out what's going on. "We had no idea Jameson was seeing someone."

Jameson, huh?

I didn't realize that's what the J in JT stood for.

His gaze flicks toward his son. There's no fondness whatsoever in his expression. Only cool disdain. That realization arrows clean through my heart. What must it have been like to grow up with a father like that?

"In fact, I didn't think he was capable of it," he muses. "The only thing my son seems adept at is wreaking havoc in a woman's life before tossing her aside."

My eyes widen at the ugly words murmured in such an offhanded manner.

Before I can say anything, even think of a scathing retort to fire back with, he leans toward me. "I'd be careful if I were you, my dear. You don't seem like my son's usual type. I'd hate for him to sully your good name." He winks before adding, "Don't say I didn't warn you."

Shock rushes through me.

Did his father really just say that?

It's only then that I feel JT's fingers bite into the skin at my waist and almost wince. I know he's unaware of the pain being inflicted.

"JT and I are just friends," I tell him in an equally cool voice.

The man snorts as if that's the most ridiculous thing he's ever heard in his life before excusing himself to talk with someone far more important across the room.

Another wave of disbelief crashes over me as I silently watch him saunter away before refocusing my attention on JT. I'm almost scared of what I'm going to find written across his face. Already, his beautiful green eyes are boring into mine.

Even though I don't want them to, they manage to steal my breath away.

Every time I'm around him, I feel myself falling a little harder. A little deeper. Becoming more ensnared.

It's not what I want. Whatever this is between us needs to remain uncomplicated.

Unfortunately, it feels anything but.

"Are you okay?" I ask.

He shrugs. "Yeah, I'm fine. Believe it or not, you actually caught him on a good day."

I cringe, hoping he's exaggerating, but I don't think so.

JT's father seems like a jackass. And I've had more than my fill of those lately.

Now that his father has disappeared, I step out of his arms, needing to put some much-needed space between us. A strange sort of energy hums in the air.

When he remains silent, only continuing to pin me in place with his gaze, I point toward my original destination.

"I should get going. I have some studying to do for tomorrow."

Not once does his attention deviate from me as he shoves his hands into the pockets of his khakis. "I have to stay a bit longer." He throws a look full of longing at the exit. "At least another hour or two."

My gaze slides around the room before getting snagged by his father. For some unknown reason, I don't like the idea of leaving JT alone when that man is still here. Which is crazy. It's not like we're involved. The plan is for him to take care of the pesky issue of my virginity.

That's it.

End of story.

And then we'll both move on with our lives as if nothing happened between us.

Easy peasy lemon squeezy.

I take a quick step in retreat, only wanting to flee the restaurant. The way he continues to stare makes my body buzz with electricity. "Well, okay then."

When he remains silent, I take another step before swinging around and rushing toward the exit that will lead to the concourse. I'm about five feet away when his deep voice slices through the chatter that surrounds us.

"Want me to pick you up in an hour or so?"

I throw a glance over my shoulder and catch his gaze.

I shouldn't.

In fact, it would probably be for the best if I took a few days to clear my head after the last forty-eight hours.

"Sure."

Damn.

His muscles visibly loosen as his lips hitch into a sexy smile. Something unexpectedly flips in my belly as possessiveness flares to life in his eyes.

"I'll text when I'm on my way."

JT

I bring the bottle of ice-cold water to my lips and watch Claire as she hugs her brother and his wife before kissing each kid goodbye.

"What the hell have you gotten yourself tangled up in now?" my brother asks.

Whatever had begun to loosen within me tenses right back up again.

When I fail to respond, he continues, "That girl seems much too innocent for the likes of you."

I wipe all expression from my face and rip my gaze away from Claire before glancing at my brother, who has sidled up beside me. Just goes to show you how preoccupied I am, because the guy weighs a solid two fifty. He's not exactly light on his feet. No matter how stealthy he's trying to be.

"We're just friends," I mutter.

He snorts. "Funny, that's exactly what she said." There's a pause before he adds, "Hmmm, I sure wouldn't mind having a friend like that." He rams his elbow into my ribs before scratching his chin. "Think she'd be interested in befriending me as well? I'm definitely the more handsome Higgins brother."

Rage crashes over me and the words shoot out of my mouth before I can rein them back in again. "Stay the fuck away from Claire. And you're right, she's too damn innocent." This last part is more or less mumbled, because it's the truth, and I know it.

When it comes down to it, I have no business doing anything with Claire Garrison.

After picking her up from that frat party Friday night and listening to her recount what happened, I feel protective where she's concerned, which is crazy because it's not like I don't want to get her just as naked as that jackass ex-boyfriend of hers.

Unlike him, I'm sure as shit not going to force her into something she doesn't want. Or isn't ready for. Hell, Friday night when I tasted her honeyed flesh and then told her to think everything over...you can be damn sure that's the first time those words have slid from my lips.

Here's the thing—Claire is different.

On some level, I've *always* known that was the case.

She's worth taking my time with. No matter how long I have to wait. I've never craved another woman the way I do her. I've never wanted to protect anyone the way I want to keep her safe.

"So that's Garrison's little sister, huh?" he asks, breaking into the turmoil of my thoughts.

The reminder has my lips wilting at the corners. "Yup."

I don't have a clue what's going on between us. Is this simply a... *deflowering*, for lack of a better word?

Or are we starting something up?

I wish I had a better handle on the situation.

But I don't. I'm flying by the seat of my pants where she's concerned.

Hasn't that always been the case?

"And the guy is cool with whatever's going on between the two of you? Because he told me in no uncertain terms to stay the hell away from both his wife and his sister."

"Sounds about right." I shake my head before saying once more, as if repeating it out loud will make it true, "I told you, we're just friends."

By the smile that simmers around his lips and the dubious expression in his eyes, he doesn't believe the load of crap I'm shoveling his way.

"How old is she anyway? Just tell me she's not jailbait."

I can tell by his speculative tone that he's eyeing her up, and it sets my nerves on edge. When Joe and I were in high school, even in college, we'd hit on each other's women. There were a handful that I showed up with that ended up leaving a party with him. And there were a few of Joe's that I swayed away. Not one damn time did I feel jealous or angry.

It was nothing more than a game. Those women didn't mean anything to either of us. But that's not how I feel right now. The comment leaves my free hand clenching. Part of me wants to grab him by the collar and—

"Twenty-one," I say with a grunt.

"Hmmm. Good to know."

He's trying his damnedest to get a rise out of me.

"Well, if you're not interested, then maybe you wouldn't mind putting in a good word for your big brother?" He flashes me a grin. "She sure is pretty. And tall." His whistle is long and low. Just enough to claw its way under my skin. "Would you just look at those long, lean legs."

All right, now he's *really* starting to piss me off.

"Stop looking at her damn legs," I grumble.

He elbows me again and jerks his head toward the crowd. "I'm certainly not the only one checking her out."

With narrowed eyes, I glance around.

Sure enough, there are about seven dudes with their gazes trained on her. I squeeze the water bottle until the plastic crumples like paper. My brother's shoulders silently shake with mirth.

Asshole.

"I've never seen you get wound up over a woman before. It's disturbing."

I thrust my hand through my damp hair and decide to level with him. "Look, I don't know what's going on. Up until a week or two ago, she couldn't stand the sight of me. But things have changed." My gaze slides back to Claire as she leans down to speak with her niece. Since she's bending at the waist, her perfect, heart-shaped ass is on display for every guy in the vicinity to ogle.

Fuck.

My brows snap together as a few of them openly admire her backside.

It takes every ounce of restraint I have not to stalk over there and drag her from the restaurant. None of my teammates have dared to approach her, but that's only because Liam has put the fear of God into them. Otherwise, there are probably at least ten dudes who would be all over her.

Thankfully, Liam shoots a few hard glares around the room, and most have enough good sense to turn away. Although there's a couple who continue to side-eye her.

Bunch of douchebags.

I don't think I've ever wanted to grab a woman and haul her ass out the door just so other men would stop gawking at her. But that's exactly how I feel with Claire. Those thoughts are enough to have me plowing a hand through my hair.

"She's a virgin," I blurt.

Shit.

I didn't mean to say that out loud.

Or maybe I did.

Maybe what I need is for my older brother to knock some sense into me before I do something Claire and I will end up regretting. Surprise morphs over his features as his gaze jerks to her.

"Shut the fuck up." There's a beat of silence. "You said she was twenty-one."

"She is."

His brows lower. He looks as pissed off as I feel, which is kind of comical.

"What the hell are you doing with a virgin? Not to mention that she's the younger sister of a teammate. You can't just fuck her and throw her away like you usually do." He looks eerily similar to our father. "You've really stepped in it this time."

I draw the corner of my lower lip into my mouth and chew it as I continue to contemplate Claire. "She just wants me to, you know, do the deed."

He gives me an *are you crazy* look before throwing an arm in her direction. "That girl can't get laid on her own?"

I quickly slap his arm down before growling, "Lower your damn voice! She's been focused on other things like school and hasn't dated much."

He folds his arms across his barrel-like chest. "Why you?" He cocks his head and narrows his eyes. "I thought she couldn't stand your guts."

"I might have said that I could make it good for her," I mumble.

He gives me a hard stare before rolling his eyes. "You know this is going to end disastrously, right?"

Yup…completely aware of it.

"Getting involved with a virgin can be messy," he adds. "They get attached. You're not going to be able to just shake her loose." His voice drops. "Not without repercussions."

I don't say it, but…I'm not interested in shaking her loose. I'm more concerned about what Liam will think than anything else. And then there's the issue that Claire views this as a short-term deal.

I want more, but I can't exactly tell her that, now can I?

All it'll do is spook her.

I need time to ease Claire into thinking of this as more of a relationship. I need her to see me as boyfriend material.

Which I've never been before.

Clearly, I've got my work cut out for me.

When Claire finally takes her leave, she sends a look over her shoulder as if she knows exactly where I'm standing and that I've had eyes on her the entire time. A hint of a smile plays around her lips before she disappears from the restaurant.

That one shared look is enough to make me forget that Joe is standing next to me until he claps me on the shoulder.

"You're fucked, dude."

Tell me something I don't know.

CLAIRE

I shove my key in the lock and open the door to the apartment. I haven't seen Holly since we attended the frat party Friday night. She wasn't home on Saturday when JT dropped me off, and she wasn't around before I left this morning for the game. We haven't had a chance to talk about everything that went down.

My guess is that she'll flip out.

As I walk inside the apartment, I notice that Holly's bedroom door is shut. She only holes up in there when she's sleeping or studying. I drop my purse on the small dining room table and beeline toward her door before knocking on it.

"Hols?" I raise my voice. "Are you in there?"

I release a breath and realize I could really use her advice regarding JT. Holly has a lot more experience than I do. She's had a slew of boyfriends over the years. So, if there's anyone who can help me navigate these choppy waters, it's my roomie.

My brows jerk together when I hear hushed voices from the other side of the door. Holly is in between boyfriends at the moment and isn't one to bring hookups back to the apartment.

I press my ear against the door. "Holly?"

"Umm, yeah. Give me a minute."

There's the rustle of covers and then more muted murmurs.

Yup, she's definitely got a guy in there.

A couple seconds later, the door cracks open. Instead of swinging it wide, she squeezes her curvy body through before slamming it shut.

She's wrapped up in a short fuzzy robe.

At four thirty on a Sunday afternoon.

It's pretty obvious what's been going on in there.

Her long, dark hair is mussed.

Color rides high on her cheekbones.

And her eyes are all bright and shiny.

Not to mention, totally satisfied.

My hands settle on my hips and a smile twitches around my lips. "Why you little hussy! You've got a man in there!"

Her eyes widen before she buries her face in her hands.

I can't help but laugh at her embarrassment. I wrap my fingers around the handle and pretend to twist it open. "I wonder who it is. Should we find out?"

She practically leaps at me and knocks my hand from the knob. "No! Don't do that."

My brows snap together. "Settle down, Hols. I was just kidding. I wouldn't do that to you." I nod toward her room. "Do I know him?"

There's a long pause.

"Yeah." She rakes both hands through her long strands and gathers them up before lifting them away from her face. "I wasn't expecting you home so early. I figured you'd probably hang out at your brother's place."

There are times when I do that, but I've got some work to finish up. I really wish Holly didn't have a dude here. I'd love to sit down and talk to her about what's going on.

But I guess it can wait for another time.

Wait a minute…I know this guy?

I drop my voice. "Please tell me it's not the guy from across the hall who keeps bothering you." I shake my head. "What happened to your rule about not shitting where you eat?"

Before she can respond, the bedroom door swings open, and Ryan stands on the other side of the threshold wearing nothing more than a pair of tight black boxer briefs. A smirk settles across his face as he leans his lanky body casually against the doorframe.

My eyes widen as my jaw goes slack. I can tell by the smug look in his eyes that what happened between him and Holly was a calculated move on his part. Considering his behavior Friday night, maybe I shouldn't be so surprised. It hurts that Ryan would deliberately sleep with my best friend as a way to get back at me. We were only together for two months, but we've been friends for three years.

Doesn't that mean anything?

More than that, I'm stunned that Holly would stab me in the back by sleeping with him.

What the hell was she thinking?

When I'd texted her Friday night, I only told her that I was taking off. I hadn't wanted to get into the specifics of our breakup in a text message. I can only imagine the twisted version of events my ex gave her.

Nausea blooms at the bottom of my belly.

I don't bother to look at Ryan. He's not the one who matters in this situation.

It's Holly's betrayal that cuts me to the bone. I really thought she had my back. That our friendship was solid. Obviously, I was wrong.

I keep my gaze focused on Holly, who looks like she wants the floor to open up and swallow her whole.

Well, that's tough shit, sweetheart.

This is a mess of her own making, and she's going to deal with it.

With me.

It takes a handful of seconds to find my voice before I jerk my thumb in Ryan's direction. "You really slept with him?"

Color scalds her cheeks as her gaze darts away.

When Holly remains silent, Ryan pipes up. "She sure did." The smirk grows into more of a nasty smile. "And guess what? She didn't make me wait two months for it either."

He reaches out and strokes a finger over the curve of my jaw before I bat his hand away. "Don't touch me."

"Now there's a familiar refrain," he says with a snort.

That comment is like a knife slicing expertly through my heart.

Holly snaps out of her trance and spears Ryan with a hard-edged glare. Although, he doesn't seem bothered by it in the least. "Can you give us a minute to talk?"

With a shrug, he steps inside before shutting the door and leaving us alone in the tiny hallway.

As our gazes lock, her shoulders collapse.

I can't imagine anything she could say that would make this situation better. "Why would you sleep with my boyfriend?"

"Ex-boyfriend," she cuts in, as if that makes the situation less egregious.

Laughter bubbles up from my lips. "Right. Exactly how long were we broken up before you screwed him?"

Her cheeks deepen a few more shades until it looks like she'll self-combust. The air that surrounds us grows thick and uncomfortable.

"It was after you took off with JT." The way she says it makes it sound more like an accusation. Like I did something wrong. "I didn't even know you'd left the party. I saw Ryan, and I asked him where you were. He said you two had just broken up and he was really upset."

I roll my eyes.

I can't imagine Ryan telling her what actually transpired in his bedroom.

"And so you decided that out of all the guys at the party, you needed to hook up with my ex of an hour or so?"

She shifts from one bare foot to another before mumbling, "It wasn't like that."

I arch a brow. "What *exactly* was it like, then?"

A heavy blanket of silence falls over us as she gnaws her bottom lip. Just when I think she won't bother with a response, she straightens her shoulders. "I've liked Ryan ever since I met him freshman year, but you're the one he was interested in."

When I open my mouth, she quickly cuts me off. "Look, I know this was a shitty move on my part and that I'm a crappy friend, but I have feelings for him." She shrugs. "And I'm not sure you ever did."

Her words knock the breath from my lungs.

As if that rationale justifies her behavior.

Holly draws herself up to her full height. "Why did you call JT to pick you up Friday night?"

Excuse me?

I'm not the one who needs to defend my actions.

"What does it matter who I called? I needed to get out of there, and I couldn't find you anywhere."

She ignores the question and bulldozes her way onward. "I thought you didn't even like the guy." She arches a brow. "And yet he's the first person you call to pick you up from a college party at eleven o'clock on a Friday night?"

The look Holly aims in my direction says that she doesn't believe it for an instant. As if there's more going on with JT than what I've admitted.

I open my mouth before slamming it shut again.

"You didn't come home Friday night. Did you stay at his place?"

"Nothing happened," I whisper.

How did this get turned around on me?

I'm not the one who did something wrong and yet, Holly is treating me as if I did.

Her eyes narrow. "You sure about that?"

"Yes." My mind tumbles back to Friday evening and Saturday morning, and I realize it's not precisely the truth.

Something *did* happen between us.

Just as those thoughts crash through my brain, I shake them loose. Holly is trying to turn the situation around on me. Like I'm the one to blame for her being a crappy friend. Not once did Holly ever mention she was into Ryan. I would never have agreed to go out with him in the first place had that been the case.

"You know what? It doesn't matter if anything happened with JT or not. Ryan and I were going out for two months. You *knew* that I was planning on sleeping with him this weekend. *You knew!*" I step a bit closer and whisper, "Did he tell you why we broke up? Did he tell you what happened in his room?"

Her expression never falters.

My heart riots painfully against my chest as I wait for an answer.

"He said that you two were messing around and you freaked out over nothing." She shrugs. "You got scared and ran out of the room."

Even though I fully expected something along those lines, it still hurts to hear what he tried to pull summed up as something so benign. And for the response to slide so emotionlessly from her lips makes it even worse.

"Yeah, that's not *exactly* how it went down. I told him to stop, and he wouldn't."

"Was he holding you down? Do you have bruises? Did you scream for help? If he *raped* you, did you go to the hospital or call the police?"

Each question she pummels me with feels like a physical blow. They suck the air right out of my lungs and make it painful to breathe. I can only stare speechlessly.

"No," I whisper. "I was able to get away. But not for lack of his trying."

As soon as the words slip from my mouth, I know she doesn't believe them.

She doesn't *want* to believe them.

A heavy sigh falls from her lips as pity fills her eyes. "You just freaked out, Claire. You've never had sex, and you got scared. End of story."

My throat constricts and it feels as if it's closing in on me. "Do you really believe that?"

She shrugs as an apologetic expression morphs across her face. "You've waited a really long time to sleep with someone, and you've been so nervous about going through with it."

I told her that in confidence, never expecting that she would use my own words against me.

"You have zero experience where men are concerned. So, yeah...I kind of believe that you made a huge deal out of nothing."

I don't think I could feel more betrayed or hurt than I do at this very moment.

She raises her hands as if in surrender. "Look, I'm sure it felt like a big deal when it was happening. Maybe it even *felt* like he was trying to do something you didn't want him to, but it didn't happen the way you think it did. Ryan wasn't trying to hurt you or force you into having sex. He was just trying to calm you down and you overreacted."

There's a moment of silence as she drops her voice. "For god's sake, Claire. He was just fingering you." She sways closer and adds, "He told me that you were wet. That you *wanted* it. But then you tensed up and started to freak out." She cocks her head. "You weren't even undressed. Your jeans were still all the way on."

My chest constricts, making it impossible to breathe. Her words are like a verbal assault, and hearing her twisted version of the truth is more shocking than Ryan emerging from her bedroom.

"Are you serious?" My body trembles with unspent emotion. "I told him to stop, Holly. I wanted him to get off me and he wouldn't."

The more I attempt to explain what happened, the more nauseous I begin to feel. Hot tears sting the back of my eyes. I can't believe that she would side with Ryan over me. She wasn't there. She doesn't know what happened, and yet she's trying to tell me how everything went down.

She's taking his word over mine because she likes him.

Holly and I have been friends since first semester of freshman year. I've confided in her about my family and my lack of experience when it comes to guys. For her to now throw it back in my face feels like being sucker punched.

If anything, she should have my back, and it blows my mind that she doesn't. Nausea roils in the pit of my belly until it feels like I might be physically ill. I band my arms around my middle, only wanting to get away from them.

All I know is that I can't stay here for another second.

JT

I text Claire that I'm on my way as I leave the stadium, but she doesn't reply.

Every time I hit a red light, I shoot another text her way.

I don't get anything other than stereo silence in response. By the time my tires screech to a halt in front of her building, I'm in a state of panic. I've texted three more times and called. There's still no answer.

Where the hell is she?

And why the hell isn't she responding?

I slam out of the Porsche before jogging to the front entrance of her apartment. I glance quickly through the directory of tenants that's located next to the buzzers.

Apartment two-seventeen.

I hit the button a few times.

But just like her phone, there's no answer.

Luckily, a couple leaves the building as I loiter near the glass door. They're so wrapped up in one another that they don't pay attention when I grab the handle and slip inside.

It's oddly silent inside the lobby as I press the call button for the elevator. Actually, I push it half a dozen times before glancing around impatiently for the stairwell. The last thing I want to do is stand here waiting for the damn elevator to arrive.

It's taking fucking forever.

I need to figure out what the hell is going on with Claire.

Just as I search the area for the stairs, I spot a pair of sneakers sticking out from behind a chair about twenty feet down the hall in a little sitting area.

Those shoes look oddly familiar.

With narrowed eyes, I contemplate them for a second or two. They look exactly like the ones Claire had on Friday night and then again today at the game.

I abandon the elevator and stalk toward the sitting area. Air gets trapped in my throat as I peek around the second chair and find Claire huddled on the floor next to it. Her face is pale and streaked with tears. There's a strange glassiness filling her eyes.

My heart riots harshly against the wall of my chest.

What the hell could have happened to her from the time she left the party to now?

"Claire?" My voice is low, strung tight with the need to understand what's going on. "What happened? Why are you sitting in the hallway by yourself?"

I don't wait for a response before squatting down and gathering her up. Once I have her secured in my arms, I press her tightly to me. When she remains unresponsive, my chest constricts.

She curls into me, burying her face against the hollow of my throat. "Can you just get me out of here?" Her voice is so thin and reedy that if I weren't listening so intently, I would have missed it. "Please?"

I turn my face toward her and press a gentle kiss against her forehead. "Of course."

Two minutes later, she's secured in my car, and we take off down the tree-lined street. Unlike Friday night, I don't bother asking if she wants to be dropped off at her brother's house. The only place she's going is back to mine.

My gut is a tangle of knots, because she hasn't uttered a sound since leaving the apartment building. This feels like déjà vu all over again. When we finally pull into my garage, I cut the engine and jump out before hustling around to the other side of the car. With a flick of the wrist, I pop open the door and pull her into my arms where she belongs.

Whatever happened must be pretty bad, because Claire doesn't protest when I lift her off her feet and carry her into the house. She lays her head against my chest as I walk through the kitchen, up the back staircase, and straight into my room. I settle on the bed with her held firmly in my arms. She feels like a lifeless rag doll.

And that scares me more than I'm willing to admit.

Claire is usually so feisty. I've never seen her so beaten down and vulnerable.

So broken.

Not even when I picked her up on Friday night was she this upset.

"You need to tell me what happened." Her silence is ripping me apart inside, and I can't take much more of it. It's almost mind-boggling how much she's come to mean to me in such a short span of time.

It feels like I'm drowning in all the riotous emotion that careens through me.

When she remains silent, I gently lift her chin until she has no choice but to meet my gaze. The tears that swim in her eyes twist my heart into painful little knots.

"Baby, tell me what's going on." There's a beat of silence before I add in a harsh whisper. "You're scaring me."

She squeezes her eyes tightly shut and inhales a deep, unsteady breath. "I don't want to talk about it."

Fuck that.

"I need to know."

A long stretch of silence follows before her shoulders slump. "After I left the stadium, I went back to the apartment to talk with Holly. I didn't realize she was in her bedroom with someone."

"Okay," I say, drawing out the word.

"It was Ryan. They slept together."

I suck in a harsh breath and try to wrap my head around what she just revealed. "Your roommate *slept* with the guy you broke up with?"

An unexpected gurgle of laughter bubbles up from her lips as she nods. There's not a shred of humor within the sound. "That's not even the worst part."

"How's that possible?"

"They hooked up Friday night after I took off with you." She pauses, allowing that to sink in. "Ryan gave her a twisted version of the truth. He told her that I was turned on. That I just freaked out because I'm a…" She gulps before forcing out the rest, "*a virgin.*" Her eyes turn glassy with unshed tears. "She made me feel like I was just some stupid, inexperienced—"

I press my finger against her lips. "We both know that's not true. All your roommate is trying to do is make herself feel better for fucking over a friend. That's it."

She pries my hand away.

"I don't know. I sat in the lobby, going over everything that happened Friday night." Confusion flickers across her pale face before she shakes her head. "Maybe she's right. Maybe what Ryan told her is the way it happened. Or at least how he saw it. Maybe I did freak out and run away because I was scared."

Fire ignites deep within my gut. It pisses me off that she's questioning her own recollection of the events. That her roommate and ex-boyfriend have managed to gaslight her.

"You know damn well that's not how it went down. You told him to stop, and he didn't. What happened is on *him*. Not you." I pause, trying to remain calm so I don't lose it. "What he almost did to you… fuck, Claire. I'd like to rip his damn throat out for it."

She bites her lip as doubt lingers in her eyes.

"You said *no*," I reiterate sharply.

Only then does she nod. "I told him to stop."

"He's an asshole. As soon as you said it, he should have backed off." I pull her closer and gently brush my lips against the crown of her head. All I want to do is keep her wrapped up in my arms until she understands she did nothing wrong.

It's a relief that she's here and safe. All I can dwell on is the panicky feelings that had surged through me when I couldn't get a hold of her. When I had no idea where she was or what was going on.

"Why didn't you answer your phone when I texted and called?"

She nestles closer. "I turned it off. I needed some time to think."

"You scared the shit out of me." I don't think I've ever felt like that in my life. It's not something I want to dwell on. Right now, I need to take care of her and make sure she's all right.

"I'm sorry. I just…" Her voice trails off and she shrugs. "I wanted to be alone."

I press another kiss against her head. All I want to do is hold her close, but maybe there's a better way to comfort her.

"How about I run a hot bath for you to soak in? Then we can get dinner figured out."

She lifts her head until her gaze locks on mine. "Okay."

I carefully rearrange her body until she's stretched out on the bed before brushing my lips against hers. With one last glance over my shoulder, I head to the massive bathroom and turn on the faucet. I've lived here for about six months, and I've never used the jetted tub. If I'm wound tight, I usually swim laps or sit in the hot tub by the pool.

I've also never brought a woman back to the house either. By the time I bought this place, I was already trying to clean up my act. It makes me happy that Claire is the only woman I've shared my home with.

Having her here, in my space, just feels right.

Once the tub is filled with steaming water, I turn on the jets before returning to the bedroom. Claire is exactly where I left her. Something painful twists in my chest. I hate to see her hurting like this. It makes me want to go find that punk and beat the shit out of him.

And that roommate of hers…

I'm not one for abusing women, but she deserves to be slapped upside the head for her part in this. What a backstabbing bitch.

I scoop Claire into my arms and carry her into the white marble bathroom before setting her on the edge of the tub. Then, I kneel to slide off her shoes and socks.

Once those have been removed, I glance up to meet her gaze. "Should I go?"

The last thing I want is to make her uncomfortable. She's been through enough as it is.

It's a surprise when she shakes her head before rising to her feet. Air gets clogged in my throat when she grips the hem of her shirt before pulling it over her head and dropping it to the marble-tiled floor.

Her gaze stays locked on mine as her fingers settle over the button of her jeans and flick it open. She drags the zipper down and slides the denim over the curve of her hips, past her thighs before the material pools at her ankles. Steadying herself against the tub, she kicks her way free of them.

This time, her bra and panties are leopard print.

Another matching set.

With a steady hand, she reaches around her ribcage and unsnaps the bra. The slender straps slide from her shoulders and down her arms, revealing rosy tipped breasts. The silky garment meets the same fate as the shirt and jeans.

A thick lump gets wedged in the middle of my throat, making it impossible to breathe as I watch her.

She's so damn beautiful.

"Will you take off the rest?" she asks quietly.

It's not a question I have to think about. Already, I'm reaching out and dipping my fingers beneath the stretchy material before sliding it down her hips and thighs until the silky panties join the pile of discarded clothing and she's completely bare.

It's so tempting to press my face against the softness of her belly. I want to stroke my fingers over every single inch of her body and nuzzle her inner thighs until she's spreading them wide. I want to stab my tongue inside her until her breath catches and she moans out her pleasure.

But I don't.

Can't.

She needs time to herself.

As hard as it is, I force myself to back away from her before jerking a thumb toward the door. "I'll go downstairs and order a pizza or something, all right? You stay up here as long as you want and relax."

As I'm about to sprint through the doorway, her voice stops me cold.

"JT?"

I glance back. "Yeah?" My voice is gruff. To see her standing there completely bare...

It's the stuff dreams are made of. How someone can look so damn innocent and vulnerable while standing naked like that is beyond me.

"Stay with me?"

Fuck.

I'm hard as steel over here.

And she doesn't need that right now.

When the urge to reach out thrums through me, I shove my hands into my khakis. "I should, ah, head downstairs and get dinner figured out."

"Please?"

Her voice is the barest of whispers and arrows right through the heart of me. How can I deny this girl anything?

"Are you sure that's what you want?"

With a nod, she holds out her hand.

I strip off my shirt and pants, sliding the boxer briefs down my legs until I'm as naked as she is.

My fingers grip hers, towing her to me. Once she's close enough, I wrap my arms around her, only wanting to protect her with my strength. I lose track of how long we stand pressed together with all my hard edges tightly aligned against her softness.

I don't think my cock has ever been this painfully hard in my life.

It takes effort to untangle myself from her and step into the steamy water before carefully lowering myself to the porcelain. My back is pressed against the curve of the tub. Once I'm situated, I hold my hand out for her to join me.

She steps between my spread legs before turning around. My gaze drops to her heart-shaped ass as she carefully lowers herself into the water. She sucks in a sharp breath as her body is fully submerged. A sigh escapes from her as she reclines against my chest and rests her head near the crook of my neck. Only then do her eyelids feather closed.

My arms slide around her ribcage as I press her closer and inhale a big breath. That's all it takes for something to settle within me, and I realize that I'm exactly where I want to be. I'm not thrilled with how we ended up here, but I'm happy to have Claire in my arms, in my tub, in my house.

It takes a few minutes for her body to gradually loosen and her breathing to become deep and even. I press my lips to the side of her neck as my hands caress her breasts. Another sigh of contentment escapes from her as I stroke her nipples before palming the softness.

"That feels nice," she murmurs.

Her voice sounds as if she's on the cusp of falling asleep.

"It does," I agree.

"I could stay like this for the rest of the night."

After another fifteen minutes, I pick up her hand and lift it from the water so I can inspect the skin. "You're turning pruney."

She turns her head until our gazes can collide. Silently, she scrutinizes me. I have no idea what thoughts are running through her brain.

"How is it that you've turned out to be so different from what I thought?"

It's a genuine question. Almost as if she doesn't understand how we arrived at this place. How we went from her barely able to tolerate me to lying naked in my arms in a matter of weeks.

Admittedly, I don't understand it myself.

There's never been a woman who made me want to be different. A better version of myself. But I find myself wanting to be that for Claire. I'd happily turn myself into a pretzel if it made her happy.

"I always thought you were a jerk, but you aren't." She blinks before adding softly, "At least, I don't think you are." She shakes her head, and I see the shards of bitterness that seep into her eyes. "Then again, I'm not a very good judge of character when it comes to men or friends."

I really fucking hate that they've made Claire question herself.

Even though her pliant body is already pressed against mine, I drag her even closer. And yet, it's still not enough.

Over the past couple of weeks, I've gotten to know her on a deeper level. It's made me realize that there's still so much more I want to discover. More than that, I want to protect her from all the assholes out there who would take advantage of her goodness and innocence.

"You didn't do anything wrong, Claire. You trusted someone who wasn't worthy of your love or friendship."

"How could I have thought he was the right one and you were wrong?"

With a sigh, I admit, "Because I was the wrong one, too. At least, at that point in time. But I've been working on myself and getting my shit together. I spent a lot of time letting things from my past dictate the future and that was self-destructive."

She nibbles at her lower lip. "What happened on the field today? You weren't playing like you normally do."

My muscles tense. The last thing I want to do is talk about my family. I don't want to invite them into our relationship. Most of the time, I'd prefer to pretend they didn't exist.

When I remain silent, she straightens and water sloshes against the sides. I panic, thinking that she's leaving the tub, leaving me, but that's not what happens. Instead, she turns, her slippery skin sliding against mine as she straddles my waist, repositioning herself so that we're facing each other. I groan as she wiggles closer until my erection is nestled perfectly against her core.

Fuck.

This situation has become entirely too dangerous.

I was able to contain myself when her delectable little backside was pressed against my junk.

But this?

Her soft, sweet little pussy cradling my thick length?

All I'd have to do is flex my hips, and I could slide right inside her warmth.

A smile curves her lips as she takes in my pained expression. My hands wrap around her waist in order to hold her still so she can't squirm around on top of me. I'm already hard as steel. She's much too tempting for me to resist.

I'm trying to do the right thing, and she's making it difficult.

With a tilt to her head, she closes the distance between us and presses her lips to mine. Another groan rumbles up from deep within my chest.

After she tortures me for a minute or two, she pulls away and asks, "Are you going to talk to me? You want me to tell you what's going on in my life, but you won't open up at all? This needs to be a two-way street, JT."

I didn't think it was possible for anything to deflate my boner.

I was wrong. Thoughts of my parents kill all those good vibes in less than fifteen seconds flat.

I don't want to think about how I started questioning and second guessing every move I made on the field until it felt like I was paralyzed with indecision. And I sure as shit don't want to talk about how my parents tear me up inside. How it's better to distance myself from my family rather than allow them to get inside my head and fuck everything up.

When she continues to search my gaze, I know she won't drop the convo.

"My family was at the game today," I mutter. "And I let them get inside my head. Especially my dad." Even though that's a simplistic explanation of the issue, I'm hoping she'll accept it and move on.

There are so many other interesting things I can think of for us—

"Has it always been like that?"

But no. Of course she doesn't.

Even though the answer to that question is an unequivocal yes, I shrug. There's a growing tightness between my shoulder blades. "You met my father earlier. What did you think?"

She doesn't even blink. "That he was an asshole."

"And here you thought you weren't an excellent judge of character," I say with a snort.

Her lips twitch just a bit. "Has he always been a jerk?"

"Since the day I was born."

"Why do their thoughts and opinions matter so much to you?"

My erection is now long gone. I'm totally flaccid. If Claire notices, she doesn't say a word. Instead, she patiently waits for me to continue.

"My brother has always been the one who could do no wrong." My mind reluctantly tumbles back to our childhood and what it was like to grow up in his shadow. I never resented him, and I wasn't jealous.

Hell, I wanted to be *exactly* like Joe.

But my father made that impossible.

Everything I did was wrong. Or not good enough.

What it came down to is that *I* was never enough.

I blink away the painful memories. "And I was the one who could never do anything right." I shrug and attempt to reel back everything I've unwittingly exposed.

God, I hate talking about them. And I hate the way it makes me feel.

Like I'm not good enough.

Like I will *never* be good enough.

Her hand drifts over my cheek before pressing her palm against it. "It must have been difficult to feel like you never measured up."

Embarrassment and pain bubble up inside. I don't like this at all. It feels like someone has cut my belly wide open and is standing there, inspecting my insides. I've spent so many years burying my emotions deep down where they're easier to ignore. It's almost painful to drag them into the light when you've forced them to live in the darkness for so long.

"Once I got older, it didn't matter so much. I tried not to put stock in what my father thought." That's easier said than done. Even now, there are times when I suspect I'm still waiting for the day my father will turn and praise me for *something* I've managed to do right even though, deep down, I know it will never happen.

The need I feel for his approval is pathetic. Part of me hates him for creating that longing. I hate myself for not being able to let it go. For not being able to walk away and never look back again.

"You're a good man, JT. It doesn't matter what they think."

"I haven't always been." My voice is low, sounding as if it's been scraped raw with the emotion she's hell-bent on dredging up.

After all these years, it finally feels as if someone sees me for the person I am buried beneath all the hype and carefree demeanor.

Her eyes pierce mine, sifting through all the secrets I keep buried within. I get the feeling Claire sees more than I want her to. More than I'm comfortable with.

"I think you've finally allowed yourself to step out of your brother's shadow and your father's image of who he thinks you are. I think the man you are today is the one you were always meant to be."

My heart stutters before pumping into overdrive.

That's exactly what it feels like when I'm with her.

I'm tired of rebelling against them. I'm tired of allowing them to get to me. To push my buttons while I react like I'm still a fucked-up teenager with a chip on his shoulder.

I'm done with that.

I'm a twenty-five-year-old man, and it's time I started acting like one.

Listening to Claire say it so succinctly, stripping bare the emotion and history, is what I've slowly started to realize myself. It's strange how she can see it so clearly when I've spent my entire life trying to wrap my head around our family dynamics.

When the need to distract her from the insights of our conversation thrums through me, my hands drift from her waist to her breasts before carefully stroking over the hard tips of her pretty little nipples. She arches as her head falls back and a soft sigh of contentment whispers from her lips.

I love how responsive she is.

"You're beautiful, Claire."

As I continue to toy with her breasts, she lifts her head until she can meet my gaze again.

"I've thought about it just like you asked me to, and I haven't changed my mind. I want you to be my first."

My cock stiffens before pressing against her softness. It wouldn't take much for me to slip inside her body. As tempting as that is, I resist the urge. When we finally make love, it's going to be slow and thorough. I'm going to take my time with her beautiful body spread out on my king-sized bed. It takes a herculean effort to tamp down my rising excitement.

"I don't want this to be a knee-jerk reaction to what happened this weekend. This isn't something that has to be decided today or tomorrow. We have all the time in the world."

She strokes my cheeks. "My decision was made before I found out about Holly and Ryan," she murmurs. "I want you to be the one."

Even though I want her more than I've ever wanted another woman, it's only fair to say it one more time. "You can change your mind at any point. I'm not going to force you into something you don't want."

Her lips lift. "I know. That's the difference between you and Ryan. I think that's what was holding me back with him. I wanted to go through with it and yet I just couldn't bring myself to do it. It never felt like the right decision. But this does. Being with you feels right."

Before I can respond, she adds, "I know this is just sex. I don't want you to worry that I'll get clingy or go into stalker mode. That's not going to happen."

My muscles tense.

Her brow furrows as the smile falls away. "I don't want you to think that I'm going to fall for you or that it'll be awkward afterward. I promise it won't be. I think we're kind of friends now, and I don't want that to change."

Her words are like an unexpected blow to my gut and nearly knock the air from my lungs.

"JT?"

I jerk my head into a tight nod before forcing my lips into a careless smile. It takes a moment for everything within me to finally settle.

She may think this thing between us is casual, but it's not. If this is the only way I can have her right now, then so be it.

"You ready to get out?" I ask, changing the subject.

She releases a pent-up breath before dazzling me with a relieved smile.

"Yeah. I'm famished."

Me, too.

But it's not food that I'm craving.

It's the girl in my arms.

CLAIRE

$\mathcal{W}$e order a pizza that gets delivered to the house and then curl up on the couch afterward to watch some bizarre reality TV show. I've seen it a few times, but it's mostly like watching a horrific car accident, which is exactly how you get drawn in.

It's all shock value.

With my belly full of cheese pizza and my eyes drowsy, I'm wrapped up in JT's arms. At the moment, there's nowhere else I'd rather be. He doesn't seem to want to let me go even for a second.

And I love it.

When we stepped out of the tub, he grabbed a towel from the brushed nickel rack before drying off every single inch of me. It was such a turn-on to have him on his knees, running the soft material over my body as he pressed kisses against my flesh.

I love the way he strokes his fingers over my skin. It leaves me in a constant state of arousal. I've made it perfectly clear that I want him to be the one, and yet he continues to hold me at arm's length, telling me to slow down.

To think it over.

Doesn't he understand that I've thought it all through?

I'm ready to do this.

It would give me a complex except that he's always hard whenever I'm nearby.

I know he wants me.

The man is a conundrum.

In the three years I've known JT, I never imagined he would treat me so carefully. Almost as if I matter. He's constantly putting my needs before his own, and that only makes me want him more. It proves just how different he is from Ryan, who I assumed was a good guy but turned out to be the opposite.

And JT, the one I could barely stand to be around, is someone I want to get to know better. He's done everything within his power to help me. To be there for me. I don't understand how I could have been so wrong about him.

It's the feel of strong fingers sliding beneath my chin and gently turning my face toward his that has me blinking back to the present. My guess is that he wants more kisses. He seems to want them all the time.

It's just another thing I love.

Instead, he surprises me by asking, "What are you going to do about your apartment?"

Everything within me stills before deflating.

"I don't know," I murmur before sucking my lower lip into my mouth and chewing it. The thought of staying there and carrying on like nothing happened seems impossible. Obviously, Holly and I can't rewind our friendship. And I don't think I can forgive her for what she said and did.

There's no way I can trust her.

"I don't think I can live with her anymore. Not after what happened."

"I don't want you there either," he says gruffly. "Especially if that jackass is going to be hanging around."

Again, I hadn't even thought about that possibility.

There's no way I can be in the same apartment with either of them.

But I'm locked into our lease for the rest of the school year.

"Maybe I can sublet my room and find something else, but that'll take time. Holly would have to agree to it as well."

Although, she can't possibly want me around any more than I want to be there. I rub my forehead as my mind whirls with possible solutions. "I could probably stay with Liam and Gia. I'm sure they wouldn't mind." My brother would be all too happy if I moved back home. "But I can't tell them about what happened with Ryan."

Silence falls over us before JT clears his throat. "You could always stay here until you find something else."

My eyes widen. I have no idea what to say to that. I'm not even sure if he's serious.

Except that his face is perfectly sober. And he's watching me as if waiting for an answer. That's when it occurs to me that this isn't a half-hearted, token invitation he's thrown out.

His offer is genuine.

"I..." My voice trails off. I'm not sure staying with JT is a good idea. "I don't know."

I don't want our relationship to become complicated. And moving in with him, even for a short amount of time, feels like it has complicated written all over it.

"You need a place to stay, and I have this entire house all to myself. It won't be a problem."

"I don't want to get in your way," I say hesitantly.

"Are you in my way right now?"

"I don't think—"

He silences any further protests by planting a kiss against my lips. "Then it's settled. You'll stay here until you find another place to live."

I don't understand how we arrived at this arrangement so quickly. I need some time to think about it. Maybe explore some other avenues.

"But—"

"Do you have any other options?" he asks with raised brows.

I don't know. I haven't given it much thought.

"No, it's just—"

Intensity fills his eyes as he gently presses my back against the couch before crawling on top of me. My legs wrap around his waist before I squeeze them, trying to alleviate some of the pressure that has throbbed to life in my core. The feel of his thick erection pushing against the V between my thighs has a whimper of need escaping from my lips as he thrusts.

"What about Liam?" I ask. "We both know there's no way he'd let me stay here."

My brother will definitely blow a gasket if he finds out I'm messing around with JT. Liam has always been super protective. Ever since he was fifteen years old, and our mother walked out on us. I might be a grown woman, but he doesn't necessarily see me that way.

No matter how old I am, I'll always be his little sister.

I also know exactly what will happen if I move in with my brother and his wife. He won't view it as a temporary situation. He hates that I moved out of the dorms and into my own apartment.

At one point, he tried to pull rank by telling me that if I didn't live at the house with him or in the dorms, he wouldn't pay for my last year of college. Thankfully, Gia slapped him upside the head and reminded him that his money didn't come with strings and that she'd foot the bill for school if she had to.

Liam caved within seconds. But that doesn't mean he was happy about it. Nor does it mean that he wouldn't seize upon any opportunity to get me back under his roof.

He enjoys his family being close, and I can't fault him for that.

So, I'd rather *not* mention any of this to him.

It's just easier that way.

JT and I don't have a relationship.

It's more of an arrangement.

He licks and nips his way down my throat as all of these thoughts circle through my head. For one fleeting moment, I wonder if he's trying to distract me.

Why would he do that?

He can't possibly want me to shack up with him.

Wouldn't it cramp his bachelor lifestyle?

Playing house with him feels dangerous.

But he's right—I don't have a lot of options.

"You're a grown woman, Claire. You're old enough to make your own decisions."

I groan as he licks and sucks at my flesh.

Ugh. I hate hiding things from my family. Not to mention that I'm a terrible liar. I feel like Liam will see right through whatever bogus story I concoct. And then he'll ferret out the truth. He's a pro at that sort of thing.

"Yeah," I murmur, distracted by the play of his mouth over my skin. "You'd think that would be the case."

"Then we won't tell him. We'll just see how things go. You might not even be here for very long. A week or two. Is there really any point in upsetting him?" He shoves my shirt up to my neck. Since I'm not wearing a bra, there's nothing to stop him from zeroing in on my breasts. He draws one nipple into his mouth, and I arch as need floods my entire body. I squirm against him, wanting only to alleviate the pressure growing in my core.

"No."

I'm so jacked up that I can't remember the question.

He focuses his attention on one breast before kissing and licking a fiery trail to the other stiff little peak. I tunnel my fingers through his thick blond hair and try to pull him closer. When he finally releases me, I feel as if I'm on the verge of exploding.

He pins me in place with his green-eyed intensity. "So you'll stay?"

I suck in a deep breath as he peppers kisses along my flesh.

"What's it going to be, Claire?"

"If you're sure that's what you want," I hedge, still uncertain if I'm making the right decision.

"I am."

"All right, then I guess I'll stay." I tack on hastily, "But just until I find a new place."

He moves up my body until his lips can align with mine. That's all the prompting I need to open so that his tongue can tangle with my own.

Once he pulls away, a satisfied smile tugs at the corners of his lips.

"Good. I'll drive you to school tomorrow and then pick you up afterward. We can stop at your apartment and pick up the rest of your stuff." His expression hardens. "I don't want you going there alone."

I'm still in the throes of passion here, and he's talking logistics?

How is he able to shift gears so quickly?

When I narrow my gaze, he chuckles.

A moment later, he rolls off me and tugs down my shirt before pulling me back into the warm circle of his arms. For some strange reason, I get the feeling I've been played, but I'm not exactly sure how or why.

When it becomes obvious that the fooling around portion of the evening has come to an end, I blurt, "So, that's it? You heat me all up only to leave me hanging?"

A delighted smile spills across his handsome face. The man looks ridiculously pleased by my reaction.

Jerk.

"You're a real tease, you know that?"

Laughter falls from his lips as he tugs me onto his lap and attempts to kiss me.

Even though I don't necessarily want to, I turn my face away. "Is there really a point in starting something you have no intention of finishing?"

Before I can grumble out the last word, I find myself flat on my back and him looming over me. Unlike Ryan, it never crosses my mind to be frightened or nervous.

"When we finally make love, it's not going to be when you've been hurt or are nursing pain inflicted by another man. Tonight, you'll sleep in my bed, and I'll hold you in my arms." He takes my lips in a searing kiss that leaves me breathless before drawing away. "Now, if you'd like me to lick that sweet little pussy because I've got you all riled up, all you have to do is ask. We both know that I'd be more than happy to." Heat ignites in his eyes, making them glow with green fire. "Is that what you want, baby?"

His dirty words are enough to have me on the verge of self-combusting.

"Yes," I whisper, barely able to push the rest out. "That's what I want."

"See how easy that was?"

He takes my lips in a kiss that nearly singes my insides.

"Are you ready to head upstairs, or are you still watching this ridiculous show?"

"What show?"

He grins. "Good answer."

CLAIRE

"So...you're not going to tell me what the surprise is?"

Gia smiles as she continues to prep vegetables for dinner. "Your brother would kill me if I did."

Doubtful. Liam loves his wife more than almost anything else in this world. The *almost anything else* being their three ridiculously adorable kiddos.

"Come on, just one small clue? You know I hate surprises."

Because nothing good ever seems to come from them.

Surprise—Mom walked out and is never coming back.

Surprise—Dad gambled away the mortgage money, and now we've lost the house.

Surprise—Holly slept with my ex-boyfriend.

I could go on, but I won't.

She shakes her head and fights back a grin.

Hmmm.

It doesn't look like I'll be able to drag whatever this so-called surprise is from Gia. The knowledge that Liam has something tucked up his sleeve only sets my nerves on edge, and I find myself fidgeting on the stool I'm seated on at the marble island.

Tonight is the first dinner that JT and I are having at my brother's house since I've been staying at his place. Just to be clear, we're not living together. This is strictly a temporary arrangement.

We're more like roommates.

Roommates who happen to sleep in the same bed.

Roommates who cuddle and kiss and do all sorts of wicked things to one another.

That being said, I find myself reiterating that this set-up is short term.

The last thing I want is for JT to think I'm getting the wrong idea in regard to what's going on between us.

When it comes to JT Higgins, my eyes are wide open.

Strangely enough, he usually changes the subject whenever I mention looking for a new place. He doesn't seem to be in a hurry to get me out of there.

Since I want the situation with Holly rectified as quickly as possible, my ex-roommate and I have been sending stilted texts back and forth. Gone is the easy relationship we used to enjoy. I told her that I couldn't continue living with her and that I'd like to find someone to sublet my room for the rest of the year. She seemed perfectly fine with that arrangement.

I hate to admit it, because it makes me sound pathetic, but I'd actually been holding out a glimmer of hope that she might come to her senses and apologize for hooking up with Ryan.

That hasn't happened.

She's expressed zero remorse.

Clearly, Holly doesn't see anything wrong with what she did or said. We've been friends for three years. I don't understand why she would choose to believe Ryan over me.

But that's exactly what she did.

We've placed an ad through a university website and will hopefully get some interest soon. I'm not going to bother looking for another apartment until I have someone lined up for this one. I've already decided not to mention the fact that I'm moving to Gia and Liam until it's a done deal.

The less they know, the better.

"How's school going so far? We haven't seen much of you this past week."

Which is ironic, since I'm just a few miles away.

"It's fine. Just trying to stay on top of everything." I've already met with the first-grade teacher I'll be working with. She seems super nice, and I'm excited to jump in. At first, I'll be observing the classroom to learn their patterns and schedules before gradually taking over more of the teaching responsibilities.

"How's the apartment? Do you and Holly need anything? The three of us could go shopping next weekend if you'd like."

I almost wince as the response trips off my tongue. "No, we're good."

"Maybe the kids and I can swing by during the week before things get busy and grab some lunch. I know Liam would love to take you out. We can eat somewhere close to campus." She flashes me a grin. "Wouldn't that be fun?"

Alarm spirals through me as I try to keep the panic from flooding my voice. "Yeah, that sounds great."

"After dinner, I'll look at my calendar, and we'll set something up. Otherwise, it'll never happen."

And wouldn't that be a shame?

"Okay."

The forced smile hurts my cheeks. I can only hope that everything works itself out and I'll find someone to take over my lease within the next week or so. After that, I can break it to Liam and Gia that the arrangement with Holly didn't work out. My plan is to tell them that we had a big fight, couldn't resolve our differences, and I ended up moving out.

It's as close to the truth as I'm willing to get.

Gia continues to chop peppers, carrots, and green beans as I glance into the family room. Max is down for a late afternoon nap, and Charlotte and Ty are watching *Curious George* on TV. Just like always, they're totally captivated. Is it terrible that I wish they were running around, acting crazy? Gia could use the distraction. I don't want her to ask any more questions about the apartment.

Or Holly.

Or that jerk—

"What's up with Ryan? He wasn't able to make it last week for dinner. Is he stopping by tonight?"

I stifle a groan.

I probably should have mentioned that we broke up. Right now, it feels like I'm keeping all sorts of secrets from Liam and Gia. And I hate it. I've always had an open and honest relationship with them.

Within the last week or so, that's changed.

"No, he won't be coming."

Silence stretches between us before she asks, "Is something going on, Claire? You seem preoccupied. Not your usual self."

Her gaze flicks between me and the veggies she's prepping.

My mouth turns cottony as she scans my face. Unsure what to say, I bring the glass of water to my lips, practically draining the entire contents. More time ticks by as I set the tumbler down and glance at my sister-in-law, hoping that she's engrossed in preparing dinner.

Nope.

Not at all.

She holds the knife in one hand while staring at me in question. When I hesitate, her eyes narrow as if she can somehow ferret out the truth just by searching my expression. Which honestly, wouldn't surprise me.

Gia is good.

Really good.

One penetrating look and I fold like a cheap house of cards. Her kids aren't going to stand a chance when they're sneaky teenagers. The woman has a sixth sense where her family is concerned.

When it becomes apparent that she won't allow the subject to drop, I decide to throw her a breadcrumb. I draw in a deep breath and decide to tell her about Ryan. Not everything, of course. I need to be careful about what I say, because this whole mess with Ryan, Holly, and JT feels impossibly entwined and difficult to separate.

"I should have mentioned it sooner, but Ryan and I broke up."

Her dark brows rise. "You're kidding. When did this happen?"

I shrug. "About a week ago."

"What?" Disbelief followed by hurt spills across her face. "Why am I only hearing about this now? Why didn't you say something sooner?"

It never occurred to me that Gia might be upset that I didn't tell her about what was going on.

My eyes widen as I stumble over my words. "I, ah, I'm sorry. I didn't really want to talk about it."

It doesn't take long for her expression to clear, morphing into one of sympathy. "I'm so sorry. I know how much breakups can hurt. Are you doing okay?"

"Yeah, I'm good. We were only together for about two months. It wasn't a big deal." Oddly enough, that's exactly how it now feels. I haven't thought about Ryan in days. And I certainly don't miss him or wish we were still together.

Honestly?

It feels like I dodged a major bullet by getting out when I did.

She nods as if weighing my words for the truth. After a few seconds of silence, she says, "Well, I'm sorry to hear that. Are you sure you don't want to talk about it?" Her gaze pins mine in place before murmuring, "I know Ryan's the first guy you've gotten serious with. First loves can be especially hard to get over."

She's right about one thing—Ryan was the first guy I allowed myself to get close to. Although, I don't think getting over him will be a problem.

"It's better this way. He wasn't the right one for me." I almost shake my head when I think about everything that happened.

JT was right—the guy is a major tool.

"That's a good way to look at it, Claire. You're certainly handling this like a champ," she marvels before setting the knife down and walking around the island. She tugs me into her arms and holds me close. "You know that I love you, right?" When I nod, she continues. "When you're ready to talk, I'll be here to listen."

I can't help but squeeze her tight. Not only is Gia like a mother to me, but a big sister as well. She fills a lot of roles in my life.

I have memories of my actual mother, Beverly, but they've faded over time. And since it was just me, my dad, Liam, and our brother, Cullum, I was the only girl in the house. Gia came into our lives when I needed a woman most, and I'll always be thankful for that.

I've spent the last six years pouring my heart out to her, seeking advice, and crying in her arms. She's always been one of my biggest advocates and supporters. No matter what happens, Gia only wants the best for me.

"Thank you. But really, I'm okay. I don't think I liked Ryan as much as I thought I did." There's a pause before I add, "Maybe I liked the idea of him more than I actually liked him."

It's funny how I'm only now beginning to realize that.

She pulls back enough to search my eyes. "Well, the offer stands. If you ever need to talk over a pint of Chunky Monkey, I'm your girl."

That comment brings a smile to my face, because we've shared more than one pint of ice cream over the years.

Her voice drops. "Can I assume that you and Ryan didn't sleep together? I think you'd be more upset about the situation if you had."

Heat blooms in my cheeks as I shake my head. She's probably right about that, and it makes me doubly glad I took my time rather than allowing Ryan to push me into something I wasn't ready for.

"Good. I'm glad you waited. When you find the right person, you'll know it. You won't second-guess yourself. It'll just feel right."

Which is exactly how it feels with JT.

God knows it shouldn't.

But there's no mistaking that it does.

She narrows her eyes. "Why do I get the feeling there might already be someone else in your life?"

I'm pretty sure that whatever color had been filling my face drains away as I shake my head. "I'm not seeing anyone."

Technically, this is true.

JT and I aren't *seeing* each other. In fact, we're not together at all. He's simply giving me a place to crash until I can find a new one. All right, maybe there's a little more to it than that.

She tilts her head and continues to study me. "Is there someone you're interested in?"

It's a blessing when the doorbell rings and interrupts our conversation. I might be off the hook for the time being, but I have a feeling that it won't take Gia long to sniff out the truth. I jump off the stool and fly toward the front entryway. It's a surprise when I don't have to fight Ty for the honors.

I'm pretty sure JT is on the other side.

How ironic is it that I used to wish he'd stop showing up for family dinners, and now I couldn't be more excited to see him?

This will probably be the only private moment we're able to grab until later this evening when we head back to his place.

Separately, of course.

I fling open the door, barely able to contain my smile. I've missed him today. All I can think about is throwing myself into his arms.

But it's not JT I find standing on the other side of the threshold.

Air gets clogged in my throat as my hands fly to my mouth.

It feels like my body has been hit by a Mack Truck. I worked myself over pretty good in practice just like I've been doing all week long. I think having Claire at the house is going to be the death of me. All I want is to bury myself balls-deep in her.

An internal battle is waged every night when I pull her into my arms. Even though she's told me that she's ready to take things further and wants me to make love to her, I find excuses to back off from taking that final step.

She's waited this long, what's a few more days in the grand scheme of things?

Except, it's entirely possible my dick will explode.

And the way she plays with me...

The way she gazes at me so intently, petting my cock, sucking, and licking it.

It's the sweetest torture I've ever experienced, and that's saying something. I haven't exactly led a chaste life up until this point.

No one has ever affected me the way Claire does.

Strangely enough, that doesn't scare me.

Maybe it should.

For the first time in my life, I feel like I have some clarity as far as my career and relationships go. I'm sure being sober helps with that. But I'm also willing to bet that it has a lot to do with Claire. I've wanted her since the first time I saw her. And now I have an actual shot.

I think that's the reason I'm set on taking our relationship slow. The last thing I want is for her to regret what we do together. Plus, I think her getting to know me—the real me—will help smooth the way when I finally break it to her that this is the real deal.

Once I make her mine, she's not going anywhere.

I roll up to the guardhouse and wave to the woman sitting behind the window before she gives me the go-ahead to enter the subdivision. Instead of stopping at home to change, I head straight over to Liam's for dinner.

After being away from Claire all day, the need to lay eyes on her pounds through me like a steady drumbeat. I should probably add that I want to do more than just lay eyes on her. I want to wrap her up in my arms and crush her to me.

Except...

I won't be able to do that at Liam and Gia's house. We'll have to pretend that there's nothing going on.

Which sucks.

The more I think about it, the less I like it.

I realize Liam is overly protective. Everyone on the damn team knows it. But sneaking around behind his back doesn't sit right with me. And I sure as hell don't want to pretend that we're barely on speaking terms.

I catch sight of Liam's house and turn into the winding drive. As I pull up near the garage, Claire and Liam are standing at the front door. My eyes widen before narrowing. There's another man with them, and he has his arms wrapped around her and is lifting her off her feet.

What the fuck is going on here?

Possessiveness rushes through me as I cut the engine and slam out of the Porsche.

They're so wrapped up in one another that no one notices until

I'm standing beside them, clearing my throat. There must be a pissed-off expression on my face because Claire's eyes widen.

Even though she tries to pull away, the dude holding onto her doesn't let go.

My hands tighten. I'm moments away from throwing a punch. I haven't smashed my fist into someone's face in more than eight months, and here I am, losing my shit outside Liam Garrison's front door.

The guy finally notices how Claire is trying to put a little distance between them because he turns and meets my stare head-on. His eyes narrow as if he understands what I am to her and doesn't like it one damn bit. It's only when Liam claps me on the shoulder that I'm able to rip my gaze away from them.

"Hey, man. This is my brother, Cullum."

That's all it takes for everything inside me to loosen. It's almost ridiculous how jacked up I got when I thought someone was trying to take her away.

Claire isn't even mine.

Not technically.

Although, for all intents and purposes, the girl belongs to me.

The emotion rampaging through me only slams home that realization.

"Cullum, this is JT Higgins."

Even though his arms are still wrapped around Claire as if to keep her away, I extend my hand.

He stares at it for a second before reluctantly shaking it. "Nice to meet you."

By the way he grumbles the greeting, my guess is that he doesn't feel that way.

Even though Claire's other brother has only just arrived on the scene, and we've never met, I think he knows *exactly* what my intentions are with his sister, and he doesn't approve.

Well, that's too fucking bad, buddy. Get used to it, because I'm here to stay.

I notice Claire subtly trying to pull away from Cullum, but he's not having any of it.

"Oh!" Claire runs her hand over her brother's cheek. "You must be the surprise Gia was talking about!"

Cullum's focus returns to his sister and his expression softens as his lips quirk into a half-smile.

I get the feeling that Cullum Garrison isn't a man who smiles easily.

"Yup, I'll be in town for about a week."

She swats his chest. "Why didn't you say something sooner? It's been so long since we've seen you!"

He hoists his lips a bit more, but it seems forced.

Claire has told me bits and pieces about her childhood. Just enough for me to puzzle together what growing up must have been like for her. I might have had a financially secure upbringing, but Claire and her brothers did not.

"Should we all head inside?" Liam asks. "Gia and the kids will be excited to see you."

The brief look Cullum spears me with says, *Beat it, dude. You don't belong here.*

Yeah, that's not happening. Wild horses couldn't drag me away from his sister.

The three siblings enter the house ahead of me. Since I'm the last one in, I close the heavy mahogany front door. As I do, I hear Gia and the kids greet Cullum with shouts of joy and laughter. It's night and day from my family. Other than Bess, no one seems particularly thrilled to see my face when I show up.

I quickly brush the thought aside, not wanting to dwell on it. The moment I walk into the kitchen, Gia kisses me on the cheek and offers me something to drink. I tell her just like I always do that I'm more than capable of getting my own beverage before pulling a glass from the cabinet and filling it up with ice-cold water.

One—I really can get my own water. I'm not a caveman who expects a woman to wait on me hand and foot. And two—I hope Cullum notices how comfortable I am in the Garrison kitchen.

Maybe I'm not family, but I'm treated like it.

As I migrate to where Claire is standing, Cullum slings an arm casually around her shoulders and hauls her close. The sly look he aims in my direction says, *Checkmate, asshole. You didn't think it was going to be that easy, did you?*

I tip my head in acknowledgment before taking a sip from my glass.

I have a feeling that this is exactly how the rest of the evening is going to play out.

An hour later, I wish I could say that I was wrong. Cullum monopolizes all of Claire's attention until dinner is served. Occasionally, she shoots me an apologetic expression when no one is looking.

I know she doesn't get to spend much time with her brother, and I'm more than happy to stand in the shadows and watch her.

Hmmm.

That sounds a little creepier than intended.

Regardless, I'll be happier when we can take off for the night, and I can have Claire all to myself.

With nothing better to do, I help Gia ferry platters out to the dining room. I'm so finely attuned to Claire's every move that I notice the second she excuses herself to use the bathroom. I give her approximately two minutes before silently disappearing down the hallway after her.

As soon as she opens the bathroom door, I pounce and drag her to the laundry room across the hall. My lips crash onto hers before she can open her mouth. A sexy little noise escapes from her as if she's missed me just as much as I've missed her.

It only spurs me on.

I've been aching to do this ever since I pulled up in Liam's driveway. And the fact that her brother has been cock blocking me the entire time is driving me fucking nuts. When she's in my arms like this, everything rioting inside me goes eerily silent, and I can think again.

"Missed you," I growl as my lips trail over the curve of her jaw before meandering down the column of her throat. I feel like I could eat her up in one tasty bite.

"I missed you, too."

I've never wanted to drag a woman back to my place more than I do right now. I want to throw all my good intentions out the window and take her like I've fantasized about.

But I refuse to do that.

The moment we're stealing will have to suffice until we can wrap up this family dinner.

"How was your day, gorgeous?" I ask instead, attempting to distract myself.

"It was good," she says on a moan.

It only reminds me of the breathy little sounds she makes when I'm devouring her pussy. Which, by the way, I could do for hours. I love those little purrs of pleasure that originate from deep within her chest.

They're sexy as hell.

The need to hear more of them thrums through me as I nibble at her throat. "Just tell me that we can take off after dinner."

"My brother's visiting. I don't think I'll be able to leave for a while."

That's not the answer I was hoping to hear, and I grunt out my displeasure. All I want to do is get her alone. That it won't be happening anytime soon has me feeling frustrated.

"We should probably get back out there before someone notices we've disappeared," she murmurs.

Damn it, I know she's right. We stay here any longer, and her brother Cullum is bound to come sniffing around.

It only makes me wonder why we're sneaking around in the first place. Claire is a grown woman and can make her own decisions regarding who she gets involved with. Whether it's a relationship or straight-up sex.

We don't need permission.

"Maybe we should just tell them what's going on." I nip at her chin with my teeth. My gaze stays locked on hers to gage her reaction.

"JT…"

The way my name slides from her lips says it all.

She doesn't want to go there.

For some reason, that just pisses me off.

No. Not *some* reason.

There's a *definite* reason.

What I want is for Claire to acknowledge that there's something happening between us. I'm not just the guy who will take her virginity. Our relationship has evolved into more than what it was a month ago, and I'm tired of pretending that it hasn't.

And I really hate the way Cullum keeps eyeing me up as if I'm not good enough for her.

Or worse…like she needs protecting from me.

He's glaring at me the same damn way I used to glare at Ryan.

"What?" I snap. My voice comes out harsher than I intended.

Instead of responding, she peppers my mouth with kisses before nibbling at my jaw.

Gahhhh.

I know exactly what she's trying to do with this tactic.

Hell, I *invented* this tactic. It's what I do every time she talks about finding her own place.

Well, guess what?

It's not going to work.

It's…

Damn it.

It's working.

The velvety softness of her tongue darts out, licking at the seam of my lips until I'm opening.

Until I'm groaning.

Until my tongue is dancing and mingling with hers.

And then whatever the hell I'd been so focused on vanishes without a trace, and there's just her and the need she stokes so easily to life within me.

CLAIRE

*A*s we sit down to dinner, Cullum parks himself next to me. It's almost comical the way he throws himself down as if we're playing a game of musical chairs and the music has just screeched to a halt.

JT shoots me a look of irritation as he settles across from me. It's become obvious that my brother is trying to keep us apart. I'm surprised that he's only just walked into the situation and is more attuned to the undercurrents swirling between us than Liam or Gia.

I can only imagine the kind of interrogation that will be launched once Cullum gets me alone. There will be questions I'm not prepared to answer. If either of my brothers figure out that I'm staying with JT at his house, they'll have the shit fit to end all shit fits.

That's a given.

My gaze slides to JT as my mind tumbles back to the laundry room.

What the heck was that all about?

Now he wants to tell people—my family specifically—about what's going on between us?

The more pressing question would be—what the hell is going on between us?

It's not like I have a clue.

I thought we were just going to sleep together. And let me be completely clear when I say that there is no way on god's green earth that I'm telling Liam and Gia about that.

Or Cullum.

I almost wince.

Is JT having some kind of psychotic break from reality?

Liam has made it perfectly clear that he doesn't want me anywhere near his teammates. The last thing he wants to overhear is one of his friends talking trash about his sister in the locker room. He doesn't want any rumors flying around about his family. And he certainly doesn't want to have a problem with one of the players. That would only bleed onto the field.

I've never had an issue with his no-fraternization rule. In all honesty, it made things easier. I didn't have to worry about shutting guys down, and they could look at me as the team little sister and nothing more.

It worked for everyone involved.

All Liam has done since he was fifteen years old is take care of me.

Take care of all of us.

He busted his ass in high school and then left college early so he could start earning a paycheck in the pros. I don't want to do anything that will hurt him or break his trust.

I'm so lost in thought that I don't realize the table has gone silent. Everyone except for Ty and Charlotte. They're still being their loud, boisterous selves. It takes another moment before I become aware that the three adults at the table are staring at Cullum.

As I study the brother closest to me in age, I realize something is wrong. My gaze slides to JT. He's staring at me with an odd expression on his face.

Sympathy, maybe?

There's no time to question it as Liam bellows from his seat at the head of the table. "You've got to be fucking kidding me! How long has this been going on for?"

My lower jaw turns slack as my gaze snaps to my oldest brother in astonishment.

Gia gasps before saying in a calm voice that belies the thick tension that fills the dining room, "I'm going to take the kids to the kitchen." With that, she gathers up their plates. "Come on. You two can sit in here, and we'll turn on a show."

It's as if both Ty and Charlotte understand that their father is angry, because they silently follow their mother into the other room. Usually, Liam takes care not to swear in front of them.

Before I can push out any questions, Cullum grabs my hand and gives it a gentle squeeze. "She's been back for about a month."

"Why is this the first time we're hearing about it? You should have called us the moment she showed up at your door."

I still don't understand what they're talking about, but the pit sitting at the bottom of my belly continues to grow as my gaze darts back and forth between them.

Thick tension radiates off Cullum as he jerks his shoulders. "Because I knew exactly how you'd react." His voice drops as he adds, "And I wanted to make sure she was actually going to stick around. There didn't seem much point in riling everyone up if she was going to take off again."

And just like that, a trapdoor opens and I'm in freefall.

It takes a second or two to catch my breath.

The reason for Liam's anger becomes crystal clear, and I can't say I blame him for it.

"What does she want, Cullum? Why is she back after all this time?" I ask with more calm than I'm feeling.

As I suck air into my lungs, my chest constricts, becoming painful. This is exactly what thinking about that woman does to me.

After she took off, I sobbed quietly into my pillow every single night for six months straight and prayed she would come back to us.

She never did.

At just ten years of age, it was unfathomable that she could just pick up and walk away.

No explanation.

No goodbye.

Nothing.

That's when Dad mentally checked out. He might have been there physically, but he was an empty shell of a human being. He drank and gambled until we eventually lost the house. It took a while, but Dad finally seems to have his shit together. The last thing we need is for her to sweep back into our lives and wreak havoc. Because that's exactly what Beverly will do.

She doesn't give a shit about us.

How could she?

You don't walk away from the people you love.

For the first time since a heavy silence has fallen over the room, Cullum spears me with wary blue eyes. "She wants to talk with you." His gaze flickers to Liam. "With both of you."

"Why?" I shake my head. It feels like there's a thick, soupy fog obscuring my vision, making it impossible to see. "Why *now*? She's been gone for eleven years."

He inhales a breath before slowly releasing it like a balloon with a slow leak. "That's for her to tell you, not me."

Liam leans forward, pressing against the table as his eyes flash with unspent anger.

Fury that has been brewing for more than a decade.

"I'm not interested in anything she has to say." He stabs his finger toward the kitchen where Gia, Ty, and Charlotte are finishing their dinner. "I have a wife and three kids, just like she did. And let me tell you, there's no damn way I could pick up and leave them." When he slams his fist on the table, the plates and silverware rattle against the polished wood.

I jump and my eyes widen. Liam has never scared me, but in this moment, he does. I've never seen him react like this.

"There is nothing in this fucking world that could tear me away from them. *Nothing!* I don't want that woman in my life, and I sure as hell don't want her anywhere near my family. You be sure to tell her that!"

When it becomes apparent that our brother won't budge from his stance, Cullum's gaze shifts to mine. The question is written clearly within his eyes.

I shake my head, surprised he would think my answer would be different. "I'm sorry, Cullum. I don't want anything to do with her either. There's nothing she can say that will make the hurt she inflicted magically disappear."

Cullum shoves away from the table before stalking out of the room. I understand he's angry with us, but there's nothing I can do about that. If he wants to let Beverly into his life, that's up to him. I won't open myself up to that kind of pain ever again.

Liam scrubs a hand over his face before rising and silently heading into the kitchen. A moment later, Liam and Gia's subdued voices fill the air, but it's impossible to make out the actual words.

And then, it's just the two of us sitting silently in the empty dining room.

I have to admit, I didn't see any of this coming.

I'm in a state of numbness and shock regarding the situation. I never expected Beverly to resurface. Not after all this time. I can't begin to imagine why she would come back. Although, one thing's for sure. Whatever the reason, I don't care. It no longer matters.

"Are you okay?" JT asks quietly.

There is so much emotion rushing through my body that I can only shake my head in answer.

He rises to his feet, and in eight long-legged strides, he reaches my side before tugging me into his arms. As he holds me close, he drops light kisses on the crown of my head and whispers, "Come on, let's go home."

I can only nod as thoughts of my mother, the woman who abandoned us, tumble unwantedly through my head.

JT

I wake up with Claire cradled in my arms. I'm starting to think I could do this every day for the rest of my life.

How crazy is that?

Pretty damn crazy, I know.

I love having her here in my home. The monstrous place no longer feels empty. I enjoy returning after practice and finding her puttering around in the spacious kitchen as she prepares something for dinner.

Know what else I love?

The way she curls up on the couch as she pours over a textbook.

The girl is so damn studious.

It probably shouldn't be so hot.

I can barely keep my hands to myself. It doesn't take long before I'm sliding them between her thighs and slipping into her panties before stroking her soft heat. It's almost adorable how she'll initially resist my efforts, only to give in after a moment or two, spreading those gorgeous legs and allowing me to do whatever the hell I want.

And touching her…

It's like nothing I've ever experienced before. I find myself wanting to give her everything.

And then some.

I want every flick of my fingers to feel amazing.

Even if that means I'm walking away with blue balls. The way she sighs my name, her soft moans filling the air makes me hard as steel.

Know what I don't like?

When she starts talking about finding her own place. I usually shut that shit down quickly. Apparently, running the flat of my tongue over her pussy is the perfect distraction.

Can't say I don't enjoy it.

But that's the thing—I can't say I don't enjoy *any* of it.

I'm in no rush to see her go.

It's almost disturbing how much I want her to stay.

Whatever this is between us, I want to keep it going for as long as I can.

I know she's worried about what Liam will think, but I'm not concerned. He'll get over whatever qualms he has about me being with his sister once he sees how serious I am.

Maybe we haven't talked about what we're doing here, but it seems fairly obvious that we're growing closer. This is more than me getting her off.

At least, it is for me.

I care about Claire.

I've *always* cared about her.

I want her to be a permanent part of my life.

At the moment, her curvy ass is exactly where I like it, which is snug against my iron-hard cock. Anytime I lay hands on her, I rock major wood. Hell, just catching a glimpse of her is enough to have me stiffening up.

She sighs as I palm her breast, strumming the nipple. She's got the most perfect breasts. I've been out with a lot of women over the years, and I've fucked a good number of them. I've always preferred women with generous cup sizes. Big, beautiful titties I could play with for hours.

Claire is the opposite of that.

She's slender.

Everything about her is slight.

From her hips and belly to her breasts, I find myself utterly fascinated.

She's the perfect handful.

And all that long hair…

I dream about what it would feel like if she draped it across my body. It's as dark as a raven's wing and just as silky-soft, falling in a thick, rich curtain down her back. I fantasize about her straddling my hips until I'm buried balls-deep within her tight body so I can wrap the length around my fist, pulling it taut until she has to arch her spine as she rides me.

Those images are enough to leave my cock throbbing as I stroke it against her ass.

A sleepy whimper escapes from her.

Over the past two weeks, I've lost track of all the orgasms I've given Claire. And yet, I haven't made love to her. It's gotten to the point where I don't know how much longer I can hold back. In the beginning, it was important to give her time.

But now, she's turned the tables. Almost as if she's trying to seduce me, if you can believe that.

Maybe there's a little part of me that wants to drive her a bit crazy until the need surging through her is the same as the one that courses through me. Maybe I want her to discover that she actually likes being around me and we can make this work if she'd just give it a chance to flourish.

My hand drifts along her ribcage and down her belly until it can slip between her thighs and find her warmth. Even in sleep, she opens for me. It's gently that I slide my fingers in and out of her body before circling her clit.

The sound that escapes from her is low and throaty.

It's music to my ears.

Her breathing picks up its tempo as her eyelids flutter open. She widens her legs as her hips rotate to the rhythm of my fingers.

"You like that, baby?" I growl against her ear.

"You know I do." She lifts her hips just a fraction. "Please…"

"Please what?"

My lips nibble at her shoulder as I stroke her pussy, playing with her body until she's on the cusp of falling apart. Just as she teeters on the brink, I pull back and leave her hanging.

I want to hear her beg. I love the desperation that fills her voice for something only I can give. Maybe I just need to hear her admit that it's me she wants touching her, stroking her sweet little pussy until she shatters into a million jagged pieces.

I haven't figured out this deep need I have for her. I just know it's there, humming beneath the surface, just waiting for a chance to break loose. From what I can tell, it doesn't appear to be going away anytime soon.

"Please, JT. I want you inside me."

I make her plead prettily a few more times until she's close to tears. Only then do I press my finger inside her heat until it's buried deep.

She gasps as I fill her.

Fuck, but she's so damn tight.

And hot.

It's like being cocooned in decadent velvet.

I can only imagine what it'll feel like when she's wrapped around my throbbing cock.

Slowly, I pump my fingers in her body. She's so damn slick. I just want to bury myself to the hilt within her.

And then stay there for days.

"Okay, baby," I whisper in her ear. "I'll give you what you need."

She rolls onto her back, and I settle on top of her. With my gaze locked on hers, I take her mouth and her arms twist around my neck as her slender legs wrap tightly around my waist until her pussy slides against my thick erection. I growl into her mouth as our tongues tangle.

"You're so fucking sexy," I growl.

"I want to feel you inside me," she pleads. "I'm ready. I don't want to wait any longer."

I press a kiss against her lips and realize that I'm finally going to give in to her demands. I want her just as much, if not more.

"Okay."

Her eyes widen. I don't think she was expecting me to capitulate so quickly. She has absolutely no idea just how difficult it's been to resist her.

To have her lying naked in my bed each night, so warm and inviting.

Begging me to take her.

This is the first time I've held off on making love—all right, let's call it what it really was—fucking a woman.

Each one walked away satisfied. But still, that's all it was at the end of the day.

What I have with Claire is so much more than that.

Exactly what?

I don't know.

It's too soon to tell. There's no reason we have to rush what's happening between us. We have time to figure it all out. In this moment, all I want to do is make sure I make this the best possible experience I can for Claire.

With a grin, I nip at her chin and skim down her body. I press kisses against her collarbone before sliding farther down and sucking each rosy tipped nipple into my mouth. I continue my descent until I arrive at my intended destination. Already her lips are wet and plump from me playing with them.

As I settle between her thighs, she widens them until every delicate inch is exposed. Claire has the most beautiful pussy I've ever seen. And the fact that she's waited so long to give herself to a man brings every protective instinct I have surging to the forefront. I've never considered myself someone who cared just how much experience a woman had. Hell, I enjoyed when a woman knew exactly what she liked and what she was doing.

In the past, I've always been careful to steer clear of virgins or women who were inexperienced. I didn't want them to get clingy or become infatuated. I wanted someone who understood that this was nothing more than a little bit of fun between the sheets. Mutual satisfaction and gratification for one night only. There wouldn't be any exchanging of numbers or midnight booty calls down the road. This wasn't going to turn into some quasi-relationship.

But that's changed with Claire.

I'd be lying through my teeth if I didn't admit that the fact no man has ever touched her turns me on like nothing else. It makes me want to pound my fist against my chest and stake my claim.

I don't want anyone else to touch her.

Hell, I don't want them to even look sideways at her.

As I stare down at her glossy perfection, I know that I'm going to take my sweet damn time. I want to draw out all this delicious pleasure until she's dizzy with it.

And then, I want to do it all over again.

When my lips finally settle on her glistening flesh, her spine bows off the mattress as her breath catches. She's so damn responsive. As I nibble at her clit, I slide one thick finger inside her. After a few lazy strokes, I add a second finger, trying to prepare her for what's about to happen. I want to make this experience as painless as possible.

Instead of shying away from my touch, she widens her legs and presses herself against me. A sigh of pleasure falls from her lips as I continue to caress her with both my fingers and mouth. I know she's getting close. I can tell by the way her breath hitches and her muscles tighten.

Just as she dances closer to the precipice, I pull back.

When she finally comes, I want my cock buried deep within her heat.

She groans as my lips feather against her one last time. The way she writhes against me is so damn sexy.

I crawl up her body before stretching out on top of her and pressing the blunt tip of my erection to her entrance. With the way I'm feeling, it's entirely possible the tip of my cock might explode before I'm all the way inside her. The realization that I'm finally going to claim her sends every primitive instinct within me hurtling to the surface.

I've never wanted to bury myself inside someone more than I do at this very moment. Even though I want to fuck her, it's so much more than that. Whether she realizes it or not, Claire is giving herself to me. Giving me something infinitely precious. The asshole she was with before might not have realized what a gift this is, but I certainly do.

I'm not about to fuck it up.

As I press forward, her eyes hold mine as if we're the only two people in the world.

"It's going to be okay, Claire. I won't lie and say that it's not going to hurt. It will. But I'll be as gentle as I can."

She nods before drawing in a nervous breath as her body tenses beneath mine.

"Relax, baby. You just need to leave everything to me."

It'll only hurt more if she allows the anxiety to get to her. I need her to loosen up and focus on the pleasure.

Even though I want nothing more than to thrust deep inside her, I keep myself under control. I hold myself up on my elbows so that my weight doesn't crush her. Carefully, I slide my dick in and out of her tight heat. Shallow strokes that give pleasure rather than pain.

It takes a minute or so for her muscles to lose their rigidity. She arches, trying to get closer so that more of my cock fills her. With each movement, I slide a little deeper until I butt up against her thin barrier.

As my cock bumps it again, I almost lose control. So badly do I want to plow right on through until I'm completely surrounded by her soft heat. It's killing me to take things slowly.

But I have to.

There isn't a choice in the matter.

It's almost as if the other women I've been with were just a precursor. Practice for this moment when it would take every ounce of self-restraint within me to make this as good an experience as I can for her.

Her pussy is nirvana. A tight, velvety fist clutching the tip of my shaft. I can't wait to feel all of her pulsing around me, squeezing me until I explode inside her.

That's the moment I realize that I've forgotten one very important detail.

A condom.

I always make sure to wrap it up.

Always.

I've never gone bareback.

As much as I don't want to, I hastily pull out. Her fingernails dig into my back as she tries to tug me down again.

"JT?"

"I'm not wearing anything," I say gruffly.

She sucks in a deep breath before slowly releasing it. "I'm on the pill."

I pause so that the tip of my cock sits at the entrance of her tight pussy. So badly do I want to slide back inside.

"I've never been in a woman without a condom." I have no idea if she believes that or not. If she's smart, she'll tell me to get something on before allowing me back inside her body. "I have some in the drawer." I jerk my head toward the nightstand. "It'll be quick, I promise."

She studies my face carefully before shaking her head. "I trust you. You haven't lied to me yet. All you've done is take care with me. I want to feel you inside me. I want to feel you *come* inside me."

With a groan, I surge back inside her body.

Her breath catches as I gently knock against the barrier again.

I pull out and ask one more time before I lose control, "Are you sure? I'll use a condom. I don't want to put you at risk."

With a nod, her nails bite into the flesh of my back as she tugs me forward, holding me in place as if she's afraid I might pull out again.

"I'm sure. I want to feel you. It's so good." She arches. "*Soooo good.*"

"Yeah, it is, baby." I lean down and take her lips before whispering, "It's never felt like this before. Not ever."

I continue to take short, shallow strokes to help prime her body. My cock is now coated with her cream, and it's the best fucking feeling in the world. When she tightens around me, her soft cries filling the air, I thrust, breaking through her virginity until I'm buried deep inside her body.

Her pussy pulses around my cock. She's so hot and tight that I lose it. I'm only able to stroke in and out a few more times before spending myself inside her. Her arms tighten around me as her name falls from my lips.

I don't think I've ever come so hard in my life.

I wrap Claire up in my arms and roll to the side until she can collapse on top of me. Her heart beats wildly against my own. My mind is hazy as I run my fingers through her hair.

Fuck.

That's the only word I can grasp onto.

That was freaking amazing.

I almost snort.

No. It was so much more than that.

As I bask in the afterglow, a drop of wetness hits my chest. It's enough to have me crashing back to earth with a painful thud. With my heart in my throat, I wrap my fingers around Claire's shoulders and lift her up until I can search her eyes.

I wasn't wrong.

She's crying.

Her eyes are filled with glassy-looking tears that twist my heart.

Fuck!

"Did I hurt you? I'm so sorry. I tried to be as gentle as I could." And here I'd thought I was being so careful. Apparently not. A teary-eyed woman in your bed is never a good sign.

Are there regrets already running rampant through her head?

I'm gearing up for full-blown panic mode when a smile trembles around the curves of her lips.

She presses her mouth against mine and whispers, "No, you didn't hurt me. You made everything perfect. Thank you."

Relief floods through me as my muscles loosen. "Are you sure?"

With a nod, she snuggles against my chest. I wrap my arms around her and hold her tight.

"It was amazing. I'm glad that I waited." There's a beat of silence. "And I'm glad that it was you."

Every drop of air filling my lungs rushes from my body as my heart constricts.

I'm glad it was me too.

CLAIRE

My phone chimes and has me surfacing from a deep sleep. I blink as everything that happened crashes back to me.

Holy crap.

That was…

It was completely amazing.

Not in my wildest dreams did I imagine sex could be like that.

Especially with JT.

My gaze slides to him. He's still sacked out beside me and snoring lightly.

God, he's beautiful.

Even though he's a man, there's something ridiculously beautiful about him. It must be all that thick blond hair paired with his light green eyes. Not to mention that gorgeous smile. Over the years, I've heard his smile described as panty-melting.

They're not wrong.

Just because I managed to keep my distance for so long, doesn't mean I was immune to his finer points or charm.

What I like most about JT is that he's not the man I assumed he was. For goodness' sake, he held me off for almost two weeks before giving in.

And you know what?

It was well worth the wait.

I can't imagine my first time being any more perfect.

He made it perfect.

I shake myself from those thoughts and reach for my cell. As soon as I glance at the screen, my brows draw together. It's a text from Holly.

Can u meet at George's around three? Have a roommate lined up. Need to sign paperwork.

I nibble at my lower lip and fire off a quick response, letting her know that I'll be there. I'm relieved that Holly found someone to take over my part of the lease and that I'm off the hook for the remainder of the rent. It also means I should start looking for my own place in earnest. I can't stay here indefinitely. It's not a permanent solution.

For a second time, my gaze settles on the man lying beside me. I startle when I find him watching me.

"What's going on?" His voice is all deep and raspy as he stretches his arms over head. The sheet slides down his body, revealing a perfectly sculpted sun-kissed chest.

My mouth turns cottony as I stare. "Holly found a new roommate, so I'm going to meet up with her at three o'clock to sign the paperwork."

His reaction is almost comical.

It's like someone threw a bucket of cold water on him. All of the sudden, he looks wide awake.

He glances at the clock on his nightstand. "I need to head over for practice, but I'll be done at three. Set it up to meet with her at four. I don't want you going there alone."

Even though part of me wants to argue that I'm perfectly capable of meeting up with my former roommate by myself, I decide not to. If I'm being honest, I don't want to see Holly alone.

I'm glad that we don't have any classes together. When we set up our schedules for the fall semester, I was bummed that none of our classes aligned. Only now does it feel like a blessing in disguise.

"Okay. I'll text and see if that works."

I don't realize he's holding his breath until it slowly hisses from between his lips.

His eyes narrow as he contemplates me. "I was expecting you to put up more of a fight. That was almost too easy."

A chuckle escapes from me as I press a quick kiss against his lips. His arms immediately snake around my body before he hauls me against him.

"I wish I could spend the rest of the day in bed with you, but I can't," he growls. "I have to get moving."

"Me, too," I admit, wishing for the same.

He presses a kiss against my neck and whispers, "Are you sore?"

I shake my head because, rather surprisingly, I'm not. I think it's because he was so gentle, making sure I was completely ready.

"Nope. Not at all." I can't resist teasing him. "Don't take it personally. Not everyone is hung like a stallion."

His mouth tumbles open as his eyes widen before they narrow. "What the hell are you talking about, woman? I'm fucking massive."

I laugh and hold up my pinkie before wiggling it around. "Itty bitty."

A growl rumbles up from deep within his chest.

Before I realize it, he flips me over and stretches out on top of me before thrusting his hips against my center.

"Itty bitty, my ass!"

When he grinds his cock against me again, I can't stop the low groan of appreciation as sensation ricochets throughout my core. "I'll show you exactly what it feels like to fuck a man hung like a stallion."

Since we're both still naked, his hard length slides deep inside my body.

"Mmm," I sigh in contentment.

"You're damn right!"

He continues to thrust, the steady rhythm driving me closer to the precipice. This time, there is no gentleness.

And I love it.

Love the roughness of it.

Just as I get ready to slip off the edge, my muscles coiled tight with impending release, JT pulls out of my body.

With a gasp, I arch my hips so that he can slide easily back inside my wet heat.

As my gaze locks on his, an arrogant smirk curves his lips.

He leans down and kisses me before rolling onto the mattress and sprawling out naked.

"Are you being serious right now?" I screech.

His cock is rock hard.

I leap toward him, intent on getting my hands on it, but he twists away at the last moment.

"Hey, what are you complaining about?" He arches a brow. "The last thing you want is some teeny-tiny dick fucking you."

He rolls from the bed. His shoulders shake as he saunters into the bathroom.

Frustration spirals through me and I pick up a pillow and heave it in his direction before flopping onto the bed.

A couple seconds later, he sticks his blond head out of the bathroom. "Why don't you get your sweet ass in here and I'll finish you off in the shower."

Poetic it is not, but I don't care.

I'm horny as hell.

Before he can even get the sentence out, I'm scrambling off the bed and racing to the bathroom.

And just like he promised, he takes care of me in the shower until we both find our release.

JT

We're camped out at a diner near campus, waiting for Claire's bitch of an ex-roommate to show her face. Like there was any way in hell I was going to let her come here by herself. When I told her that, I expected her to put up a fight and was pleasantly surprised when she didn't. I think she was relieved when I insisted on accompanying her.

I'm just glad she gave in so easily.

What was I really going to do if she didn't?

It's not like we're a couple. I have zero pull where she's concerned. The girl is completely free to do what she wants, which is exactly why it's time to have a little *come-to-Jesus* meeting about the state of our relationship.

Especially after what happened this morning.

I'm tired of coasting along.

I need to know what's going on between us.

Is this thing just casual?

A sexual experiment of sorts?

I don't have a clue.

I just know that what I feel for Claire grows stronger with the passing of each day.

And I want more.

As I play with her fingers, a soft smile curves her lips.

There's a ball cap pulled low over my eyes so I don't get recognized. I don't want to be bothered when I'm with Claire. Normally, I don't mind going out and shaking a few hands, snapping some pics, or signing some autographs. Like everything else in my life, that feels different too.

I just want to be alone with her and don't want distractions.

As soon as we wrap this up, I'm hustling her back to my place so we can sit down and hash out all the questions that are floating around at the back of my head. Ironically, I've never been one to slap a label on a relationship. Hell, I've never really wanted a relationship, but Claire has changed all that.

She's all I can think about.

I just want to lock her ass down tight and know she's mine.

I want to know if she feels the same way I do.

Maybe then I'll finally be able to sit back and chill out a little bit.

We can fill Liam in on what's been going on. There isn't going to be any more sneaking around and hiding.

I'm done with that.

And I sure as hell didn't like the way her brother was staring at me like I didn't have any business being near her. I wanted to tell him that I've done way more than just look at his sister.

Except, I don't think that would have gone over well with anyone.

Especially Claire.

So, I sat there and kept my trap shut.

"After this, I thought we could go back to my place and talk," I say.

One dark brow rises across her forehead as she fiddles with the straw in her drink. "What do we have to talk about?"

"I was thinking that we should discuss what's going on between us."

A silent beat passes as she stares. Her mouth opens as if she's going to say something before her gaze flickers behind me. The color drains from her face as she snaps her mouth closed.

I swing around, willing to bet that the ex-roommate just walked in.

By the shock that fills Claire's face, she must have brought jackwad with her.

Fury bubbles up inside me.

Those two are the biggest fucking asshats I've ever met in my life. It's like they're intent on inflicting as much pain as possible. I honestly can't figure out why they'd want to do that.

The ex, maybe.

He's got to be bitter about losing her.

But the roommate?

I don't get it.

Thank fuck I insisted on coming with.

I know Claire can handle herself.

Hell, I've had a front-row seat to just how scrappy she can be.

But I'm here for support. I've got her back and I'm not going anywhere.

Since I'm seated across from Claire, I decide to move next to her instead. I don't want her ex anywhere near her. And I know she doesn't want that either.

As I slide from the booth, my gaze locks on his. He stumbles to a halt before straightening his narrow shoulders. My attention stays pinned to his as I slide in next to Claire and wrap an arm around her body before tugging her close.

Her former roommate drops down across from us. Jackwad takes a seat next to Holly. All I know is that he better keep his fucking mouth shut. The fact that he even dared to show his face has me wanting to smash my fist into it.

Without a word in greeting, Holly pulls the paperwork from her purse and slides it across the table. "Her name is Sydney, and she's planning to move in on the first of November. She'll pick up your share of the rent and utilities and will keep the lease until the end of May."

As Claire picks up the documents and begins to read through them, I notice her hands tremble. Without any further questions, she digs out a pen from her purse and signs the papers before sliding them back toward her ex-roommate.

Hopefully, after this, she won't hear from either of them again.

"I'll let you know when I'm going to move the rest of my stuff out," Claire says.

Holly nods but other than that, there's absolutely no emotion on her face. She's obviously not sorry for anything she said or did. Apparently, Claire's friendship didn't mean all that much to her. The need to protect her thrums through me, and I pull her just a bit closer.

I hope she realizes that she's better off without either of them in her life.

When I lift my gaze, I notice her jackass of an ex staring at me with an ugly twist to his lips.

My body goes whipcord tight. "Is there a problem?"

He shrugs, but the sneer doesn't falter. "Just curious if you've banged her yet."

His glittering gaze slices to Claire, who sits immobilized beside me.

"Is he the reason you wouldn't sleep with me?" When she remains silent, he continues in a snide tone. "Were you spreading those pretty legs and putting out for him?" He chuckles before smacking his forehead. "What the hell am I talking about? Of course you weren't."

His gaze shifts to me again as he jerks a thumb toward Claire. "Don't waste too much time on her, man. She's one frigid bitch. Better take care so your dick doesn't get frostbite."

Before I can suck in a breath, I'm out of my seat and grabbing him from across the booth. I'm not cognizant of anything other than my fist slamming into his face.

Once.

Twice.

Three times in rapid succession.

The feel of my knuckles plowing into the flesh, cracking bone, is one that's completely satisfying.

It's only when Claire screams and yanks frantically at my arm that I spare a glance in her direction.

A dazed expression mars her face as if she can't believe what just happened. As I become aware of my surroundings, I realize that a crowd has gathered. People have their phones out and are taking videos.

I swear under my breath and look down at the asshole I just punched. He's crumpled on the floor, holding his nose. Blood drips down the front of his shirt and onto the scuffed-up linoleum.

Fuck.

CLAIRE

I stand off to the side as JT talks with the police. Holly and Ryan are speaking to another officer about twenty feet away. Ryan holds a towel filled with ice against his nose. His other hand waves around wildly.

None of this feels real. Any moment, I'm going to wake up and all this will have been a bad dream.

Except, deep down, I know that isn't going to happen.

It's like I blinked and complete chaos exploded around me.

Without a doubt, JT shouldn't have gone after Ryan. But I can't deny that my ex was looking for a reaction.

Well…the asshole got one.

Even though I was loath to do it, I explained to the officers what happened with my ex a few weeks ago and what he said to me in the restaurant. I don't want JT to get into any trouble over this incident, but I have the feeling that's inevitable. There were too many people with cell phones shooting videos and taking pictures. If they hadn't realized who JT was when the fight erupted, they certainly know who he is now.

It's only a matter of time before the video goes viral.

If it hasn't already.

There's a thick crowd of onlookers that have gathered on the sidewalk. Even though the cops keep telling people to move it along, most continue to linger. I just hope a news crew doesn't roll up and start shooting footage.

That would make an already terrible situation even worse.

More than anything, I want to get out of here, but I can't leave without JT.

It's my fault he's in this mess. I never should have mentioned the meet up with Holly.

"Claire!"

I whip around as both of my brothers jump out of Liam's pearl white Cadillac Escalade.

My mind blanks.

I open my mouth to say something, but nothing comes out. JT glances at me before his gaze snaps back to the cop he's speaking with. With a nod, he pulls off his ball cap and plows a hand through his thick blond hair.

A moment later, he makes his way toward me.

The three of them arrive at the same time.

My gaze flickers from Cullum to Liam. "What are you doing here?"

Liam's brows snap together. "What happened with JT and Ryan is all over the place." He jerks his head toward one of the cops. "The police called. They recognized your name and thought you should have family pick you up."

Unsure what to say, I remain silent. Liam's eyes narrow before bouncing between me and his teammate.

JT Clears his throat. "Liam—"

My brother's gaze cuts to him before taking a step in his direction. "What the hell are you doing here with Claire?"

My heart clenches.

JT doesn't spare me a glance. "There was a problem with her roommate, so she's been crashing at my place."

I blanch.

Liam's eyes widen. For a long, silent moment, he stares at his teammate as if the words aren't computing in his brain.

My brother's expression turns thunderous. "What do you mean, Claire's been staying at your place? Why would she do that?"

Liam's gaze swings back as if he's waiting for me to refute what's just been said.

How did this situation become an even bigger mess than it was five minutes ago?

Why the hell did JT open his big mouth?

This is hardly the time or place for that conversation.

"What's he talking about, Claire? Why would you move out of your apartment?" He plows a rough hand through his dark hair. "The last time I checked, you could barely tolerate being in the same room with JT. And now you're staying with him?" When I remain silent, his gaze bounces between us, looking for someone to fill him in. "What the hell is going on around here?"

I bite down on my lower lip until the metallic taste of blood seeps into my mouth. "I…" My voice trails off into nothingness.

I have no idea what to say.

My tongue darts out to moisten my lips as I plead, "I don't want to do this out on the street. Can we go home and talk?"

Liam ignores me as his gaze slices to his teammate. "Did you sleep with her?"

JT sucks in a harsh breath before gradually expelling it back into the atmosphere. "It's not like that."

"See? I told you something was going on between them!" Cullum folds his arms across his broad chest. He might not play professional football, but he's still tall and muscular.

A mixture of annoyance and anger flickers across Liam's expression. "Be quiet! You're not helping the situation!"

"Something happened with Holly," I blurt. "And I couldn't continue living at the apartment. JT was just letting me stay with him until I could find a new place. That's it." From beneath my lashes, I shoot JT a silent apology.

Hurt swirls in his eyes and for a heartbeat, I wonder if he'll tell Liam the truth.

"Yeah man, that's all there is to it. I was just doing her a favor," he finally mutters.

The expression on Liam's face says he doesn't believe either one of us. But he wants to.

It's there in his eyes. He wants desperately to believe nothing happened.

His attention turns back to me. "So why didn't you just tell us what was going on in the first place? Why go to JT?"

I hate lying to him, but it feels like the easiest way to smooth over at least part of this mess. I don't want to ruin his friendship with JT. Especially over something that was, from the very beginning, just sex.

I decide to go with bits and pieces of the truth.

"I wanted to handle everything on my own. Ryan and I broke up and then he started dating Holly. I couldn't stay there anymore."

Liam's eyes widen as he shakes his head and holds up a hand. "Wait a minute, you and Ryan broke up? When did this happen?"

"A few weeks ago."

I just hope he doesn't ask about the circumstances surrounding the breakup. I can't go there with him. Especially with Ryan standing no more than thirty feet away. Liam will literally kill him. And Cullum will happily hold him down while he does it.

I can't allow that to happen.

Ryan isn't worth it.

It takes a few seconds for his face to soften. "Why didn't you tell us what was going on? You didn't have to handle all this on your own, Claire. We're family. We're supposed to be there for one another."

"Because you would have wanted me to move in with you guys," I say with a sigh.

"And that would have been so terrible?"

"Of course not, but I knew it would make it more difficult to move out again and get my own place. I really like having my own apartment, Liam. You didn't want me to leave the dorms. If I ended up moving in with you guys, you would have wanted me to stay put."

His fingers rise to stroke his jaw as he grudgingly admits, "Maybe."

He folds his tatted arms across his chest. "You still should have told me the truth." He jerks his head at his teammate. "That doesn't explain how you ended up staying with him."

I suck in a breath before glancing at the blond man. It only takes one look to realize that JT is pissed at me for not coming clean and telling Liam the truth.

But what *exactly* is the truth?

We're not together.

We're certainly not involved in a relationship.

I asked him to take my virginity. And, as of seven o'clock this morning, I'm no longer a virgin.

So where does that leave us?

I'm not about to tell my brothers that JT and I have been fooling around and had sex.

It's none of their business.

"We ran into each other and got to talking. He offered to let me stay in one of his guest rooms for a few weeks until everything got worked out." I point toward the restaurant behind us. "I was here to meet up with Holly and sign the sublease agreement."

Liam refocuses on his teammate. Instead of thanking him for his hospitality, my brother grunts, "You better not have taken advantage of her."

JT's voice is completely devoid of emotion when he replies, "It's just like she said, man. We've become friends over the past few weeks. Nothing more." He flicks a cold glance in my direction. "You know I'm not into relationships. I was just doing you a favor by letting her stay. That's all it was."

His words cut me to the quick, but there's nothing I can do about it.

"Well, now that I know what's going on, you can just stay with us until you find another apartment." He adds, "And I fully expect you to find your own place soon."

I force a smile. "I've already started looking."

"Good, I'm glad that's settled." Liam jerks his head toward one of the cops. "I'm going to make sure that everything is taken care of so we can get out of here." He claps JT on the shoulder. "I appreciate you looking out for her. Claire means everything to us. So, thanks."

"It wasn't a problem."

"All right, I'll be back in a minute. I don't want to leave you here. You're in this mess because you were defending Claire." His expression sobers. "I'm glad you didn't let her come here by herself." He glances between us before shaking his head. "I wish you would have filled me in on what was going on."

"You're right," JT says. "I should have mentioned that she was staying with me. At the time, it didn't seem like a big deal. Sorry about that."

Is that how JT truly feels?

Was he simply doing me a favor by letting me stay at his house for a few weeks?

After another moment, both of my brothers walk away to speak with one of the police officers, which leaves JT and I to stand awkwardly on the sidewalk by ourselves.

For the first time in weeks, I'm not sure what to say to him. I'm at a loss for words. He must feel the same way, because he shoves his hands into the front pockets of his jeans. Even though his gaze holds mine, it's shuttered, and I have no idea what he's thinking.

The easy camaraderie we've found is no longer there.

"I'm really sorry." I gesture to the restaurant. "I don't want you to get into trouble over this."

His eyes stay fastened on mine before he shrugs. "Everything will be fine. It doesn't sound like Ryan is going to press charges."

No, I don't think that will happen either. Not since I threatened to press charges of my own.

The more seconds that tick by, the more expansive the gulf feels between us.

My tongue darts out to moisten my lips. From the corner of my eye, I watch my brothers walk back to us. There's no time to clear the air.

"All right, we can go," Liam says before turning to JT. "They're releasing you. No charges are being pressed."

When he glances toward Ryan and Holly, I can't help but do the same. My ex looks pissed off.

"I have the feeling there's more to the story than what you've told us," Liam mutters.

My gaze flies to his.

When he continues to stare, I murmur, "I'm really tired. Can we get out of here, please?"

For just a moment, I'm not sure if he'll press the issue.

I breathe a sigh of relief when he shrugs.

"Yeah, let's get out of here before the press catches wind of it." Liam mutters, "Not to mention the front office. Your ass is in enough of a sling as it is. This will definitely push them over the edge."

JT doesn't bother with a response. At this point, he won't even look at me. Something twists painfully beneath my breast.

I wish I could ask Liam to give us a few minutes alone so we can talk, but he's already suspicious. My gaze flickers toward Cullum.

The way he watches us with a knowing expression…

He's just waiting for the opportunity to prove that he's right regarding my involvement with JT. Until I know exactly what we are, if anything, there's no point saying a word. I refuse to make the situation worse than it already is.

"Maybe I should ride back with JT so I can get my clothes and books." I have no idea if he wants that, but we need to talk. And if it doesn't happen now, I don't know when it will.

"How about we swing over on the way home, Claire-Bear?" Cullum's blue eyes drill into mine. "Then you can pick up all your stuff."

Well, hell.

There's nothing more for me to say.

Not without rousing suspicion.

"Sure, okay," I reluctantly agree. "That works."

I glance at JT, hoping for some kind of insight into his thoughts, but his expression remains blank. I have no idea what he's thinking or if he even cares that we seem to be over. Maybe he's secretly relieved that I'm moving in with Liam. Maybe I was nothing more than a distraction, and now that he's taken my virginity, he can move on.

My heart explodes with pain.

"All right, man. We'll see you back at your house." Liam claps JT on the back. "Thanks again for everything."

Not once does JT's guarded gaze touch mine. It's like I'm no longer there.

"I told you before, it wasn't a problem."

JT takes off as I stay with my brothers. I can't stop my gaze from trailing after him, wishing that I were leaving with him instead. The further away he gets, the more torn up I feel about the way everything ended.

Because I think that's exactly what happened.

We ended.

As the three of us walk toward Liam's Escalade, Cullum slings an arm around my shoulders and hauls me close.

I stumble as he whispers in my ear, "You sure know how to pick them, don't you?"

I say nothing to that statement, because he's right.

I certainly know how to pick them.

JT

$\mathcal{C}$oach throws the newspaper down in front of me as I sit on the other side of his desk. I don't have to glance at it to know what I'm going to find. Unfortunately, I've already seen the photograph.

Actually, there are several circulating.

It didn't take long for the video to explode all over the internet. Every entertainment and gossip website had it splashed across their home page, not to mention all the sports channels that have picked up the story and are now running with it.

I almost snort at that.

Story...

What freaking story?

Although try telling Claire's ex that. I think that douchebag has been interviewed on five different stations already and that was at eight o'clock this morning. It's probably more by now. Every time he tells the tale, it becomes more embellished.

More outlandish.

He's soaking up all the attention this has brought him.

What a piece of shit.

All I can say is that I never liked the motherfucker. Not from the first moment I laid eyes on him. Although, it's a little hard to feel vindicated when all the progress I've made during the past eight months has been blown to shit by a twenty-second clip of me attacking a kid half my size and punching him in the face.

It may have felt good in the moment, but not so much anymore.

"JT," Coach snaps. "Are you paying attention to one damn word I'm saying?"

The fact that he looks on the verge of stroking out has me sitting up a bit straighter. "Sorry."

Unsure what to do, I run my hands through my hair.

I've already apologized.

Half a dozen times.

But that doesn't stop the words from sliding off my lips again. "I'm really sorry about all this. The situation got out of control before I could think about what I was doing."

That's not true.

I knew exactly what I was doing.

Should I have hit that douchebag?

Especially in such a public setting?

That's a tough call.

I'm willing to bet the front office and the coaching staff would unanimously agree that the appropriate response would have been to walk away like a pussy with my tail tucked between my legs.

Am I sorry that I lost my shit?

I guess.

Maybe.

Listening to that guy talk smack about Claire had me totally snapping. Even thinking about that weasel makes my hands clench with the need to hit him all over again.

Coach shakes his head in disappointment. "What the fuck am I going to do with you, Higgins?"

That sounds like more of a rhetorical question, so I keep my trap shut.

The woman who runs my PR told me not to respond to the press no matter what, so I'm only being quoted as saying repeatedly *no comment*. It doesn't exactly paint me in the best light.

Everyone from the general manager of the team on down is unhappy. Apparently, you screw up one time in eight months, and suddenly you're on everyone's shit list. Although, I can't say that any of my teammates are pissed. Liam let it be known right away that I was protecting Claire.

So, at least there's that.

As of yet, I haven't reached out to her.

I just can't. Not right now.

I have no idea where we stand. After listening to her explain to Liam that we're nothing more than friends, I offered her a place to stay, and that's the extent of it.

Here's the thing—that's exactly what she kept telling me the entire time we were together.

That it was sex.

That I was just taking her virginity.

How many times did I shut down her attempts to look for an apartment?

At least half a dozen.

So, maybe this *was* strictly about sex as far as she was concerned.

How the hell do I know?

Coach reams me out for the next ten minutes.

There's a good chance this will be the straw that breaks the camel's back and I'll end up getting traded at the end of the season. I can tell he's starting to wind up again when there's a knock on his office door.

I don't bother to turn around to see who it is.

At this point, it doesn't matter.

I just want this meeting over with, so I can move on with my day.

Coach waves whoever it is into his office, and I sit up a bit straighter when my father waltzes in. I'm sure there's a look of surprise written across my face. If I was already having a fucked-up day, it just nosedived.

The steely look in his eyes tells me that it's about to jackhammer to an all-time new low.

I didn't think that was possible.

What the hell is he doing here?

"Hey, Jimmy," my father greets. "Do you mind if I have a few words alone with Jameson?"

Well, shit.

This doesn't bode well for me at all.

He called six or seven times this morning, and I let it go straight to voicemail. Looks like he brought the ass chewing to me.

"Yeah, sure. Maybe you can talk some sense into your boy."

My father grimaces as if those words actually cause him pain. "Doubtful."

Coach rises from his chair and quietly shuts the door behind him. My father glares as if I'm a piece of shit on the heel of his expensive wingtips before folding his arms across his chest.

"Couldn't be bothered to pick up the phone when I called?"

My gaze stays trained on him as I shrug. Once again, I'm reduced to a sulky fourteen-year-old punk in his presence. It makes me gnash my teeth in silent aggravation. "Been busy."

"Yes, I can see that. Your antics are plastered all over the papers and television."

"Not to mention the internet."

Christ…I should really learn to keep my big mouth shut.

All I can say is that the man brings out the worst in me.

His eyes narrow as he snaps, "You think this is funny?"

"It's not funny at all," I admit wearily.

"Your damn right it's not. I spoke with Stu today."

Even though those words surprise me, I don't let it show. Because that's exactly what he's waiting for.

A reaction.

Stu Stermfield is the General Manager of the organization. They've been friends for years. Ever since my father coached in Green Bay.

He allows those words to sink in before saying in a careful tone, "I think it might be best for everyone involved if you cut ties after the season and looked elsewhere for a team."

I arch a brow.

My father really is a pompous asshole if he thinks he has that much pull around here. Even with all his clout, he's no longer in charge. He's a glorified old-timer who's trotted out for meet and greets. He waves to the fans, shakes a few hands, signs some autographs, and tells a couple of stories.

That's it.

"All you've done since arriving in Green Bay is tarnish the Higgins name and make a laughing stock out of the family. Your mother and I are fed up. We've had enough. It's high time you moved on."

"Excuse me?" Laughter gurgles up in my throat. "You *actually* spoke with Stu about trading me? You want me out of Green Bay that badly?"

Instead of answering my question, he sighs.

It's a long, drawn-out sound.

"From the very beginning, you were a difficult child. Always demanding so much attention from everyone. Always trying to keep up with your brother. Always wanting to steal the spotlight. You were such a goddamn nuisance." He shakes his head as if he can't understand any of it. "I'd hoped that once you were older, you might outgrow those childish tendencies and start acting like a mature adult, but that has yet to occur. Your career and how you've chosen to conduct yourself aren't befitting to the Higgins name. It never was. And clearly, it never will be."

There's not one single drop of emotion to be found within his icy expression. It's as if we're nothing more than strangers. Actually, he'd probably be filled with far less animosity if we were.

"Your mother and I have grown weary of your antics. At this point, we feel it's best to walk away."

Walk away?

What the hell does that even mean?

I keep my jaw firmly locked so that it doesn't fall open. The last thing I want is to give him the satisfaction of seeing that his barbed darts have struck a chord with me.

I've never understood my father's hatred.

I just know that I've always felt it.

He's made damn sure of that.

It's almost laughable that I spent so many years doing anything I could to please him. I tried to be the best at everything just so he'd give me a crumb of affection, and yet he's always stingily withheld it.

I remember sitting in the kitchen with Bess after a game or when I'd bring home an A on an exam. Without fail, she would make my favorite dinner and snickerdoodle cookies in celebration. We would sit at the kitchen island, just the two of us, and talk. She'd tell me how pleased my parents were with my accomplishments, but deep down I knew her words were a lie.

"Why?" The question slips out before I can rein it back in again.

It's only then that I realize how tired I am of holding all this poison in. First, I tried to please him and then I tried everything in my power to piss him off. If I couldn't have positive reinforcement, I was hell-bent on seeking out negative attention in its place. That turned out to be so much easier than trying to earn his accolades.

Well, I'm done with that.

I should have washed my hands of him years ago. Buried somewhere deep down, I've been holding out hope that our relationship would reach a turning point. That he'd finally see me for the man I've grown into and the accomplishments I've earned over the years.

That hasn't happened.

Today feels like the first time I've come to a place of acceptance regarding what I've secretly been waiting for and that it will never come to fruition. I don't need his love or approval.

There's only one person who matters to me, and I've backed away from her because I was unsure of where we stood. I was afraid to put myself out there any more than I already had. I was afraid she'd turn away, just as my parents have repeatedly done my entire life.

"Why?" He seems genuinely puzzled by the question.

"Forget it, Dad." I rise to my feet, realizing that it no longer matters. I'm ready to end this farce of a relationship.

His brows draw together as he scowls. "Sit down, Jameson. I'm not finished with you."

I ignore him and move toward the door. "Actually, you are."

He grits his teeth and points toward the chair I've just vacated. "Sit your ass back down right now!"

A gurgle of laughter escapes from my mouth. "Or what?" I tilt my head. "What *exactly* are you going to do?"

His jaw slackens as his fingers clench and unclench uselessly at his sides. I'm not worried that he'll try to take a swing at me. My father may be a lot of things, but he's never once laid his hands on me. He's a lot more cowardly than that. He would much rather beat me down verbally than strike with his fists.

And I've had enough.

Before he can respond, I close the distance between us.

"You know what, Dad? I think you're right." I keep my tone level because I want him to hear me. I don't want anger and hurt to cloud my message. "Distance is exactly what we need. All you've done my entire life is beat me down. Whatever happens from this point forward is none of your concern. I absolve you of all responsibility."

His mouth starts to work as if he's gearing up for an argument.

I cut him off before he can begin. "That's what you've wanted, right? Well, now you have it."

With that off my chest, I head for the door. Each step I take has the weight of the world falling away.

I've never felt so free.

It only makes me wish that I would have swept him from my life years ago.

Just as I'm about to step over the threshold, he calls my name. I turn and cock a disinterested brow in his direction.

"I'll have your belongings boxed up and sent over."

"Don't bother. There's nothing you have that I want."

And then I'm gone.

A million pounds of weight fall away as I leave the office behind.

CLAIRE

"Hey." Cullum holds out a bottle of water as he stands next to the lounger I'm sitting on. I take it before setting it on the small wooden table next to me. "You've been out here for a while. Everything okay?"

I shade my eyes against the shining autumn sun before staring up at my brother. Even though my life is in total upheaval, it's still good to have him here. With his work schedule and my course load, we don't get the chance to see each other as often as we'd like.

Although, thinking about that reminds me of the reason behind his unexpected visit. Since I don't want to discuss JT with my brother, I decide to tackle that issue instead.

"So, where's Beverly been all this time?" I can't even bring myself to call her Mom.

She isn't my mother.

She walked away from that responsibility more than a decade ago. I never thought I'd see her again. It's strange to think that she's back after all this time and wants to be a part of our lives.

What did she really expect would happen?

That she'd pick right up where she left off?

That we were going to welcome her back into our lives with open arms?

I almost snort, because that is *so* not going to happen.

In fact, I can't even imagine it.

That's how far-fetched the notion is.

What surprises me most is that Cullum is willing to entertain the idea of having a relationship with her. He had the toughest time adjusting to her absence. You might assume I would have suffered most because I was the lone girl in a house full of men, but that wasn't the case at all. Even though Liam stepped up and took responsibility when our father couldn't, Cullum is the one who ended up working full time while he was still in high school so we could scrape together enough money to pay the bills.

Life wasn't easy for him.

And for a long time, he was pissed off about that.

Sometimes, I think he still is.

Cullum sighs. It's a deflated sound that emanates from deep within his chest.

"Just around, I guess."

Even though there's nothing amusing about his answer, a gurgle of laughter escapes from me. "Just around, huh? Awesome."

Cullum lowers himself onto the wooden lounger beside me, and we silently stare at the crystal-clear water of the pool as it rocks gently with the breeze.

"What does she want?" She must want *something* from us. Why else would she bother showing back up more than a decade later?

The weight of his stare falls on me. "She wants a chance to get to know you again."

And just like that, everything within me shuts down.

"It's a little too late, don't you think?"

"It doesn't have to be," he says.

I turn and meet his gaze. "I disagree. I think it's *much* too late for her to pop back into our lives and expect that we've been sitting around, eagerly awaiting her return."

"She doesn't think that, Claire."

With a shrug, I reach for the bottle of water. My throat is parched and it's starting to ache. I unscrew the cap and bring the bottle to my lips before guzzling down a third of the icy cold liquid.

It does nothing to make me feel better.

"I wouldn't know what she thinks, because I was just ten years old when she walked out of my life." Even though it's not necessarily true, I add sharply, "I barely remember the woman."

"I remember her," he whispers.

His softly spoken words leave me gutted. I want to reach out and take him into my arms, but I don't. Unable to hold his gaze, I shift mine back to the pool.

"She wants to see you."

"Sorry to disappoint, but I have enough going on in my life. I don't need to complicate it by opening myself up to her again."

The woman has some nerve showing up out of the blue. She leaves when I'm a kid and then wants to waltz back in eleven years later like nothing happened?

No. It doesn't work that way.

"Is JT Higgins one of those complications?"

Rather than answer him, I smash my lips together.

My silence in no way deters him. "I know something's going on between you two. Liam may be fooled, but I'm not. I see the way he looks at you." He bumps my shoulder with his broader one. "And I see the way you look at him in return."

"I don't want to talk about it, Cullum. Whatever *was* going on isn't anymore. So, there's no need for you to worry." Forcing out those words is surprisingly more painful than I expected.

"Who says I'm worried?"

My gaze snaps to his.

One of his brows is cocked.

"The night you arrived…" My voice trails off. "It seemed like you were intent on keeping us apart."

He puffs up his already broad chest. "I'm your big brother, Claire. I'm supposed to keep guys away from you." He gives me a look that says *duh*. "It's kind of my job."

I blink.

"Plus, the media made him out to be a douchebag player." His expression sobers. "That's not the kind of guy you should be involved with."

"Are you saying that you've changed your mind about him?" I ask, trying to understand where he's going with this conversation.

He mulls over the question. "Maybe. I guess from what I've observed over the past couple of days, it seems like he cares about you a lot." He flashes a lopsided smile. "He certainly took care of the asshole you were involved with."

I inhale a sharp breath and massage my temples.

Ryan…

Labeling him as an asshole is being overly generous in my opinion.

Cullum doesn't know everything that went down between us. If he did, my older brother would probably kill him. That being said, I would dearly love to strangle Ryan myself. He's been all over the media.

Giving *his* side of the story and playing up the part of injured victim.

It pisses me off just to think about it.

I can only wonder for the umpteenth time how I could have been so wrong about him. I've known Ryan for three years, and he's always been nice. Not once did I suspect that he would force himself on me or hurtle ugly words like he did at the restaurant. And now, he's taking advantage of the situation with JT to get notoriety in the press.

It's disgusting. I hate to admit just how right JT was about him.

JT…

For the first time in weeks, he's backed off. I haven't heard a word since I packed up my stuff with Cullum and Liam looking on.

The press is happily tearing him apart right now.

I hate that I did this to him. He wouldn't have been at the restaurant or gotten into an altercation with Ryan if it hadn't been for me.

"Do you care about the guy?" Cullum asks, interrupting the whirl of my thoughts.

"Yeah, I do." I'm tired of lying to my family. It feels good to finally come clean.

At least with one person.

"Then what are you going to do about it?" He cocks his head. "Because the way I see it, you kind of shit all over the guy when he was only trying to protect you."

I stare at my brother and realize that he's right. Instead of telling everyone the truth when all hell was breaking loose, I continued to lie.

To JT.

My brothers.

And myself.

Maybe I was afraid to admit that I'd fallen for the bad boy of football. Or maybe I was afraid that he wouldn't feel the same and I'd end up getting hurt again.

I mean, we are talking about JT Higgins here.

He's not exactly a shining example of monogamy or relationship longevity.

"I don't know," I whisper in confusion.

Cullum slings an arm around my shoulders and hauls me close. "You're a smart girl, Claire Elizabeth Garrison. You'll figure out what's best. You always do." He drops a kiss on the crown of my head. "You didn't get this far in life by being a dumbass."

My lips tremble with a smile.

I think this is exactly the kick in the pants I needed.

CLAIRE

*I*t takes a couple of days for me to work up the courage to talk with JT.

Fine, I'll admit that I dragged my feet, hoping he would reach out first, so I wouldn't have to.

That hasn't happened.

So here I am, leaning against his silver Porsche in the nearly empty parking lot. It's just about three o'clock in the afternoon. Practice should be wrapping up any minute. The more time that slips by, the more frayed my nerves become. I go back and forth in my head, wondering why I came up with this cockamamie plan in the first place and if I should go home.

Although, it feels much too late to turn tail and run at this point.

Plus, I kind of don't want to.

I need to see this through.

I need to tell JT exactly how I feel. And if it doesn't turn out the way I'd hoped, well... I tried. Right? I put myself out there for someone I truly cared about.

This is probably the scariest thing I've ever done.

My heart thunders painfully against my ribcage and my mouth

feels cottony. There's a small swarm of butterflies trying to wing their way to life inside the confines of my belly.

This sucks.

Big time.

By the same token, it feels exhilarating as well, because I'm going after what I want.

And what I want is JT.

After ten agonizing minutes, guys trickle out of the stadium. A few recognize me and wave before calling out greetings. I've been around most of them for three years, so even without Liam, they know me. Most see whose car I'm leaning against and shake their heads before flashing big, toothy grins.

"Maybe we should stick around so we can watch Higgins get the shit kicked out of him by Garrison," Collin McTavish calls out with a laugh.

"Not like I haven't wanted to do it myself a time or two," Grady Bradford shouts.

"Tell JT it was nice knowing him," someone else says with a chuckle.

"Guess we'll be looking for a new defensive end after Garrison gets a hold of him," yet another deep voice chimes in.

"Claire, you trying to get Higgins killed?" a player asks.

The more guys that stroll past, giving me sly looks and yelling out smartass comments, the more jacked up I become. Just as I consider jumping back inside my car and getting the hell out of here, I catch my first glimpse of long blond hair.

Even though he's about eighty feet away, I feel the moment his gaze collides with mine. His feet grind to a halt for a moment or two before he's once again on the move.

My gaze coasts over his lean body, taking in the navy T-shirt stretched tautly across his broad shoulders and wide chest. The way the cottony sleeves hug his bulging biceps has a burst of arousal exploding in the pit of my belly.

Or maybe it explodes lower.

Much lower.

Have I mentioned how much I love his arms?

Even though it's only been a few days since I last laid eyes on him, it feels like forever. We spent the last couple of weeks getting to know one another and exploring each other's bodies.

I miss it.

I miss *him*.

More than I even realized until this moment.

When JT is no more than five or six feet from me, he grinds to a halt. His gaze never wavers. The intensity of it has every thought fleeing from my brain. I came here with a plan in mind.

A whole speech worked out in my head.

And now I can't remember a single word of it.

When I remain silent, my fingers twisting together nervously, one of his brows slinks upward.

I blurt out the only thing I'm able to grasp onto. "I'm so sorry, JT."

It's definitely not the long-winded speech I'd mentally rehearsed half a dozen times on the way over, but it is what lies in my heart.

I *am* sorry.

Sorry that I inflicted pain.

It had never been my intention.

He cocks his head. His blond hair gets ruffled by the autumn breeze that blows through the nearly empty parking lot. The urge to close the distance that separates us and run my fingers through the long, golden strands thrums through me. I have to clench my hands so I don't do exactly that. A week ago, I wouldn't have thought twice about reaching out and touching him, but so much has changed between us. We aren't in the same place.

"What are you sorry for?" he asks.

"For lying to Liam and Cullum about our relationship and keeping it hidden." I pause, hoping he'll jump in and save me from my awkward verbal fumbling, but he remains silent. "And I'm sorry for not being honest with you about how I felt."

"And how do you feel?" he asks.

I suck in a deep breath, knowing I need to push out the words.

Whether he breaks my heart or not, I need to tell him the truth.

"I went into this arrangement only wanting to get rid of my virginity. I didn't want it to be more than that." I search his gaze, but his expression remains shuttered. I have no idea if what I'm saying means anything to him. "Even though I tried not to fall for you, I did." There's a pause before I admit, "Whatever this is between us, I don't want it to end. I don't want *us* to be over."

There.

It may not be poetic or well spoken, but it's how I feel.

When he remains silent, a painful lump settles in the middle of my throat as all my hope sinks to my toes. Instead of telling me what I want to hear, what I'm desperate to hear, he reaches out and captures my hand before towing me to him until his arms can wrap around my body and I'm crushed against his chest. He drops a kiss against the crown of my head as I lift my chin until I'm able to meet his gaze.

"We're not over, Claire. Not by a long shot. I was trying to give you a bit of space. Some time to think everything through."

That's all it takes for my knees to weaken with relief. If he weren't holding onto me so tightly, I'd collapse on the pavement at his feet.

"You kind of left me hanging there for a moment," I mutter.

He smacks a kiss against my mouth as a smile hovers around the edges of his lips.

"I needed you to open up and tell me how you were feeling. Honestly, I had no idea. At every turn, you let me know that it was just sex, and you were moving out and moving on as soon as I took your virginity. I hoped it wasn't true, but I didn't know."

I glance away as shame spirals through me because he's right— that's *exactly* what I did.

"I'm sorry. I think I was just trying to protect myself. I didn't want to end up getting hurt again."

"I know, baby. Trust me when I say that I'll do everything within my power not to hurt you." His fingers slip beneath my chin to lift it until his gaze can capture mine. "You understand that, right? For three years, it's been you. Now that I actually have a real chance at making this work, there's no way I'm going to blow it."

His lips crash onto mine and I'm swept away in a sea of desire.

Everything around us fades to the background. All that matters is being in JT's arms, where I belong.

We only break apart when someone clears their throat. I turn my head, only to meet Liam's narrowed stare. His tatted arms are crossed over his chest as he cocks a brow.

Instead of waiting for JT to explain the situation, I jump in and do what I should have from the very beginning.

"I lied to you and I'm sorry about that. JT and I have been seeing each other for a couple of weeks." I gulp before slowly pushing out the rest. "And we're going to continue seeing one another."

I wait for an explosion.

It's a surprise when there isn't one.

Liam has always been so protective. I know it's because he loves me. And I appreciate it, I really do. As a family, we've always been close, but he can't continue to shield me from everything.

The longer he remains silent, the more nerves prickle at the bottom of my belly.

"All right," he says.

My mouth drops open. I'd braced myself for a massive fight, and there's...*nothing.*

It all feels a bit anti-climactic.

"All right? That's it? No screaming or yelling?" I jerk my thumb toward JT. "You're not going to beat the crap out of him?"

"Is that what you want? Because it would be a pleasure to do it."

I toss my hands up. "Of course not. But you've always made such a big deal about me staying away from your teammates. I just assumed you'd have an issue with this."

"All I've ever wanted is for you to be happy, Claire. If JT makes you happy, then I won't say a word about it. He's a hell of a lot better than the other guy you kept bringing around," he says with a snort.

My eyes widen. "You didn't like Ryan? But you never said a word..."

His lips quirk at the corners before he taps his index finger against the side of his head. "That's a little something called reverse psychology. You should check it out."

I roll my eyes. "So, you're totally fine with us seeing each other?"

"Yeah, I'm fine with it." His gaze shifts to JT and he smirks. "But that doesn't mean I'm not going to beat his ass out on the field every chance I get for going behind my back and seducing you."

Color flares in my cheeks. "He did not *seduce* me!"

"Just try it, old man. We'll see who gets their ass beat on the field."

"By the time I'm done with you, you'll be sorry that you ever looked sideways at her," Liam says with a chuckle.

JT's expression sobers as he glances at me. "Not possible."

Even though my brother grunts in response, he looks pleased with the comment.

"All right then, I'm heading home for dinner." Liam's eyes touch upon both of us. JT now stands behind me with his arms wrapped around my shoulders so that my back is pressed against the strong wall of his chest. "I expect to see you both there."

We nod.

It is Thursday, after all.

And tradition is tradition.

Especially in the Garrison household.

Just as my brother strolls to his Escalade, which is parked a few rows over, he adds, "And don't think for a minute that she'll be moving back to your place, Higgins. That isn't going to happen on my watch."

I glance up at JT before sighing. "You know he's serious about that."

"Yup, I do."

There's a beat of silence before I ask, "So, you still interested in dating me?"

He shifts me in his arms until we're once again facing each other. "Sweetheart, it's going to take more than Liam Garrison to get in the way of me being your man."

I twine my arms around his neck and rise up onto the tips of my toes before pressing my lips to him. As I do, I realize how right everything feels. Even when I was trying to keep my distance, fighting the attraction I felt, it was always JT I wanted.

It was never my intention to hang onto my V-card this long. I wasn't waiting for the perfect guy to come along and sweep me off my feet.

And yet, that's exactly what happened.

Somehow, the guy I'd always thought was totally wrong for me ended up being absolutely perfect.

EPILOGUE

JT

The sun is just peeking over the horizon as I wake with Claire in my arms. By the slight snoring, she's still sleeping soundly. No matter where we are or what we're doing, I have this insatiable need to be as close to her as possible.

We've been together for six months now.

Contrary to what Liam said, she spends every night at my place, in my bed, wrapped up in my arms. It's exactly where she belongs. Instead of looking for an apartment close to campus, she decided to stay with Liam and Gia, making it much easier for her to spend time with me.

After about four months of Claire going back and forth, and tired of not holding her in my arms when I fell asleep at night, I finally pulled Liam aside and told him that I had every intention of marrying his sister.

Not now.

Not anytime soon, since Claire just turned twenty-two and hasn't even graduated from college.

But that's my plan.

Rather surprisingly, he was cool with it.

I think he sees just how much loving her has changed me, which in no way means that he didn't keep his word about beating my damn ass on the field that first month. That motherfucker got me good a couple dozen times. And I let him, hoping it would help him get over any lingering objections he might have about us being together.

After that, I started hitting back.

Something powerful contracts in my chest as my gaze falls on Claire.

It blows my mind just how much I love her.

I spent years hopping from one woman to another, never bothering to get to know any of them. One was just as interchangeable as the next.

But Claire…she's different.

I don't know why.

She just is.

The very first moment I laid eyes on her, I realized it.

Three years ago, a relationship would have never worked. I was nowhere near ready for the kind of commitment we now have. It only goes to show that everything worked out the way it was meant to. I thank my lucky stars every single day that she finally gave me a chance to prove that I could be a man worthy of her.

That I could be different from the man she met all those years ago.

I nibble at her earlobe until she stirs in my arms. A little sigh of pleasure escapes from her softly parted lips as I continue to nip and kiss her flesh. Her sleepy eyes feather open as a smile curves her lips.

"Hey, you." Her voice is all low and gravelly, full of slumber and sexy as hell.

If my cock was stirring to life before, her raspy voice has it going rock hard in an instant.

"Did I wake you?" I ask innocently.

Her smile widens. "I can't think of a better way to wake up in the morning than with your lips on me."

She turns her head until our mouths can align. It's Saturday morning and we've got the entire day stretched out ahead of us. Hell, we could laze about in bed for hours if we wanted.

Can't say that idea doesn't hold a certain amount of appeal.

Maybe we'll take a nice long soak in the tub…*afterward*.

As I kiss her, she shifts until every curve is pressed up against my hard lines.

I pull away enough to ask, "You know I love you, right?"

"I love you, too." Her eyes soften as her hand rises to my face to trace the sharp angles and planes as if committing them to memory.

I need her to know what's in my heart. What's always been in my heart. I don't want to take one second with her for granted.

"You mean everything to me, Claire. I can't even begin to imagine my life without you filling it. You've become my everything."

She searches my eyes before pushing against my chest until I'm rolling onto the soft linens. Before I can ask what she's doing, she climbs on top of me and straddles my pelvis with her naked body.

Her hands settle on my cheeks before stroking them. "Baby, I love you more than anything. I'm yours, and you're mine, and nothing will ever change that. I promise."

My gaze holds hers captive as I reach up and brush aside the long strands of her dark hair so that I can cup her breasts with my palms. Gently, I knead the softness. After a few minutes, her head lolls back and a sigh of pleasure falls from her lips.

"Mmm, I love the way you touch me."

"Not half as much as I love doing it," I whisper.

She shifts until my hard length slides deep inside her pussy. Every single time I'm inside her sweet heat, an intense feeling of home-coming echoes throughout my being. It's a sense of rightness I've never experienced before.

It's as if being cradled inside her body is where I belong.

Where I was always meant to be.

Claire Garrison is my everything.

She completes me in a way I never expected.

Or imagined possible.

She's my other half, my home, the love of my life.

I spent three years watching her from a distance. I yearned for something that could never be mine, something I wasn't ready for.

But I'm not that guy anymore.

Claire makes me want to be the very best man I can.
A man worthy of her.
And now that I am, I'm going to hold her close and never let go.

* * *

Thank you so much for reading If You Were Mine!
If you enjoy football romances, check out The Campus Series. For a
sneak peak at Campus Player, turn the page!

Want to read Campus Flirt for free?
Join my newsletter and get this free novella -)
https://BookHip.com/BMXXLBA
Want to read the free prequel to Heartless?
Join my newsletter and get it here -) https://BookHip.com/
RZSTWWG
(Turn the page for a sneak peek at Heartless!)

CAMPUS PLAYER

DEMI

"*M*orning, Demi!" Gary, one of the stadium custodians, calls out with an easy smile and wave as he saunters toward me. "Up and at 'em bright and early this morning, I see."

My heart jackhammers beneath my ribcage from the twenty-minute run as I flash him a grin. "Always!"

"You have a good one! I'll see you tomorrow!"

Since I've already moved past him, I holler over my shoulder, "Same place, same time!"

Even with *The Killers* pumping through my earbuds, I almost hear the deep chuckle that slides from his lips. Our morning greetings are a ritual three years in the making. I've been running through the wide corridor that leads to the stadium football field since I stepped foot on campus freshman year. This will be something I miss when I graduate in the spring. Five days a week, I'm up at six, logging in a four-mile run before returning home, jumping in the shower, and heading off to class.

At this time of the day, the stadium is still relatively quiet, with only a few people wandering the hallways. There's something both serene and eerie about it. I've been here on game days when there are thirty thousand fans packed shoulder to shoulder, rooting on the

Western Wildcats football team. Three-fourths of the stadium filled with black and orange is an amazing sight to behold. Football is a religion at Western. Unfortunately, the same can't be said for the women's soccer team. We're lucky if there are a couple of hundred spectators in the stands.

I've come to terms with it.

Sort of.

I keep my gaze trained on the light at the end of the tunnel and push myself faster. As soon as I burst out of the darkness, bright sunlight pours down on me, stroking over the bare skin of my arms and shoulders. It's late August, and summer is still in full swing. A whistle cuts through the silence of the stadium, and my gaze slices to the field. Nick Richards has been head coach of the Wildcats for the last decade. He also happens to be my father.

Two days a week, the guys are up at six in the morning for yoga. Dad is a big believer in flexibility. Even though I'm winded, a smirk lifts the corners of my lips. Watching two-hundred-and-eighty-pound linebackers contort their bodies into Downward-Facing Dog, the Warrior II Pose, and the Cobra is enough to bring a chuckle to my lips. Some of the guys actually like it, but most grumble when they think Dad isn't paying attention. Little do they know that he sees and hears everything.

My father catches sight of me and flashes a quick smile along with a wave in my direction. He has a black ball cap pulled low and aviators covering his eyes. There's a clipboard in one hand as he paces behind the instructor.

When I point to the field, he shakes his head. He might make the guys do yoga, but he refuses to participate. Something about old dogs and new tricks. Every once in a while, I'll tell him that he needs to get out there and set a good example for the team. He usually shoots me a glare in return.

Every Wednesday night, Dad and I get together. Our weekly dinners became a thing when I moved out of the house and into the dorms freshman year. He's busy coaching football, and my schedule is packed tight with school and soccer. Getting together once a week is the best way for us to stay connected. It doesn't matter if we're in the middle of our seasons; we always make time for each other. Especially since Mom lives in sunny California. After eighteen years of marriage, she got fed up with being a distant second to the Western University football program. She packed up her bags and walked out. I hate to say it, but Dad didn't notice her absence for a couple of days. Which only proved her point. Now she's remarried, learning to surf, and is a vegan. I visit for a couple of weeks during the summer before soccer training camp starts up at the end of June.

Even though it's only the two of us, our weekly dinners are set for three people.

I tell myself to stare straight ahead and not glance in his direction.

Don't do it!

Don't you dare do it!

Damn.

My gaze reluctantly zeros in on him like a heat-seeking missile. Long blond hair, bright blue eyes, sun-kissed skin, and muscles for miles. And he's tall, somewhere around six foot three.

I'm describing none other than Rowan Michaels.

Otherwise known as the bane of my existence.

My dad discovered the talented quarterback the summer before we entered high school and took him under his wing. Which has been...aggravating. In the seven years since, Rowan has become an irritatingly permanent fixture in my life. He's the brother I never wanted or asked for. He's the gift I wish I could give back. He's the son my father never had but secretly longed for.

On a campus with over thirty thousand students, one would think that avoidance would be easy to accomplish. That hasn't turned out to be the case. Somehow, we ended up in the same major—Exercise Science. I get stuck in at least one class with the guy each semester. This time it's statistics, which is a requirement. Three times a week, I'm forced to see him. And then there are the weekly dinners at Dad's house.

Every Wednesday, Rowan shows up without fail.

It's so annoying.

No, *he's* annoying!

Our gazes collide, and electricity sizzles through my veins before I immediately snuff it out and pretend it never happened.

I am not attracted to Rowan Michaels.

I am not attracted to Rowan Michaels.

I am not attracted to Rowan Michaels.

Maybe if I repeat the mantra enough times, it'll be true. That's the hope I cling to. I've made it through the last seven years trying to convince myself of this. I only have to get through our final year together, and then we'll go our separate ways—me to graduate school or maybe to the Women's National Soccer League, and Rowan to the NFL. He's one of the most talented quarterbacks in the conference. Hell, probably the country. There is little doubt in my mind that he'll be a first-round draft pick come next spring.

Trust me when I say that Rowan Michaels fever is alive and well at Western University. His fanbase is legendary. The guy is a major player.

Both on and off the field.

Girls fall all over themselves to be with him. They fill the stands at football practice, show up at parties he's rumored to be at, and basically stalk him around campus.

It's a little nauseating. Don't these girls have any self-respect when it comes to a hot guy?

I wince at that unchecked thought.

Fine...I'll begrudgingly admit it; he's good-looking.

I shake my head as if that will banish the insidious thoughts currently invading my brain. Enough about Rowan. It's time to focus on the reason I'm at the stadium at this ungodly hour. I rip my gaze from him as I hit the cement staircase. After half a flight, all thoughts of the blond quarterback vanish from my mind. How could they not when my quads, glutes, and calves are on fire, screaming for mercy as I force myself to the nosebleed section. By the time I finish, my legs are Jell-O, and I still have a two-mile run back to the apartment I share with my best friend off-campus.

I give Dad a half-hearted wave before leaving. It's the most I can muster. His lips quirk at the corners as he shakes his head. He thinks I'm crazy. At the moment, I can't argue with his assessment of the situation. Although, it's the extra training I put in that helps me run circles around the other team in the second half of the game.

The jog home feels like it will last forever. By the time I unlock the apartment door, I'm ready to collapse. I beeline for the shower and jump in before it's fully warm. My skin prickles with goose flesh, but it feels so damn good. Twenty minutes later, I'm dressed and ready to take on the day. My hair has been thrown up in a messy bun, and I'm making a protein smoothie that will fuel me for my morning classes.

Just before taking off, I poke my head into Sydney's room. I know exactly how I'll find her, and that's buried beneath a small mountain of blankets. She doesn't disappoint. We met the summer before freshman year in training camp and have been besties ever since. She's the yin to my yang. The peanut butter to my jelly. The Thelma to my Louise. Where I'm more introverted and cautious, she's loud and boisterous. She's been known to leap without necessarily looking at what she's jumping into. Every so often, it gets us into trouble. Sydney and I have lived together since sophomore year. I gave up trying to cajole her ass out of bed for a six o'clock run after the first week of us cohabitating when she nearly took my head off with an alarm clock.

"It's that time again," I sing-song obnoxiously, "rise and shine."

There's a grunt and then some shifting from under the blankets that tells me she's alive.

When I chant her name repeatedly, each time escalating in volume, she growls, "Get the fuck out!"

"Awww," I mock, "that's so sweet. I love you, too."

Sydney snorts before a hand snakes out from beneath the blankets to give me a one-fingered salute. Then she grabs a pillow and tosses it in my general vicinity. It falls about five feet short of its mark.

I stare at the dismal attempt. "If you're trying to cause bodily harm, you'll have to do better than that."

"Piss off."

"All right then." I shrug. "See you after class." With that, I close the door behind me.

My farewell is met with another indecipherable mouthful. If this weren't something we went through on the daily, I'd worry she was in the midst of a stroke. Sydney is definitely not a morning person. She's more of an early afternoon person. Another thing I've learned over the years? The action of waking up to a brand-new day is a gradual process. She's like a bear rousing prematurely from hibernation. It's not a pretty sight. She's lucky I don't take her insults personally.

I grab my backpack from the small table crammed into the breakfast nook area along with a coffee before heading out the door. The apartment I share with Sydney is located three blocks from campus, which is highly sought out real estate. We're fortunate Dad is friends with the guy who manages the building. It's probably one of the only perks of having a father who is a head coach of a college football team.

You'd think there would be more, but you'd be wrong. Honestly, being Nick Richard's daughter is more of a hindrance than anything else. People assume you receive special treatment on campus, from professors, or that you have an in with all the football players.

Or worse...

Much worse.

After a bunch of ugly—not to mention untrue—rumors circulated freshman year, I've done my best to distance myself from the Wildcats football team. They're a great bunch of guys, but I don't need all the ugly gossip and speculation that comes along with being friends with them.

As I reach Corbin Hall, the mathematics building for my stats class, my gaze is drawn to a clump of students standing around outside the three-story, red-brick building. In the center of that crowd is Rowan. I don't have to see him physically to know that he's close. The muscles in my belly contract with awareness. It's like a sixth sense. One I wish would go away. He's the last person I want to be cognizant of.

As I jog up the wide stone stairs to the entrance, my gaze fastens on him. A smirk twists the edges of his lips, and my eyes narrow before I drag them away and yank open the door to the building.

Relief rushes through me as I step inside the air conditioning and disappear from sight.

"Hey, Demi, wait up!"

I turn at the sound of my name before slowing my step. The dark-haired guy jogging to catch up smiles before falling in line with me.

Justin Fischer.

He's a baseball player and teammates with Sydney's boyfriend, Ethan. We've been seeing each other for about a month. It's still casual at this point. With school and soccer, I don't have a ton of time to invest in a relationship. He seems to understand that and isn't pushing to be more serious.

When he leans in for a kiss, I angle my head. At the last moment, he tilts in the opposite direction, and we end up bumping teeth instead of locking lips. With a grunt, I pull away and chuckle. My fingers fly to my mouth to make sure I haven't chipped a tooth.

Maybe I've been reluctant to admit it to myself, but that kiss sums up our relationship perfectly.

Awkward and a step out of sync with each other.

"Sorry," he murmurs with a slight smile. I search his face and wait for any telltale sign of sexual chemistry to ping inside me. Unfortunately, my insides remain completely unfazed, which is disappointing but not altogether unexpected. I had a sneaking suspicion when we first got together that it might turn out this way.

"No problem," I say, hoisting my smile and brushing aside those thoughts.

"I haven't seen you for a couple of days," he remarks as we turn a corner and continue walking.

"It's been busy." Which isn't a lie. School might have recently started, but the academics at Western are rigorous. And being a Division I athlete is more like a job. If you're not ready to put in the work, don't bother showing up. There's no half-assing it around this place.

"When's your next game?" he asks.

"Tomorrow at six." My gaze flickers in his direction. Not that I expect him to come, but...

Fine, so maybe I do. If he wants to be my boyfriend, then he needs to show a little support.

His dark brows draw together. "That sucks. I've got a mandatory study hour I have to attend."

I shrug off the disappointment. It's another nail in the coffin of this relationship as far as I'm concerned. "That's cool. It's not a big deal."

"But I'll see you tonight?"

Oh. Right.

Tonight.

Well, damn. In a moment of weakness, I threw out an invitation to join our Wednesday evening dinner. It's one I now regret. If only there were a gracious way to rescind the offer.

"If you're busy, I totally understand—"

"Are you kidding? No way." With a grin, he shakes his head. "I wouldn't miss it for the world. I'm looking forward to meeting Coach Richards."

Great. So this is more about my father than me? Exactly what every girl wants to hear.

I force a brittle smile. "Awesome. He's excited, too."

That might be something of an overstatement.

Justin nods toward the end of the corridor. "I better get moving. Professor Andrews is a real stickler for punctuality."

"Yup. See you later."

This time, when he leans in, our lips align perfectly. The kiss is nothing more than a fleeting caress. There and gone before I can sink into it.

And I'm left feeling...absolutely nothing.

I bury the disappointment where I can't inspect it too closely before giving him a wave as he takes off. For a moment, I stand rooted in the hallway and watch as he disappears through the crowd. There's nothing to distinguish Justin from the thousands of guys who look exactly like him on campus. He's of average height and build with dark hair and espresso-colored eyes. He's nice enough. Although, if I'm completely honest, he's a little self-absorbed. He talks about baseball all the time. If Ethan hadn't introduced us, he's not someone I would have looked twice at. We don't have a ton in common.

As much as I hate to admit it, this relationship has probably reached its expiration date.

Now it's a matter of pulling the plug.

Ugh. I hate breakups. Although, it's doubtful this will end up destroying him. I'll have to make it through tonight and figure out the rest.

With a sigh of resignation, I head to the classroom and find a seat tucked away in the far corner of the small lecture hall. A lanky guy I recognize from a few of my other classes settles beside me. He flashes a dimpled smile as we empty our backpacks.

The tiny hair at the nape of my neck rises seconds before Rowan enters the room. It's like my body knows when he's within a thirty-foot radius. I glance at him from beneath the thick fringe of my lashes before shifting away. Air becomes wedged in my lungs as I wait for him to take a seat. And it won't be next to me because I'm—

"Hey man, would you mind moving?"

Surrounded on both sides.

Damnit. I'm hoping the cutie next to me will tell Rowan to go take a flying leap.

What? It could happen. Not everyone at this university is enamored of the football-playing god. Although I realize the odds aren't stacked in my favor. Rowan is the most recognized athlete on campus. People fall all over themselves to accommodate him.

It's a little sickening.

Okay, maybe more than a little.

"Sure, no problem, Michaels." The guy next to me hastily packs up his books before vacating the desk. Unable to ignore him any longer, I glare as Rowan slides onto the seat next to me.

"Did you really think you could evade me that easily?" Laughter brims in his deep voice. A voice, I might add, that does funny things to my insides.

"One can always hope, right?"

"Oh, answering a question with a question." He leans closer, eating up some of the much-needed distance between us. "I like it."

I roll my eyes as his lips stretch into a satisfied grin. Irritation bubbles up inside me when sexual tension blooms at the bottom of my belly. Or maybe that tension has settled a little lower.

It's definitely lower.

I'm tempted to swear like a sailor. How is it possible that I feel nothing for the guy I'm actually dating, and yet my pulse skitters out of control for someone I don't even like? It's so freaking ironic. It's been this way since we met, and nothing I do stomps it out. I can try to fool myself into believing it's not there, but that doesn't make it any less true.

It's a relief when Professor Peters takes his place at the podium and clears his throat. Once he's captured everyone's attention, he delves headfirst into the probability of dependent and independent events.

Grateful for the excuse to ignore Rowan for the next fifty minutes, I open my textbook and concentrate on the lesson. Just as the blond boy fades into the background, his bare knee bumps into mine. Electricity ricochets through my entire being. I glance at him to see if he's noticed the strange energy we always seem to generate and find his ocean-colored gaze fastened to mine.

My guess is that he does.

Damnation.

Want to read more of Demi & Rowan's story?
Check it out here -) https://books2read.com/u/mYAxqV

Download the free novella Campus Flirt here -) https://bookhip.com/
BMXXLBA

HEARTLESS

SKYE

"*Y*ay! The bitches are back together again, and tonight we ride!" Lanie wraps her arms around me and squeezes tight. "It's been too long, girl! *Way too long!*"

A reluctant smile curves my lips. "I know. It's good to be back." The circumstances surrounding my return are less than ideal, but I'm happy to see Lanie again. She's been my best friend since middle school, and I've missed her. FaceTime and texting are nice, but it's not the same as talking in person. She links her arm through mine as we walk across the open field.

I glance at the cute cowboy boots that adorn her feet. When she told me that we were going to a field in the middle of nowhere, I didn't believe her.

That was my first mistake.

Second mistake?

Not going with sturdier footwear.

Instead, I'm wearing a pair of flimsy sandals. They're cute as hell, but that's not going to do me a whole lot of good across this terrain.

Lanie insisted we celebrate my return by dragging me to a bonfire in a farmer's field. Already, the place is crawling with drunk-off-their-asses, barely legal adults. Shouting and raucous laughter fill the balmy night air.

Even though I know it won't do me any good, my gaze coasts anxiously over the ever-swelling crowd. Nerves dance across my spine as I silently pray Hunter will be absent from the revelry. Or, if he is here, we'll somehow be able to avoid one another.

If I know Lanie—and I do—she'll be up my ass to cut loose and have fun. How can I do that when Hunter and I now attend the same college? At any given moment, I could turn a corner and smack right into him.

The thought of that happening makes me nauseous.

As much as I want to play it cool and act like my ex-boyfriend doesn't matter, the words slip from my mouth before I can stop them. "You don't think he'll be here, do you?" I shoot her a look that's rife with concern.

Lanie doesn't bother to ask who I'm referring to. She doesn't have to. She's all too aware of my past. She had a front row seat to our relationship and its demise.

"I don't know." She pauses and pops her shoulders into a careless shrug. "Maybe."

"What?" My feet grind to a halt as my mouth dries, turning cottony. I'm barely aware of the blades of straw poking my feet through the leather sandals. "But you said—"

Her expression hardens, transforming into one of impatience. "Even if he *is* here, the chances of you running into him are slim." She waves an arm toward the massive group of students who have gathered to mourn the end of summer by drinking themselves into a stupor. "Look around. Half the university is here. There's no way you're going to see him, Skye, so stop worrying about it and live a little."

My teeth sink into my lower lip before I suck the fullness into my mouth. No matter what Lanie says, I'm going to worry.

When I remain silent, my best friend plants her hands on her hips and glares. Here comes Lanie's version of tough love.

"Would you rather sit home by yourself on a Saturday night

because you're too chickenshit to show your face? Afraid that you *might* run into Hunter Price?"

I'm sorry, is that really a question?

From the annoyed expression that flickers across Lanie's face, I decide to keep those thoughts to myself.

"Skye Elizabeth Sinclair!"

I wince as my full name cracks through the air. It brings an unpleasant image of my mother to mind. This is what I get for living with someone who isn't afraid to call me out on my bullshit. Maybe I should have taken Dad up on the offer to live with him.

I decide to go with something close to the truth. "I was hoping to avoid him for a while," I mutter. "That's all."

And when I say a while, *what I really mean is forever.*

Is that really too much to ask?

Lanie sighs as her expression softens. Marginally. "I know, but you're going to run into him on campus or at a party eventually. It's inevitable. Accept it and move on."

I snort.

Easy for her to say. Lanie doesn't have any ghosts from her past that are ready to jump out and scare her.

I have a carefully constructed plan in place for the year. It involves lying low and flying under the radar, so Hunter doesn't even know I'm here. "Yeah, I guess..."

Unwilling to let me backslide, Lanie loops her arm through mine and pulls me toward the growing group of partiers. "It'll be fine. I promise."

Unfortunately, my bestie isn't in a position to guarantee me anything, and we both know it.

The closer we get to the party, the more my anxiety ratchets up. At least night has fallen. The only light emanates from the bonfire that flickers in the distance and the stars that twinkle across the dark velvety sky.

For the time being, I'll remain vigilant. There's really nothing more I can do.

I inhale a deep breath before carefully blowing it out.

Maybe Lanie's right, and I'm making a big deal out of nothing. It's been three years since we've seen each other, and a lot has happened since then. We've both moved on with our lives. I'm sure he's forgotten all about me. As those thoughts circle through my head, my shoulders loosen from around my ears, and my heart stops thumping a painful beat.

The moment we reach the outer ring of people, Lanie is swept off her booted feet and spun around in a tight circle like a rag doll. Her short floral dress flies around her thighs. Laughter rings throughout the air as her arms slip around her boyfriend's neck.

Jaxon Conway has a typical football player's physique. He's a mountain of a man—tall, broad in the shoulders, and muscular. He looks like he could easily bench press Lanie's VW Bug. I would be intimidated by him, but he's quick to laugh and has warm brown eyes. He's like a teddy bear—big and gruff on the outside but tender and mushy on the inside.

"Missed you, babe," he growls.

"It's only been a couple of hours since we saw each other!"

"Doesn't matter," Jax complains. "I still missed the hell out of you."

"Aww." Lanie's voice softens, becoming dreamy. "I love you so much."

"I love you more," he responds with enough heat to melt the panties off Lanie's body.

Ugh.

Make it stop.

These two are so sickeningly sweet that I get a toothache every time I'm around them. Although, if anyone deserves a good guy, it's Lanie. Like most girls in their early twenties, she's dated her fair share of assholes. Jaxon is almost too good to be true. Kind of like a mythical unicorn that sprang to life. He's an athlete who isn't interested in screwing as many girls as he can get his hands on.

Ever since I rolled into town a few days ago, Jaxon and Lanie have been glued together at the hip. I get the feeling he'll be our unofficial third roommate for the year.

Know what's been getting a lot of use?

My noise-canceling headphones.

Most nights, those two sound like they're auditioning for a porno. Let's hope it calms down soon.

Jaxon and Lanie coo at each other before their mouths fuse, and they start going at it like a pair of cats in heat. I clear my throat and glance everywhere but at them. If we were hanging out at the townhouse, this would be my cue to exit stage left. But we're not at home; we're in the middle of a field a few miles from town. There's nowhere for me to go, and no one for me to talk to.

Awkwardness descends as I flick a piece of straw from my shirt.

Maybe I should take this opportunity to grab a beer. There must be a keg around here somewhere. You can't have this many college kids congregating in one spot and not have alcohol. That would be considered sacrilegious, right?

With any luck, by the time I return, Jaxon and Lanie will have stopped mauling each other long enough for us to move on with our evening. It's not like he's being shipped off to war tomorrow and they'll never see each other again.

Sheesh.

My gaze meanders to them in hopes that they've gotten their fill of each other.

Nope. The face sucking has become even more intense. Any moment, clothing is going to spontaneously combust from their bodies.

I don't really want to be around when that happens.

So…a beer it is.

Not that either of them is paying me the least bit of attention, but I point toward the mass of bodies that have multiplied in the fifteen minutes since we've arrived. "I'm going to grab a drink." When my words are met with kissy noises, I say, "Try not to miss me too much while I'm gone."

Lanie waves a hand absently in my direction as they continue to get it on.

"Okay then," I mumble before reluctantly taking off on my own.

The number of people gathered here is a little overwhelming.

Lanie's right; half the university must have shown up. Everyone is talking, laughing, and drinking. In other words, they're having a great time.

Me, not so much.

It takes a good ten minutes to find the keg. Or maybe I should say *kegs* since there are six of them next to the back end of a midnight black pickup truck blasting music from massive speakers. I can barely hear myself think over the thumping bass. Then again, maybe that's for the best. It's a relief to get out of my head, even for a few minutes.

I locate the line for the beer and take my place at the end of it. I'm not much of a drinker, but I need something to smooth out all of the rough edges so I can relax and enjoy myself.

My flesh prickles with awareness, and I run my hands over my arms to banish the disconcerting sensation. I glance around, scouring the crowd for one face in particular but don't see him anywhere. That alone should alleviate my anxiety, but it doesn't.

My parting with Hunter wasn't what one would call amicable. I don't blame him for being hurt and angry. Whether Hunter understands it or not, I did what needed to be done. As painful as it was, I'd do it all over again. I loved Hunter more than life itself.

A part of me still does.

Probably always will.

If everything I've read online is true, then my sacrifices have been well worth it. Hunter will get snapped up in the NFL draft before graduating this spring. Ever since I can remember, that's been his goal. If one person deserves for all his dreams to come true, it's Hunter Price. Unwilling to dwell on my ex, I shove him from my mind and take in the scene before me.

People are gathered together in groups, greeting one another as if they're long-lost friends who haven't seen each other in decades. It's surreal to be surrounded by so many people yet feel so removed from it all. As if I'm more of an observer than a participant. Other than Lanie and Jaxon, I don't know anyone else. I'm sure people from high school attend CU, but I lost touch with most of them after I moved away.

By the time I make it to the front of the line, I'm antsy and ready to head back to my friends. Even if they're still going at it. Which is really saying something. I'd much rather stand around as a third wheel than be an island onto myself. I dig through my front pocket and hand over a couple of bucks in exchange for a blue plastic cup before it's filled to the rim with golden liquid.

The cute guy manning the keg flashes me an easy grin as his eyes drift over my body. When he's finished with his perusal, his gaze once again settles on my face. Kudos to this guy for not gawking at my boobs like he's never seen a pair of D cups before.

"Here you go, beautiful," he says, handing over the cup with a gallant flourish.

This little bit of silliness lightens my mood. "Thanks."

Our fingers brush as I take the Solo cup from him.

"Next time, cut to the front of the line." He gives me a flirty wink. "I got you covered."

I flash him a grateful smile. Maybe tonight won't be so bad after all.

With my drink in hand, I'm ready to make my way back to Jaxon and Lanie. Only now does it occur to me that they could have moved from the spot where I'd left them.

Who's to say I'll even be able to find my way back?

A knot of unease settles at the bottom of my belly. My fingers go to the purse slung across my chest. It's big enough to hold my phone, but that's about it. I could always shoot Lanie a text, but who knows if she'd hear it. And I have no idea how to navigate my way back to our apartment. The unsettled feeling that had taken up residence in my gut turns into full-on nausea.

Only now do I realize that walking away was a bad idea. I should have stuck to Lanie and Jax like glue. But standing around and watching them make out felt pervy.

And not in a good way.

With those thoughts swirling through my brain, I spin around and slam into a wall of impenetrable muscle. The impact knocks me off-balance, and I stumble back a step. Before I can fall, strong hands reach out and grab my shoulders, yanking me forward. My breath catches, and my heart pounds at the narrowly avoided tumble.

I shake my head to clear it as beer sloshes over the rim of my plastic cup and spills onto the ground at my feet. I'm lucky it didn't end up down the front of my top or the shirt of the unsuspecting person I plowed into.

How humiliating would that have been?

Ugh…I don't even want to think about it.

"I'm so—"

My voice falls off as I glance up, my gaze colliding with narrowed blue eyes. Hunter quickly sets me free as if his fingers have been burned. Neither of us breaks eye contact. All of the raucous noise of the bonfire dies away until it's just the two of us standing alone in the middle of a dark field.

This is the moment I've been dreading.

My eyes roam over his face, cataloging the myriad of changes that time has wrought. When I walked away, Hunter had still been a boy, his lean muscles beginning to thicken. Now the transformation has been complete, and he's a full-grown man. Hunter has always had size on his side, but somehow, he's managed to grow both taller and broader. He must be somewhere in the vicinity of six three or four. I have to crane my neck to hold his gaze. The graphic T-shirt he's wearing stretches tautly across the wide expanse of his chest and hugs the chiseled strength of his biceps. It's enough to make my mouth dry and my knees soft.

If I have one weakness, it's for thickly corded arms. All that tightly harnessed power waiting to break free…

A shiver of desire scampers down my spine before I stomp it out.

Unaware of the effect he's having on me, Hunter's deep voice cuts through my thoughts.

"What are you doing here, Skye?"

It's the harshness of his tone that has my gaze snapping back to his as heat floods my cheeks. I can't stop myself from staring. The little bit of cyberstalking I've done over the years has in no way prepared me for coming face-to-face with my ex-boyfriend. He's grown into his dark looks, becoming even more of a heartbreaker than he was in high school.

My tongue darts out to smudge my parched lips as nerves dance along my skin. I search Hunter's eyes, looking for any hint of softening, but there's none to be found. His gaze is as frigid and detached as I imagined it would be. The tiny kernel of hope that our time apart would be enough to heal our past wounds shrivels and dies inside me.

There is no forgiveness in his heart.

But then again, did I really expect there would be?

Maybe. It would have made coexisting on campus for the next year so much easier.

It's obvious from his terse behavior that Hunter would prefer to pretend I never existed in the first place. As much as I would love to give him that, I can't. Unforeseen circumstances have forced me home.

I straighten my shoulders and attempt to keep my voice level. I don't want him to hear the slight tremble that is working its way through my body. "I transferred to Claremont for my senior year."

His shadowed jaw ticks as he clenches his teeth. *"Why?"*

The way he bites out that one word leaves me wincing.

I take a quick step back and lift my chin, not wanting him to see how much power he still holds over me. Time has done nothing to diminish it. "That's none of your business."

Whether Hunter realizes it or not, he still owns a piece of my heart. It's better for both of us if he never suspects the depth of my feelings.

His hands tighten into fists as he closes the little bit of distance that I've managed to put between us. Instead of scrambling back the way every instinct is clamoring for me to do, I hold my ground until we're standing toe-to-toe. My heart pounds a painful staccato against my breast as his harsh breath feathers across my parted lips.

There was a time when I couldn't get close enough to Hunter.

Now I can't get far enough away.

Sorrow floods through every fiber of my body that it has to be this way between us. Next to Lanie, Hunter was my best friend. He was my first everything.

Date.

Kiss.

Love.

Heartbreak.

Everything we once shared has been blown to pieces, and we're nothing more than strangers. Actually, what we are is much worse. His animosity is palpable. It radiates from him in suffocating waves that threaten to choke the life out of me.

"You shouldn't have come back," he growls. "You don't belong here anymore."

That may be true, but there's nothing I can do about it. I'm here. And I'm not going anywhere.

I shift my weight and force myself to say, "Claremont is big enough for the two of us."

"No, it's not. Stay the fuck out of my way, Skye." His eyes flash with barely suppressed hostility. "You won't like the consequences if you don't."

Before I can summon up a retort, he stalks away. Rooted in place, I track his movements until he fades into the crowd. Not once does he turn around and acknowledge my presence. I've been dismissed. Relegated to the black hole that is our past.

Once he disappears from sight, my knees weaken as the pent-up breath rushes from my aching lungs.

I haven't been on campus for a full seventy-two hours, and in Hunter's eyes, I'm public enemy number one.

Want to read more of Hunter & Skye's story?
You can do it here -) https://books2read.com/u/m2Moq7

Download the free prequel (Heartless Summer) here -) https://bookhip.com/RZSTWWG

ABOUT THE AUTHOR

Jennifer Sucevic is a USA Today bestselling author who has published twenty-four new adult novels. Her work has been translated into German, Dutch, Italian, and French. She has a bachelor's degree in History and a master's in Educational Psychology from the University of Wisconsin-Milwaukee. Jen started out her career as a high school counselor before relocating with her family and focusing on her passion for writing. When she's not tapping away on the keyboard and dreaming up swoonworthy heroes to fall in love with, you can find her bike riding or at the beach. She lives in the Michigan with her family.

If you would like to receive regular updates regarding new releases, please subscribe to her newsletter here-
Jennifer Sucevic Newsletter (subscribepage.com)

Or contact Jen through email, at her website, or on Facebook.
sucevicjennifer@gmail.com

Want to join her reader group? Do it here -)
J Sucevic's Book Boyfriends | Facebook

Social media links-
https://www.tiktok.com/@jennifersucevicauthor
www.jennifersucevic.com
https://www.instagram.com/jennifersucevicauthor
https://www.facebook.com/jennifer.sucevic

Amazon.com: Jennifer Sucevic: Books, Biography, Blog, Audiobooks,
Kindle
Jennifer Sucevic Books - BookBub

www.ingramcontent.com/pod-product-compliance
Lightning Source LLC
Chambersburg PA
CBHW051138190726
48290CB00006B/1893